Child *from the* Ashes

By:
J. R. KESLER

ISBN: 1450595278
ISBN-13: 9781450595278

This one is for Cathie. Always there for me

Books by J.R. Kesler

Trash Baby
Billie
Love Means Nothing

PROLOGUE

Pain, fear and loneliness were all the little boy knew. It seemed as if he had spent his entire short lifetime huddled in a corner. To be noticed meant more pain. In his memory no one had ever loved him or held him or cared about him. His universe was a small, filthy apartment. Just him. . . and the man.

The boy was covered with bruises and lacerations. Open, running sores marked his body. Two of his ribs had been cracked and then healed. Rope burns scarred his wrists where he had been tied to the kitchen table. His left arm had been broken but, by some miracle, had repaired itself.

His fleshless body showed bones just beneath the skin. His meals were scavenged from barely edible leftovers from the table and out of the refrigerator. Warm stale beer and shriveled baloney made an occasional meal for him.

He had fared a little better until about a year ago because a woman had been in the apartment and she had made sporadic attempts to feed him. An infrequent glass of milk would appear before him and an occasional bowl of soup would make a feast. The woman even kept him from being beaten so often. Whenever she heard the man's drunken footsteps on the stairs she would shove the boy into a closet. If she were too slow in hiding him, the man would begin abusing the child shortly after coming in the door.

The woman was often the target of the man's fists, especially when she was trying to protect the boy. One day her

interference infuriated the man to a new level of rage and he
punched her repeatedly in the face. When he was finished, she
lay crumpled in the corner, nose at an odd angle, blood running down her unconscious face. The man kicked her once and
stormed from the apartment.

The boy stared down at the inert form of the woman then
curled up beside her on the floor and cried himself to sleep.
When he awoke hours later, he discovered the woman was gone.
Had he been old enough, he would have known that the empty
dresser drawers gaping open in the bedroom marked the woman's swift, panicky departure. He never saw her again and his life
became much worse from that day on.

The pain and fear had become such an integral part of the
child's existence that he was on the brink of being lost forever.
To survive, his mind was looking for a hiding place, a sanctuary
from which he would never have to return. He would eventually
become an animal, not a tiny little boy waiting to be cuddled
in some mother's arms. The chances of his ever being a normal
person were rapidly dwindling.

Even though he was four years old the boy could say but a few
halting words. He could not speak about the terror that gripped
him when the man was around nor of his need for someone to care
for him. Since he had never been loved, he could not give form to
the emotion. It lay dormant, a subliminal need that nudged him
awake in the night, searching for this undefined craving.

He heard the man coming now, listened to him stumbling
up the apartment stairs as he did most nights after he'd had
too much to drink. The boy dashed into the bedroom to hide.
The man's erratic walk, sewer breath and red-rimmed eyes were
always signals for unusual savagery. When he was drunk, the
man lost what few inhibitions he had and was capable of indescribable cruelty.

Frantic with fear, the child fled to his room, a cornered animal looking for a way to escape. He could hide under the bed

again but the man always found him there and would drag him out by the hair. Once the boy had held onto a bed leg and the man had torn out patches of his hair until he was forced to let go. The beating had been worse that night.

The boy ran into the closet seeking the ancient steamer trunk covered with old dirty clothes. He knew the trunk was empty because the woman had stored things in it and the woman was gone. Prying open the lid, he dove into the trunk and burrowed beneath a mildewed blanket left in the bottom. The old, musty smell and absolute blackness terrified him. He heard the front door slam, the muttered cursing, then a querulous hollering.

"Hey, you little bastard! Where you at? You better get your goddamn ass out here where I can see you!"

When the man heard no response, he began searching the apartment. He was glad when the kid would hide. His drunken, sadistic mind made a game of it. Hide and seek and then beat the little fucker.

The boy tracked the sounds as the man stalked him. The suspense, the claustrophobic blackness were becoming more than he could stand. By the time the man was in the bedroom the boy was whimpering, little panting sobs full of overwhelming fear that the man heard when he paused by the closet door.

"So there you are, you little shit! I'm gonna make your sorry ass pay for not comin' when I told you to!"

Awkwardly he flipped the trunk lid open. He grabbed the boy by the back of the tattered tee shirt, threw him out of the closet, then followed, pulling his belt from his pants. The sheer terror of the hunt had made the cowering child urinate in the frayed, little underwear that hid his genitals. Again and again the belt lashed out and burned him across the tiny shoulders. He screamed and tried to crawl under the bed, but the man would have none of that. The child tried to protect himself by rolling up onto a little ball but this just increased the man's fury. A kick to the ribs knocked the breath from the boy's lungs. The acrid stench of the man's sweat and fetid breath were overpowering.

"God damn it, you better quit tryin' to hide from me!" he yelled.

The man jerked back the small head and slapped the boy across the mouth with the back of his hand and blood spurted from a tear in his lower lip. A second blow made his nose bleed. Seized by a sudden inspiration, the man ceased the beating.

"I'm gonna fix it so's you can't do no more hidin' on me," the man said as he staggered off toward the kitchen.

The boy heard him rummaging around in cupboard drawers. Seized by panic he dragged himself to his feet in his desperation to get away from the torture. He had never before tried to get out of the apartment but now he was too terrified to lie there and wait for more.

Suddenly the man spotted the running child and staggered forward to intercept him. He stumbled over one of the kitchen chairs instead, lacerating his shins. By the time he picked himself up the boy was struggling with the doorknob. As he jerked the door open the man was upon him, twisting his hair viciously, paying the kid back for the bruised legs.

Intent on his revenge, the man barely heard the sound coming from across the hall. The boy and the man looked up in surprise at the woman staring at them, her hand poised in the act of inserting a key in her door. All three were momentarily frozen into silence. The look on the boy's face, the blood running from his nose and mouth, brought the woman to life.

"What's going on?" she stammered.

"None of your fucking business, lady!" the man spat at her as he pulled the boy back into the apartment and slammed the door.

CHAPTER 1

Brian Tanner was on an Emergency Room rotation in the third year of his pediatric residency when he first saw Stevie Sanderson. The nurse brought the child into the examination room and set him gently on the exam table. The little boy looked up at Brian with fear and sadness in his eyes while holding his right arm close to his chest. His lower lip oozed blood and a bruise blossomed hostilely on his left cheek. The pain he felt was terrible, but that was almost incidental. He did not know *why*. The boy was only four years old and already he had seen more suffering than most people experience in a lifetime.

Brian knew Stevie, even though he had never met him before. He felt the boy's fear and pain as though it were his own. He and the child were kindred spirits and Brian ached for the child. Carefully he picked the boy up from the examination table, wrapped his arms around him and rocked him slowly.

The little boy didn't respond, lying stiff and frightened in Brian's arms. There would be no response other than fear, Brian knew. He put the boy back down on the table then began examining his injuries.

Finished, he picked up the registration document and glanced through it a second time. The triage nurse had written that the child had fallen down the stairs at the apartment building where he lived. Brian snorted in disgust as he tossed the clipboard and chart onto the supply cabinet near the exam table. The sound of it landing on the metal top seemed harsh in the silence of the room. He looked over at the woman who had come into the cubicle with the nurse. She was unkempt and dirty, hair stringy and unwashed, with an ill-fitting dress hanging on her skinny frame. Her face reflected a lifetime of frustration.

Brian's continued scrutiny made her uneasy. Finally he asked, "Are you the mother?"

"Yeah," she replied.

"How did your boy get hurt?"

"He and some other kids was playin' in the hall and he accidentally fell down the stairs. There ain't no carpet on 'em so he got banged up pretty bad."

"How many times has he fallen down those stairs?"

"What d'ya mean?"

"I mean, how many times have you beaten up on this little boy and then said he fell down some stairs?"

The nurse looked away in embarrassed silence. She had heard from the other nurses about Dr. Tanner's occasional tactlessness but hadn't seen it herself.

"You got no right to say that," the mother said sourly. I bring my boy in to get fixed up and you say somethin' terrible like that. I could sue you for talkin' to me that way."

The woman was trying hard to show righteous indignation, but her eyes would not meet Brian's.

"Lady, nobody gets bruises on the face like that by falling down stairs," Brian said. "Look at this mark on his cheek. Do you expect me to believe that somebody's fist didn't do that? Not too likely. I can see why you had to bring him in by the way he's holding his shoulder. Did you also notice that he didn't cry out when I picked him up? He was more frightened of me than he was of the pain."

"Listen, Dr. Know-It-All, just get the hell away from my boy! I'm gonna take him outta here and find a hospital without a prick like you."

Brian was about to respond when the nurse interfered, "Dr. Tanner, this isn't the way to handle the problem. Let's take care of the child and worry about the other later."

Brian fought his anger and finally nodded in agreement.

"Mrs. Sanderson, your son is more important than our disagreement. I want you to go back to the waiting room while we take care of Stevie."

The woman's face reflected her attempt to weigh the alternatives. She was not a person to whom deep thought came easily. Finally she decided on the easiest course of action. She had been through this situation too many times but had always talked her way out of them.

"All right," she said, "but you're gonna be sorry you talked to me like that."

Brian ignored her comment and turned to the nurse, "Julie, would you escort Mrs. Sanderson out of here. On your way back get me a suture tray and send up an order to have some x-rays taken of that shoulder."

When the nurse returned a few minutes later, Brian set about repairing the damage as carefully as he could. Much as he hated it, there was more suffering ahead for the boy. Suturing the lip was the worst part even though he numbed the area before he began. There was just no way to avoid hurting and scaring the little guy while he stitched the torn sides of the lip together. He had to have a second nurse come in to help hold the boy down while he did the work. Stevie screamed and writhed as he fought these new enemies.

Brian hated what the boy was going through, but he had no choice. When he was finished, he talked soothingly to the child, trying to explain what he had done, but Stevie just recoiled in fear. He had been hurt too often for one soft voice to have any effect. Brian turned sadly to the nurse.

"Have Stevie taken up to Radiology for that x-ray and then have him admitted. Make it stat. If anything's broken, we'll take care of it yet tonight. When you're done, have Mrs. Sanderson come back to the consultation room. I want to talk to her some more."

The nurse looked uneasy. "Are you sure you want to talk to her? You know that hospital policy says you aren't supposed to accuse anyone if you suspect child abuse. It's our job to contact our Social Services Department and they're responsible for reporting anything we document to the Protective Services Department downtown. You're just going to put us in a bind if you confront her anymore."

"Just do what I told you," Brian said brusquely.

The nurse shrugged and left the cubicle. She returned a short time later and said, "Mrs. Sanderson says for you to go to hell. She's not going to talk to you. I really think you should leave her alone."

Brian turned angrily from the nurse. Finally he said, "Okay, document everything and send it to Social Services. I don't want that little boy hurt anymore."

He turned and walked slowly out of the cubicle.

Another hour of patching and mending the usual assortment of E.R. trauma passed. Brian looked at his watch. Almost midnight and nearly time to go home. He suddenly realized how weary he was despite the fact that he had worked only fifty hours that week. Even though there was a constant flow of misery and mayhem, the hours were more predictable so most of the residents didn't mind the E.R. rotation. It beat the eighty hours they often put in each week. Brian liked the E.R. assignment because of the need for high energy and immediate action.

He looked again at his watch. Before leaving for the night he wanted to find out the results of the x-rays on Stevie Sanderson's shoulder. He went to the nurse's station and noted with surprise that the x-rays and report were already there. Somebody in Radiology had screwed up and shown unusual efficiency, Brian thought.

He took the films out of their over-sized envelope as he went into one of the small workrooms beside the nursing unit. He stabbed two of the plastic sheets under the view-box clamps and switched on the light. Brian traced the skeletal outline of Stevie's little shoulder with his finger to find the area of separation described on the brief report from Radiology.

After making sure that a clavicle strap was put on the boy and leaving instructions for his admission, Brian left for the night. He would make sure that the parents were dealt with when he came back the next day. He wanted to be personally involved in the case. He knew from experience that in a majority of these incidents, the authorities merely gave the parents a slap on the wrist and then returned the child to them, often to be beaten yet again.

That wasn't going to happen this time. Not if he had anything to say about it.

CHAPTER 2

Brian descended the steps to the lower level of Genesis Medical Center, headed for the employee locker room. Genesis was a two hundred and eighty-five bed acute care facility that specialized in OB/GYN and pediatric patients. It was less than ten years old, though, and provided the best atmosphere of all the Lansing hospitals he worked at during the various rotations his residency required. Since he was a pediatric resident, he spent much of his inpatient experience there.

The locker room was empty except for an OB/GYN resident by the name of Mark Duncan, just toweling off after a shower. No Neck he was referred to, or just Neck, because of the fact that the shoulders on his two hundred and sixty pound, six foot five frame started at the back of his head and sloped out at such an alarming angle that buttoning the neck of a regular shirt became virtually impossible. The few dress shirts he owned had been specially tailored to cope with the muscles bulging around his shoulders.

Neck had been an All Big Ten linebacker at Ohio State as a sophomore. He had blown out his left knee twice before abandoning his professional football dreams. Medicine became a new obsession. His choice of OB/GYN as a medical specialty seemed somehow perverted to his football buddies.

Brian himself was six foot one and a hundred and ninety-five pounds but he always felt dwarfed by Neck. Brian had been a pretty good athlete back in high school, but knew he stood as much chance in a fight with Duncan as goose-down in a whirl-wind. After playfully tussling with Neck at a resident picnic and being body slammed to the turf in a remarkably short time, Brian had gone out of his way to make sure Mark Duncan was always his friend.

"On call tonight, Neck?" Brian said.

"Yeah, just cleaning up after a messy one. With a little luck I can catch some z's upstairs. There aren't any others ready to pop very soon that I can see."

"How was this one messy?" Brian said.

"Four hundred and twenty pound mama with a C-section. Had to cut through more layers of fat than I've ever seen before. Hard to imagine a woman that big would have too small a pelvis to accommodate a vaginal delivery. The lady was with child for seven months before she even knew it, if you can believe that. I can't picture any guy impregnating her, or even wanting to. Her husband must have a tool as long as your arm in order to make contact. Not to mention a serious control of his gag reflex. On the other hand he's probably a matched set with her. There's someone for everyone. Part of the Maker's sense of humor."

"How's the baby?" Brian asked.

"Twelve pounds, fourteen ounces. Much bigger and we could make a tight end out of him. If he takes after mama, though, he'll just be the world's largest paperweight. Some kids just don't stand a chance, you know?"

"Yes, I do know," Brian said simply. "Well, see you later, Neck. Take care."

"You too, Brian," he replied.

Brian retrieved his jacket from his locker and headed for the door. The gray tiled floor echoed his footsteps off the walls as he walked down a deserted back corridor. The hall emptied out a single door onto the physicians' parking lot at the rear of the three story white brick building. The November evening was crisp but he didn't put on his coat. His bondo buggy Kharmen

Ghia sat forlornly in a pool of light under a tall goose-necked security lamp, looking a blotchy red. The door creaked open as he got in and fired up the engine. Good for another hundred thousand miles, Brian lied to himself.

The route Brian took from Genesis in East Lansing to his apartment in the northern part of Lansing was relatively quiet at the post-midnight hour. He wended his way through back streets, not being in any mood to dodge the traffic of Michigan State students out late on Grand River Avenue in quest of pizza, beer and hormones on a Friday night.

The ancient Ghia puttered along unenthusiastically but dependably. He could have afforded better but he was saving as much of his resident salary as possible to open his own office when he completed his training in June, just eight months away. Of course there was always the $76,000 in school loans he was paying on each month as well. Brian spent much of his infrequent spare time moonlighting in the various hospital emergency rooms and urgent care centers around Lansing.

He felt the tension knotting his shoulders as he reflected on Stevie Sanderson in the E.R. He had been purposely avoiding those thoughts because of the rage that always lay in wait just beneath the surface. There had been times when the rage had escaped and it was not something Brian could allow anymore.

The Hidden Tree Apartment complex sat sixteen buildings and sixty-four units strong at the end of a winding road that led through a sparsely wooded area several blocks east of where U.S. 127 bisected the city of Lansing. Considering the relative cheapness of the rent, the units were remarkably free of losers. Geezerville it was often referred to because of the number of retirees inhabiting it. Brian knew that his two-bedroom apartment on the second floor would cost him almost three times as much over near the MSU campus.

The Ghia expired reluctantly several seconds after Brian turned off the key, coughing asthmatically, then shuddering a final gasp as Brian got out. A wind had come up and Brian felt its chill deepen his depression. He missed his mother as he did every night. He wasn't a mama's boy; it was just that she was a very special person who had been his best friend for most of his life.

He climbed the interior stairs to his apartment and let himself in. The silence greeted him like a black cloud. He looked at the kitchen clock and decided it was too late to call Cincinnati.

Brian didn't want to call just then, anyway, because he knew his mother would hear the depression he would be trying to hide from her and then she would be concerned for him. Eight months, Brian reminded himself, and then the two of them would open his peds clinic and take care of children and everything would be okay again.

Maybe a snack and Sports Center on the tube would lift his spirits. The refrigerator revealed a wasteland of molding leftovers and bare shelves. Anger bubbled to the surface then was gone. He didn't have the energy to sustain it. He took a quick shower and headed for bed.

He felt overwhelmingly alone. As he lay there in the darkness with his hands behind his head he heard the boy calling out to him for help . . .

. . . "What's going on?" the woman stammered.

"None of your fucking business, lady!" the man spat at her.

With that, he pulled the boy back into the apartment and slammed the door.

The beating went on for only a short time after that. The sudden exposure had sobered the man to the point of making him cautious.

The woman knew what was happening. When she had first moved into the apartment two months before, she had tried to ignore the sounds, to convince herself that it was none of her business. It was getting to her more and more of late, though, to a point where she found herself weeping while trying to shut out the shouting and crying and pain-filled screams. She had used up all of her excuses for doing nothing, but still she hesitated. Several times recently she had been at the point of reaching for the phone to call the police, but then the noise would cease.

She had never seen the boy before, only heard his cries. But now the battered little face, the terrified eyes, haunted her. She tried watching TV but the mindless drivel just added to her oppression. She undressed and attempted sleep, but even a sleeping pill couldn't blot the horror out. By dawn, she was frantic with the need to do something.

All that morning she searched for a solution. It had to be the police. There was no avoiding it. She grabbed her coat and headed for the door because she had to talk to them face to face. The phone was no good. They wouldn't believe she wasn't a meddling, nosey neighbor if she just called.

As she was about to leave, she heard the door slam across the hall. She opened the door a crack and watched the man shamble up the corridor and disappear down the stairs. His ratty looking jacket and greasy baseball cap seemed to indicate he was leaving the building.

It suddenly occurred to the woman that she had to get into the man's apartment. The thought frightened her, sending tremors through her bowels and weakening her knees. She crept cautiously across the hall and pressed her ear against the door. She heard nothing; no sounds came from the little boy. She had to see him, to know if he was all right.

She checked the stairs again, went to the edge and listened carefully. The man must be gone. She went back to the door and tried the knob. Locked. She knocked tentatively, hoping the boy would open the door. She assumed no mother was around since she had never seen any evidence of a woman about the apartment. She knocked again, louder this time. Again no answer.

She descended the three flights of stairs to the building manager's apartment and knocked on the door. Getting no response, she rapped louder and more insistently. Noises of someone stirring inside filtered through the door and then a bleary-eyed, belligerent man opened the door. His hair and shirt were rumpled from sleep. His breath preceded him, a nearly visible yellowish-green miasma that contaminated the air in front of him.

"Yeah?" he said irritatedly.

"Mr. Myers, I need the key to apartment forty-one. The man hired me to clean it on the weekends but he forgot to leave me the key when he left this morning."

"Come on! That no-good bastard didn't really hire you, did he? He's two months behind in his rent. What's he doin' wastin' money to have it cleaned?"

"I don't know anything about the rent, Mr. Myers. I've been cleaning it for the last five Saturdays and he's paid me every time. I'd appreciate it if you'd loan me the key."

"Listen, lady, I'll let you use it on one condition. You tell that shithook if I don't have his rent in my hands by Monday, I'm evictin' him. I hope he don't pay. I'll be glad to see the last of that guy. Drunken bum."

"Okay, I'll tell him. May I please have the key?"

Reluctantly the man disappeared inside. She watched the excess of ingested calories challenging the tensile strength of the man's undershirt as he walked away. She knew there was a Mrs. Building Manager and could not comprehend the union. There would be nothing short of the threat of disembowelment with a rusty spade that would ever make her mate with a base life form like the Manager.

Key in hand, she bustled back up the stairs. She knocked one more time, just to be sure. Still getting no response, she unlocked the door and peeked in. The apartment was dark. Reaching in, she fumbled along the wall for the light switch. Light sprang from the single globe in the middle of the ceiling. She spotted cockroaches scuttling for cover in the kitchen area. Surveying the room, she was appalled at the filthiness. Dirty dishes and clothes were scattered everywhere and the smell of garbage and refuse permeated the place. Revulsion blended with hatred for the man when she thought of the boy sentenced to a childhood with that pig of a man. Pity for the boy brought tears to her eyes.

The boy was nowhere in sight. The woman crossed the apartment to the bedroom, listening as she went for sounds of the man's unexpected return. Flutters of adrenaline pounded at her heart. She was frightened, but she had to see the boy. She had to. Cautiously opening the bedroom door, she found the room dark, except for a few shafts of sunlight coming through tacky old curtains on the window. She switched on the overhead light. A short cry escaped her lips.

"My God! Oh, Sweet Jesus!" she cried out.

The boy was tied to the foot of the bed. Blood had dried and then crusted on his mouth and chin. Red-black streamers of it blended in with the gray, torn tee shirt.

Tears ran down her face as she hurried and knelt beside the little boy. He was scarcely aware she was there. A dull, glazed look had replaced the terror of the night before. His lips were cut and swollen from the blows he had received. She began to untie him, noticing that the circulation had nearly been shut off in the hands, leaving them an ugly purplish hue. The woman felt a sudden savage fury toward the man. She had never known such hatred. It consumed her, leaving her stunned by its intensity.

Holding his bony weightless body, she carried the boy out to the living room and laid him on the filthy, aged couch. Examining the boy's injuries more closely, she knew she had to get clean towels and medication to take care of the cuts and bruises. There was no use looking around in the pigsty that surrounded her. She labored to her feet and hurried across to her apartment. In the bathroom she gathered the items she needed and started back toward the hallway.

Busy with her task she hadn't heard the man return. She heard him now, though, across the hall through the open door. He was shouting, enraged at the boy.

"How'd you get loose, you little shit!" he yelled.

The boy was lying on the couch where the woman had put him.

"I'm gonna tie you up good this time so's you for sure won't get loose," the man said and grabbed the boy by the arm.

The woman had heard enough. She grabbed the baseball bat she kept in the corner nearest the door. She had bought it at the sporting goods store downtown and kept it for protection. The neighborhood was starting to get rundown and a woman living alone was vulnerable to the vermin that inhabited the area. Physically, she was a big woman, five feet seven inches and one hundred seventy pounds, and exceptionally strong from a lifetime of hard work.

Fear and fury blended as she screamed at the man, "You bastard, leave that baby alone! You've hurt him enough!"

The man looked up in surprise and dropped the boy back on the couch. Recognizing her, he screamed, "Hey, you damn bitch! What are you doin' in here? Who d'ya think you are, interferin' in my business? You better get outta here before I kick your fuckin' ass!"

Even at this time of day he had been drinking. The woman saw him coming for her, fists balled up, ready to hit her. Instinctively protecting herself, she struck out at him. Too drunk to dodge the ball bat, the man took the blow on an upraised arm.

He grunted in pain. "Goddamn it!" he yelled at her.

Committed now, the woman swung wildly, flailing desperately, afraid the man would recover enough to grab her. Fear and rage added strength to the clubbing.

One swing hit him in the ear, another flush on the mouth and yet another on the temple, driving his head sideways. Blood spewed from his torn lips as he screamed obscenities at her. His right arm was now useless and he couldn't coordinate himself enough to block all the blows with his left. Finally, unable to retaliate, he fell to the floor, drawing himself into a ball, hoping to avoid any more shots to his head. He pleaded for her to quit, whimpering in his pain.

Breathless and awash with hate, the woman looked down with loathing at the child beater. She swung with all her might at the man's rib cage as he lay curled up before her. The wind gushed out of his lungs as the bat crunched into his side, breaking one of his ribs. He lay flopping soundlessly on the carpet like a beached carp, trying desperately to suck air into his chest.

The woman was trembling, an overload of adrenaline causing her to shake uncontrollably. She had to leave soon before her legs gave out. She looked over at the boy. He was staring down at the man as if burning the sight into his memory. She knew she couldn't leave the boy alone there. Stepping over the man, she lifted the boy tenderly and ran from the apartment. She locked and chained her door, hoping it would be enough if the man tried to get into her apartment.

She staggered across the room and collapsed into the rocking chair, holding the child close for comfort. Realizing the enormity of what she had done and frightened at what the consequences might be, she held the boy, sobbing, rocking and waiting. Her heart felt like it was coming out of her chest. She laid the bat beside her, ready if she needed it again.

The little boy's skinny arm wrapped itself around her neck, holding on for dear life to the first sign of gentleness he had ever known. They remained that way the rest of the afternoon, waiting for the pounding on the door. . . .

CHAPTER 3

The Ghia ground contemptuously and refused to start. Eventually the battery gave up its last spark of life, leaving Brian frustrated, angry and seeing visions of twenty-dollar bills floating at an alarming rate from his wallet to the cash register of a fifty-dollar an hour mechanic. He felt a certain impotence when it came to cars, his mechanical aptitude grinding to a halt shortly after being able to fill the gas tank and changing the oil at a jiffy lube place.

It was Saturday morning and he was looking forward to his workout at the YMCA out on Haslett Road, then a brief stop at Genesis to check on Stevie Sanderson and several other children he had admitted through the E.R.

Brian often went into the hospital on his days off even though it wasn't required. He had a fairly limited social life and no steady girlfriend, although he was a good-looking guy. His sandy blond hair and lean muscled body often had the nurses salivating. There was plenty of sex available in the hospital but Brian wasn't especially interested in the involvement. The title, M.D., frequently acted as an aphrodisiac with many of the female employees. Brian had seen some physicians who were so unattractive they could frighten a rabid dog but their power and income had brought women to their beds in amazing numbers.

Brian had been in love once back in college and it had ended badly. It wasn't time yet to risk himself again. The girl he was looking for was out there someplace waiting. At the right time he would find her.

Brian went back inside his apartment and called a tow truck from a garage that had been recommended to him by one of the other pediatric residents who had heard the Ghia in action. Brian hitched a ride with the tow truck driver to U.S. 127 and got off at the bus stop. He hoped to be able to make enough connections to get close to the Y. After using the Nautilus equipment for an hour, he'd hit the sauna and whirlpool, then head for the hospital.

Maybe when he was done at the hospital, he'd stuff his gym bag in his locker and walk home. It was less than ten miles if he took some short cuts. Maybe grab a bite on the way.

The CATA bus came humming into view fifteen minutes after Brian had propped himself against the bus stop sign. There were only three other people on the bus, Brian noted as he paid the driver and grabbed a seat near the front. Brian sat staring out the window at the gray day. Three giant smokestacks from the Board of Water and Light power plant dominated the skyline just west of the white-domed State Capitol building.

Two stops later Brian found reason to wish he had taken a cab. The door hissed open and two jerk kids got on. One was a Mexican, the other white with a dangling cross earring and a shaved scalp. Baggy jeans drooping beltless halfway down their asses. They were both about Brian's height but thinner. The white kid had a case of acne so severe it looked like he had been sunbathing in a hailstorm. They were loud and obnoxious from the moment they entered the bus, their presence the emotional equivalent of throwing dog feces into a fan.

Brian watched them saunter back down the aisle. They paused by a young black woman who glanced up at them nervously. They sat down directly behind her and began making comments. Brian couldn't hear most of what they said but their tone was obvious, with frequent obscenities surfacing like sulfur bubbles in a pond.

There were bullies everywhere, Brian thought. Sociologists and psychiatrists and ministers could give you plenty of reasons why these people were victims of their circumstances and their parents, but Brian didn't care. He hated their type and could find no excuse strong enough to forgive them. There were right ways and wrong ways and it didn't take a Rhodes Scholar to know the difference.

In a short time the woman got up and came forward a half dozen rows and sat down again. She was barely seated before the human slugs came down the aisle and sat behind her again.

"Hey, puta, you too good to sit by us or somethin'?" the Mexican kid said.

"Yeah, pretty damn insultin'," the white kid added. "You wanna give us a kiss to make up for it?"

The woman looked at Brain, eyes wide like a doe caught in the glare of car's headlights. He nodded her toward the empty seat beside him. Relief flashed across her face as she rose quickly and came toward him. Brian stood and let the woman in past him.

"Hoo, shit! What's this?" the white kid said as the two of them came forward and were about to sit down behind Brian who stood and faced them.

"Sorry, guys, these seats up front are saved for some friends of mine," he said.

"The spook your girlfriend or somethin?" the white kid said.

Brian ignored him and stood in the row behind the woman, protecting her. At the same time the bus came to a halt at the next stop. The doors opened and an elderly man labored on and sat down across the aisle from Brian. The woman in front of Brian suddenly arose and headed for the door. The two toughs decided they would follow.

Brian stepped in front of them, blocking their progress while the woman went down the steps.

"What you doin', asshole?" the Mexican said.

"Let her go, guys. You've had your fun."

"Hey, who the fuck died and left you in charge?" the white kid said.

Without warning, he took a swing at Brian. The kid was a punk and Brian knocked the blow aside then used the kid's momentum to drive his face into the metal bar that framed the back of the seat beside them. The sound of flesh crunching against metal sounded sickening. The kid sat on the floor looking stunned and draining blood from his nose.

Brian turned and watched the Mexican lean over and fumble at his pant leg. When he stood, a six-inch knife blade protruded from his fist, aimed toward Brian's belly. Brian knew he was in trouble. He didn't know any moves to counter a knife thrust. He backed up slowly, looking quickly about him for a weapon. He suddenly felt a hard object tap him on the thigh. When he glanced down, he saw a long barreled flashlight in the bus driver's hand.

Quickly he reached behind him and grasped the flashlight. Just as the Mexican thrust the knife forward at him, Brian brought the club down on the outstretched forearm. He could tell by the cracking sound and the scream of agony from the Mexican kid that he had shattered the radius.

"Ah, you fucker, you broke my arm!" the kid wailed, sitting on the floor, holding his wrist in his lap.

"You want me to call the depot and have them send the cops?" the bus driver said.

"No," Brian replied. "Just go a few more blocks so they don't mess with the woman, then dump them off."

Brian picked up the knife and put it in his gym bag, all the while watching the two kids. The white kid had snot and blood draining from his nose. The Mexican held his broken arm in his lap.

"You don't have to be animals, you know," Brian said to them. "You have a choice."

They ignored him, nursing their wounds and their hatred.

CHAPTER 4

Brian's whole body was trembling from muscle fatigue by the time he got to the hospital. The adrenaline and anger left from the confrontation on the bus caused him to overdo the weights and reps on the Nautilus equipment at the Y and left him exhausted by the time he finished. He took a taxi to Genesis and grabbed some lunch in the cafeteria before going up to the Peds floor.

As he was about to finish, a surgery resident by the name of Stephan Demarco hurried up to the table where Brian was seated.

"Hey, Brian, great, glad you're here. I need a favor. You're just the right guy, no one will be suspicious of you."

"What are you up to, Stephan? You aren't still trying to get even with one of those head nurses, are you? If you are, I don't want any part of it. I'd just get on their list like you are."

"Don't be such a chicken shit, Brian. This is simple stuff. Doesn't have anything to do with Amy, Beth or Diane. Just a little joke on a nurse in PICU. No one will know you're a part of it."

Demarco sat down in the chair beside Brian and carefully revealed the contents of a small paper sack. It was a clear plastic specimen cup with a label containing a name on the side.

"Looks like a urine sample," Brian said, sitting back in his chair, body language distancing him from Demarco.

"It's apple juice. All I need for you to do is sneak it into the lab outbasket in PICU just before I go in."

"What for?" Brian said uneasily.

"Just hang around for a few minutes and you'll see. Thanks a bunch, Brian. See you up there in about ten minutes, okay?"

Not waiting for a reply, he got up and hurried off. Stephan Demarco was addicted to practical jokes, only a few of which were not in serious bad taste. He was also seriously addicted to women. Stephan the Stud, loved females but often used only the brains he had that were surrounded by pubic hair in dealing with them. As a fourth year surgery resident he was thought of as a prime catch by many of the nursing personnel until they realized he was only interested in doing the horizontal mambo and not developing a monogamous relationship. He was a relatively handsome guy who's only real physical flaw was a hairline that was starting further back on his head with each passing year. The expanse of forehead had caused Stephan a problem several months back.

The Amy, Beth and Diane he had referred to were the Head Nurses in Delivery, Gyn Oncology and the Neonatal Intensive Care units. In an incredibly volatile mixture of arrogance and stupidity he had been bedding all three at the same time, believing, in a burst of ignorant optimism, that none of the women would find out about the others' involvement with him. His biggest crime had been to make noises about marriage in order to convince the young ladies to surrender their virtue. The hospital grapevine, of course, travels at the speed of light so it wasn't long before Amy, Beth, and Diane were each in turn plotting Demarco's demise.

Beth got in the first shot one morning when Stephan was just finishing up being on twenty-four hour call in the Surgery Unit. After participating in a five-hour repair of a leaking aneurism, Stephan had fallen fast asleep in the Resident Call Room. Stephan was notorious for sleeping nearly to the point of death when he was exhausted, a trait Beth was relying on. Having prepared herself ahead of time with indelible dyes from the Lab,

Beth had invaded the Call Room and proceeded with her artwork on Stephan's expanding forehead area.

When he awoke five hours later and wandered through the hospital on his way to the locker room, he was met by stares, laughter and pointing fingers. Distressed by the attention he was getting, Stephan darted into a restroom to see if he had serious bed head or blood dripping from his eyes. It was much worse he discovered in the mirror. Beth had used multi-colored stains to paint a flower-like design on his forehead that had the words **AIDS VIRUS** printed below them. Stephan scrubbed furiously at the artwork, nearly peeling skin away but the picture remained. He was forced to wear a ball cap or surgery cap for over a month before the scarlet letters faded.

Amy wasn't far behind. Unfortunately for Stephan, he again fell asleep at the end of a long surgery. Thinking himself safe in the Pediatric Unit, he had crawled into a crib hidden in a back storage closet and curled up for a nap as he had begun to do after the AIDS incident. He had heard the other two women were still after him. A thoughtful young nurse had given him some of her hot cocoa as he had left surgery. The sleeping pill that he had unknowingly ingested took him to an even deeper level of sleep.

The crib where he was napping had a hard plastic top with metal bars that locked into place for the children's protection. Amy had added a few chains and locks to complete the job.

When Stephan awoke in the middle of the night he found himself trapped in the crib, parked inside the hospital laundry, which was closed until morning. Amy had planned well, calling in a favor from one of the other surgery residents, who also happened to dislike Demarco. When surgery had required the on-call resident to be present, the other resident responded. Meanwhile Stephan's beeper kept going off in his mini-prison from which he could not escape. Amy had gotten other nurses on the third shift to page Stephan at fifteen to twenty minute intervals throughout the night. The hospital marketing manager had gotten a picture for the monthly newsletter just before the maintenance man cut away the locks to release Stephan.

Stephan's fear of the third reprisal, this time from Diane, had only slightly modified his behavior, however, as Brian was finding out. If ignorance was bliss, then Demarco was a happy man.

Reluctantly Brian left the cafeteria headed for PICU. He wanted to get rid of his "urine sample" as quickly as possible and distance himself from whatever Demarco was up to. As he walked through the corridors toward the elevator Brian passed nurses, x-ray techs, a housekeeper and a security guard going for lunch. He reflected as he did each day about how much he loved the hospital atmosphere. Regardless of their flaws, there was a feeling that emanated from hospitals that said people were important, that healing was something worth dedicating your life to.

The Pediatric Intensive Care Step Down Unit was located at the end of the north corridor through a set of double doors. There were ten monitored locations that fanned out from the nursing station so that there was line-of-sight location on each patient. There were currently four cribs and three beds filled with sick, injured and dying children. Over-bed monitors displayed the flawed rhythms of the young hearts beating beneath them.

Brian was going to just sneak the apple juice specimen into the Lab outbasket and then go check on Stevie Sanderson but his curiosity got the better of him. The basket was located on the counter in front of the nursing station just inside the double doors from the step down pediatric unit. The only one in the immediate vicinity was Rebecca Bentley the Ward Clerk.

She looked up as he approached. "Oh, hi, Dr. Tanner. Are you on today?"

"No, I was just checking on a couple of patients that came through E.R. last night. Will you get me the chart for Bobby Jacobson?"

"He's doing okay, I guess. Dr. Samuelson was just here. Still want the chart?"

"Yeah, I guess. Just curious about x-rays. Bikes and cars don't mix well, do they?"

"You said it," Rebecca replied.

As she turned around to get the chart from the carousel Brian took Demarco's specimen from where he had been hiding it below counter level and quickly put it in the Lab basket. He took the medical record that Rebecca handed him and strolled away from whatever Demarco was about to pull. Shortly afterward the Head Nurse, Karen Gross, materialized beside him on her way to the nursing station. She frowned slightly as she passed.

"Brian," she said simply.

"Hi, Karen," he replied, feeling like someone who had just robbed a bank with all the video cameras going.

He had been reading the information in the chart he had gotten for only a few minutes before Stephan came through the double doors and into the nursing station. Stephan pulled out a chart and began going through it, stopping at the lab section. He wrote something quickly in it as he stood behind the Ward Clerk.

"Hey, Rebecca, I don't see the lab results on Bed Three over there. The girl with the diabetes we did the valve replacement work on. I wanted a urinalysis done. It was a stat order."

"I don't remember that one," she replied.

"I put it in last night. Are you saying no one put it in?"

"Not that I know of. Maybe it's still in the outbasket."

"Well, check it for me. This is ridiculous."

Rebecca went to the outbasket and came back with the specimen cup that Brian had just placed there.

"I'm sorry, Doctor, but it's still here. I don't know how that happened."

"Holy smokes, someone's in trouble! I need to know that little girl's sugar levels right now."

"Is there a problem, Rebecca?" the Head Nurse said.

"Uh, there don't seem to be any lab results back on Bed Three that Dr. Demarco ordered. The specimen is still here," Rebecca replied.

The head nurse took the specimen cup and went to the counter behind them and put the cup down. With her back to them, she took out her pen and wrote on a slip of paper then came back.

"Well, why don't you just run it down right now, Rebecca," she said. "That extra-stat slip should get it done in a hurry."

"I can't wait that long," Demarco said. "Here, give the thing to me. Fortunately they showed us how to take care of these problems during the lab rotation. There's a way to approximate the sugar content with a simple taste test."

"You're kidding!" Rebecca said. "No way a taste test!"

"Sure it's easy. I'll show you."

Demarco pried the lid off the specimen cup and sniffed the contents like a wine connoisseur, then put it to his lips and drained the cup in one long pull. The look that came over his face was not one that Brian had expected. There was acute distress rather than smug enjoyment.

With that the Head Nurse came up to him with another specimen cup with the lid removed.

"That's amazing, Dr. Demarco. Well, if you can do it I sure can. You'll have to tell me what I expect to taste and how to evaluate the sugar levels."

With that she also drained her cup.

"Interesting. Who'd have ever thought a child's urine would taste like apple juice."

With that Demarco bolted for the restroom located just outside the double doors. They could hear his retching from there.

"How'd you know?" Brian asked them.

"Stephan flaps his lips too much. He's always so pleased with himself. He told someone of his trick and it got back to us.

We've been keeping an eye out for him since then. I must say I'm a little surprised that you were helping him out."

"Sorry about that, Karen," Brian said. "By the way, what was in the cup you switched and gave to him?"

"More apple juice with some salt and other things to change the taste. Also some Ipecac." She laughed at the thought.

"So that's why he's puking," Brian said with a grin.

"Yup, brings things up in a hurry just like it's designed to."

They were all laughing uproarishly when a nurse came quickly through the double doors of the step down unit.

"Oh, good, Dr. Tanner, you're still here. I thought I saw you go through. Hurry, we've got a boy who's getting ready to crash and burn!"

Brian dashed after the nurse, following her into one of the semi-private rooms just down the corridor and up to a crib.

"What have we got?" Brian said hurriedly.

"Five month old boy with RSV Bronchiolitis. Respiration at one hundred a minute, heart rate over two hundred. Oxygen levels are dropping. He's been in a sixty-percent oxygen tent but he's getting worse."

Brian could see the child's obvious distress as he approached. The dyspnea, difficulty in breathing, and grunting respirations were evident. Brian noted the asthma-like symptoms caused by the viral infection. They manifested themselves by constriction of the upper and lower airways in the tiny boy. He was so small that there would be no reserves. The retraction of the boy's body around the lower rib cage and clavicles showed that he was in deep trouble. If something wasn't done and very quickly, he would likely die.

Brian borrowed the nurse's stethoscope and put it to the child's small chest and listened to the decreased air exchange and respiratory wheezing. The boy was turning dusky and cyanotic. In a short time he would go into respiratory arrest.

"Let's get him into PICU! Hurry!" Brian said.

He and the nurse pulled up the side rail to the crib and raced with it into the intensive care unit.

"Karen," Brian said to the Head Nurse, "I'm going to intubate him. Get the stuff will you?"

Karen returned with a peds trach kit and an ambu bag. Another nurse came shortly afterward, pushing a respirator.

"I called the Respiratory Therapist earlier," the first nurse said. "He should be here shortly."

Holding the small face in his hand and careful of the child's throat, Brian inserted the endotracheal tube. When he was finished, Karen attached the ambu bag, which Brian then used to breath for the baby. Karen then got the ventilator ready, with help from the O_2 therapist who had just arrived. Together they ran an arterial line to check the blood gases. Ventilator in place, a tech who had been summoned from radiology ran a portable chest x-ray to make sure the endotracheal tube was situated properly below the vocal cords and above the carina.

The urgency in the air was almost palpable as they worked on the tiny child before them. A life was fluttering at their fingertips and no one was willing to let it go.

"Set the ventilator with a PEEP of four, respiration rate of forty and the oxygen at a hundred percent," Brian said. "Let's see how the little guy responds."

They continued to work on the child for nearly half an hour before the color began to return to his skin and there were overt signs that he was recovering. Brian was satisfied with the boy's progress as he backed away from the crew surrounding the infant. The tension that had been surrounding them began to ease.

"Who's the attending, Karen?" Brian said.

"Dr. Addison isn't it, Gayle?" Karen replied.

"Yes," said the R.N. who had come for Brian.

"Give him a call for me and let him know what we've done, will you? I'll be out on the peds floor for a while. That's where I was headed before I was so rudely interrupted," Brian said in jest.

"Lousy timing for sure," the respiratory therapist said. "I was right in the middle of a good sandwich when I got the call on this little turkey. I don't want some celestial discharge to ruin my appetite. Tell the kid that."

"Pretty inconsiderate of the him all right," Gayle, the R.N., said.

"Probably just trying to get attention is all. Most likely turn out to be a serious brat when he grows up," the Head Nurse said.

Brian was about to throw in another comment when they heard an angry voice to their rear.

"Hey, that's my son you bastards are making big jokes about! What the hell kind of people are you anyway?" a man said.

"You're the father?" Brian said to a young man facing him, hands on hips.

"Damn right I am," he replied.

"You really shouldn't be in here," Brian said.

"Yeah, so I can't overhear you making jokes about my son dying, eh?"

Brian put his hand on the man's elbow and guided him toward the door.

"Let's talk in the hall, sir, so we won't disturb your son."

Together they walked down the corridor that bisected the step-down unit.

"What's your name, sir?" Brian said to the man who appeared to be in his mid twenties. His well-worn work boots and jeans spoke of manual labor.

"Bill Jenkins," the man replied, face still an angry red.

"I'm Brian Tanner. Let me tell you what you were hearing back there, Mr. Jenkins. There isn't anyone who cares more for these kids than we do. That's why we chose the careers we did. You just have to understand how incredibly overwhelming it is to have some child's life in your hands. Whenever a child dies, it eats at your insides. We dilute the tension in cases like your son's by inserting our own callous humor. It's the way we deal with it.

If we couldn't rid ourselves of the fear of that baby dying, we'd have to look for a different job. Can you understand that?"

The man looked slightly mollified. "Well, all right, but it just doesn't seem right somehow."

"I understand and I apologize for your discomfort."

"Is Scotty going to be all right?"

"I think so. We're doing everything we can. He's hooked up to the ventilator so he won't have to do his own breathing until he's better. They'll watch him every second. Okay?"

"All right. Thanks." The man held out his hand and Brian shook it.

"Why don't you hang out in the waiting room for awhile until Mrs. Gross, the Head Nurse, comes out and gets you? It won't be long."

Brian patted the man on the shoulder before going back in PICU to give some last minute instructions. After doing that, he went toward the general Peds wing to check on Stevie Sanderson. He approached the Ward Clerk seated at the desk and asked for Stevie's chart.

"I'm sorry, Dr. Tanner, you just missed him. The father came and got him and checked him out without discharge orders. I feel bad for the boy; the dad seems like a real loser. Cussed us all out and told us to get his kid, he was taking him home."

"How long has he been gone?" Brian said.

"Just got on the elevator. Melinda's taking the boy down in a wheelchair. The guy didn't even want that but we told him it was hospital policy and that we'd call Security if he didn't cooperate."

Brian hit the stairs running, heading down the three floors to the discharge area. At first he thought he had missed them but then he saw a nurse with a wheelchair and a man walking behind them as they rounded a corner into the discharge lobby. Brian ran to catch them. He looked at the child in the wheelchair to make sure it was Stevie before he blocked their path. The little boy looked all shrunken and frightened.

"Oh, hi, Dr. Tanner. What's up?" Melinda said.

"Hey, who the hell are you, gettin' in our road?" said the man accompanying the child. He was unshaven, greasy hair matching oily, torn jeans. About Brian's height but heavier.

"Are you the father?" Brian said.

"None of your business. Get the hell outta our way."

"No one discharged your son, sir. He needs further attention."

"He'll get it at home. I didn't ask no one to put him in this place."

"On the contrary, you're probably the one who put him here." Brian's temper was nearing the surface and he fought to keep it under control.

"Listen asshole, I don't know or do I give a rat fuck who you are but get outta the way before I move you," the man said.

"I wouldn't even try it if I were you," Brian said. "I'm not some helpless little boy that you can beat on. If you don't take that boy back upstairs, I'll make sure you're prosecuted for child abuse."

The man made a big mistake at that point and came around the wheelchair, apparently to remove Brian from their path. Had he known Brian, he would have realized that the last thing you did was touch him in anger. He put his hand on Brian's chest and gave him a shove. At that point Brian's temper blew. He grabbed handfuls of the man's windbreaker, flannel shirt and chest hair, wheeled him around and body-slammed him into the wall. The man's head bounced forward and the air gushed from his lungs.

"You son-of-a-bitch!" he gasped at Brian. "I'll fucking sue your ass!"

Before Brian could reply, he heard the cry of alarm from the nurse. He also spotted several people walking toward them. The man struggled to get free but was held captive against the wall.

"I want you to leave your son here," Brian said to the man. He needs the care."

"Kiss my ass! Let me go or I'll have the cops on you."

"Sure you will," Brian said.

Brian felt a hand on his arm and turned his head to see the nurse, Melinda, looking up at him.

"Dr. Tanner, should you be doing this?" she said.

His shoulders slumped forward and he reluctantly released the man.

"No, probably not," he said. He turned back to the man. "You won't change your mind?"

"Get fucked!" the man said and pushed past Brian and up to his son in the wheelchair.

Brian followed them through the exit to the covered portico where an aged Chevy Caprice was parked. Brian recognized the mother sitting in the passenger side. She got out as her husband approached with the wheelchair. Brian watched her eyes widen with alarm as she spotted him. She got quickly out of the car and helped Stevie from the wheelchair and into the back seat of the car. Brian watched the little boy wince as his arm hung helplessly in the clavicle strap.

"Don't hurt that boy again," Brian said loudly to both parents. "I'm warning you!"

The father shoved the empty wheelchair violently across the walk and into the side of the building. It bounced away and tipped on its side. As the man got in the driver's side he gave Brian the finger. Smoke from squalling tires blended with blue-black exhaust as the man sped off.

Brian pounded his fist into the window of the door they had exited from, sending flashes of pain up his arm. He hit it a second time to punish himself. He should have been able to save the boy. Brian stared off toward the south, seeing nothing but the debt he still owed . . . .

. . . . The woman awoke with a start, clasping the boy instinctively to her. For a few moments she was disoriented, not comprehending how the boy came to be there. As the sleep evaporated from her mind, she began to understand. Glancing quickly at the door, she noted that the chain was still in place. She half expected to see it kicked open, the man forcing his way in to wrest the child away. The pale yellow light coming in the front window told her that the sun was disappearing for the day.

The longer she sat there, the more uneasy she became. She had to do something, anything. She couldn't just sit there, waiting for the pounding on the door. She would deal with that when the time came. Not wanting to wake the boy, she got quietly to her feet and placed him on the couch. What a frail little bundle he was! No flesh, just sunless skin tightened by hunger. She wished she were a man. She'd go back across the hall and beat the hell out of that bastard again. Hatred came surging up afresh.

She was afraid for the boy. How could she prevent that monster from getting hold of the child again? It would just be more of the same. She'd have to take the poor, abused little thing to the police to show them what had happened to him. She wouldn't even wash the blood off his face.

She left the boy on the couch and went to put on her coat. Cautiously she unlocked the door and opened it a crack to peer across the hall. Strangely, the door to the man's apartment was wide open. She listened carefully for some sound, but heard nothing. She moved closer, curiosity slowly overcoming her fear.

Moments of indecision passed. She went back to the couch and looked down at the child. His eyes were open. Apparently he had awakened while she was checking the hall. He was staring at her with fear and confusion. The woman could almost see the scars on the little boy's soul. Under the best of circumstances it would be hard to repair the damage.

"I'll be back in a second, honey. Hazel has to go out for just a little bit. Don't be afraid. I'll be right back. Okay? I'll lock the door so you'll be safe."

Securing the door behind her, she stole slowly across the hall, key held ready in her sweaty hand in case she had to get back into her apartment in a hurry. Cautiously she peered around the edge of the door. The room projected an air of abandonment. The pigsty was essentially intact but certain things were missing. The portable TV she had noticed before was no longer on the battered coffee table.

Hazel entered the room and listened. Not a sound except for her own nervous breathing. It seemed evident that the man was gone, not just for the day, but for good. In spite of the appearance of abandonment, though, she still needed to be sure. Moving quietly, she opened the bedroom door and peeked in. Dust motes floated on stiletto rays of light piercing the cracked blind. Dresser drawers hung open, completely empty. She went through the bedroom, looked in the closet then checked the bathroom. Nothing remained that belonged to the man. The only things left in the bedroom were two small, dirty-gray tee shirts, a tiny, torn pair of underwear and a little pair of infant sized socks that did not match. The blankets on the floor told her where the boy slept at night. Sorrow tore at Hazel's throat and tears sprang to her eyes. She could only guess what he had lived through.

She turned and headed back to her apartment. An idea was beginning to take shape in her mind. At first she rejected the thought, but it came back unbidden. The more she examined it, the more plausible it sounded and the more excited she became. It appeared as if the brute was gone for good. The humiliation of being beaten by a woman, or the chance to be rid of the boy, may have prompted the leaving. Who knew? She prayed that he was gone forever.

But if he was gone, what would she do with the boy? Taking him to the police was not a good idea. They'd either try to find the father, or put the boy in a foster home. It didn't seem likely that they'd let her keep him, a single fortyish woman with a little boy. Not likely at all. But the more she thought about it, the more she wanted the boy. He needed her but she needed him just as much. God had sent them to each other.

Hazel was starting to feel the beginnings of a mid-life crisis. In her mind she was already an old maid. No man had ever come along who bothered to look beyond her homely exterior to see the person who lived behind it. She often felt desperate at the thought of growing old alone. A few men had passed through her life. One or two might have married her, but they didn't meet her standards. They were the kind who would sit around all the time in their underwear, drinking beer, watching TV and hollering for her to hurry up with the damn supper.

Hazel was a big woman and not remotely attractive. She had thin, brownish-blonde hair, beginning to go gray. She wore it brushed around and pinned neatly back out of her eyes. She had the vaguest suggestion of a mustache, which she hated, but not enough to use a depilatory cream. She carried what is diplomatically referred to as an ample bosom. They had been called tits when she was younger, but now she sadly acknowledged that they had turned into a bosom.

Hazel had been alone since she was seventeen, after her father had been killed in an auto accident. Her mother had earlier died of cancer when Hazel was eleven. Hazel had loved her father dearly and his death left a giant void in her life. She had no close relatives and her father's insurance wasn't enough to live on for long. She only had a high school education and no skills so the only jobs she could get didn't pay much and were usually physically demanding. She had been a waitress, a checkout clerk at a super market and a saleswoman at a cut-rate shoe store. She had worked at a ton of other jobs that she preferred to forget. She was often frustrated, a woman of some intelligence and initiative forced to do scut work for a living.

For the last eight years, though, she had found her niche in life. She had gotten a job as a nurse's aide at St. Thomas

Memorial, one of the larger hospitals in the city. She worked in the oncology unit, taking care of the cancer patients. It was a sad, ugly place to work, with patients rotting and dying in too great a number. But she stayed there, year after year. She didn't have anyone of her own to love so she expended all of her caring on the patients. Changing bedpans, sheets, dressings, soiled gowns, whatever it took to help the people live and die with dignity, she did with such affection that each person felt better just by her presence.

She longed for someone of her own to love, but lately she had given up hope of ever finding him. Some mornings she would wake from a dream in which her husband was holding her and telling her how much he cared for her. Sometimes children were in the dreams, sitting on her lap or just playing on the floor as she watched them. When the dream faded as she awoke, the sadness was almost more than she could bear.

When Hazel unlocked and opened the door to her apartment, the boy was no longer on the couch where she had left him. He was huddled in a corner, watching her, his arms wrapped firmly around the baseball bat.

She went to him, knelt down and looked into his eyes. They were blue-gray, surrounded by purple. He began to whine and cringe, a cornered animal. He had no idea what to expect.

"Give Hazel the bat, honey. We won't need it again. That man has gone away and I'm going to take care of you. You won't see him ever again." Hazel prayed she was right. She would do everything in her power to make sure.

Reluctantly the boy gave up the bat as she gently pulled it from his grasp. She picked him up and put him on the ledge that was her hip. She noticed again how pitiful he was. She headed immediately for the kitchen. She would begin by healing the body; his mind was going to take much longer.

She started to say something to him again and suddenly realized that she didn't know what to call him.

"What's your name, honey?" she asked softly

He looked at her without comprehension.

"Your name. What is it?" Pointing to herself, she said, "My name is Hazel. What is yours?" She repeated and pointed at him.

Understanding came to him. He pointed to himself and said, "Little Shit."

Hazel was taken aback. "No baby, that's not your name. It can't be."

The boy nodded and repeated, "Little Shit."

Shaking her head sadly, Hazel carried him with her into the kitchen, put him on the counter near her and began to fix something to eat. Reassuringly she placed a large-fingered hand on the bony, blue-veined leg hanging over the edge. His gray, yellow stained underwear sagged with age.

As she began to fry the bacon and eggs, she thought about a name for the boy. The only man she had ever loved and respected had been her father. She was sure he would have been pleased to know she wished to pass his name on to this forlorn little creature.

She turned to the boy and said, "I don't think Little Shit is a very good name for such a nice little boy. How about if I call you Brian? Brian Tanner." She repeated the name, savoring the sound. "My dad's name was Brian and he'd want you to use it."

Telling Brian about her dad, Hazel failed to notice that the eggs were frying to a crisp. By the time she turned back to them, they were ruined. Disgustedly she threw them in the trash pail under the sink and returned to the refrigerator for more. She turned around to see that Brian had jumped down from the counter and was rooting in the garbage pail for the burned eggs. She ran to him in horror, grabbing his hand as he was stuffing the blackened remnants into his mouth. "You don't have to do that, baby! Hazel will fix more."

The boy perceived the sudden grabbing as hostility and recoiled in fear. A cry came to his lips and he tried to run.

Gently she held him, enfolding him in her ample bosom. "You don't ever, ever have to go hungry again, honey. I'll feed you so good, you'll just bust all your buttons."

Feeling his need to flee subside, she gave him a gentle hug and put him back on the counter and started the eggs again. She gave him a glass of milk and a cookie to stay his hunger. Milk dribbled out of the corners of the glass and down his chin as he hastily drank.

Brian didn't understand what was happening. The man was gone and this big, gentle woman was here. She had given him the first affection of his life, but he was still scared.

He had been afraid for so long, he didn't know how not to be. In a way, Brian was lucky that he could function at all. Inside his wrecked little body was a fighter, though, a spirit that had been too tough to stamp out. The mental resources he had needed to survive were exceptional. But, Hazel had gotten to him just in time.

The bacon, eggs, toast, jelly, orange juice and milk were dazzling to his tongue. He ate more than his stomach could cope with and he vomited the whole thing up a half hour later.

CHAPTER 5

The Medical Arts Center, or The MAC as everyone called it, is a medical education corporation located at the southern edge of Michigan State University in East Lansing. It is a cooperative venture of the various hospitals in the area along with the College of Human Medicine at MSU. The purpose of The MAC is to provide education and training to MSU med students and nearly a hundred residents specializing in Family Practice, Surgery, OB/GYN, Psychiatry and Pediatrics.

All the administrative offices and program directors were located at The MAC, which is where Brian was headed on Tuesday morning. Monday he had received a phone summons from the Peds secretary requiring his presence at the office of Don Santonio, M.D., the Peds program director, at precisely 10:30.

Santonio was an aloof man who seldom involved himself in the day-to-day activities of his residents. A summons to his office was never for the purpose of talking about the Detroit Pistons need for a center or the Lions lack of coaching skills. He was, however, an outstanding physician and teacher with a national reputation for running an excellent peds program. Brian had felt lucky in getting one of the slots available through the annual residency-matching program, even though it took him away from his home in Cincinnati where he had gone to college and med school.

Brian arrived for his appointment at 10:25. Peds residents were never late for appointments with "Saint Tony" as he was called behind his back. His secretary ushered Brian into the office and closed the door behind him. Santonio ignored Brian for a few moments as he gazed through a medical record sitting on the desk in front of him. He was a rather diminutive man who compensated for his total baldness with a full beard and mustache. The effect was as though his hair had been sucked from his scalp and deposited on his face, which was dominated by a nose that kindness would describe as substantial. His ex-wife, on the other hand, often informed her friends she used to park her BMW in one side of it and a snowmobile in the other.

He looked up at Brian and reached for a single piece of paper on the corner of his pathologically neat desk. He held it up for Brian to see.

"Do you know what this is, Dr. Tanner?" he said.

Brian shook his head. "No," he replied.

"This is a hospital incident report describing a severe case of rectal cranial reversal," Santonio said.

Brian furrowed his brows in question. "I'm not sure what you mean, Dr. Santonio."

"It says here you had your head lodged firmly up your ass last Saturday."

The light went on and Brian nodded. "The father," he said simply.

"What the hell were you thinking, putting your hands on the man like that?"

"He wouldn't leave his son there. I believe the boy has been abused by his parents and I wanted him to have at least a few days to be . . . free."

"There are proper ways to handle these things, Doctor. This sure as hell isn't one of them. If you take to beating up on every parent you suspect of child abuse, you'll unfortunately be a very busy man. Busy and ineffective. You'll also wind up in court and probably out of the profession before you're thirty, which, in your case, is only a year or two away." He paused, gathering wind for his sails. "I won't have it, Brian! You're one of the best and brightest residents I've seen. Besides that, you really care. You're not in medicine for money or power or prestige. You will touch a lot of lives before you're through and I won't let you screw that up."

"I'm sorry, Dr. Santonio. I just wanted to help the boy."

Santonio handed the incident report to Brian.

"What do you want me to do with this?" Brian said.

"Down at the bottom there's a place for recommendations for follow-up to the incident being reported. You'll notice a time and a person's name written there. You have an appointment with a social worker at Genesis by the name of Kristin Grey. She's an MSW with a background in handling child abuse cases. The *right* way."

"I've seen the *right* way before, Dr. Santonio, and the abuse goes right on happening. The courts and all those social worker types don't even make a dent in the problem. Sometimes they just make things worse."

"It must be difficult walking with your head so deeply imbedded in your anal orifice, Dr. Tanner. Keep that appointment. That's an order. She's a good-looking broad. It'll be worth the trip just for that. She'll be giving me progress reports on you so work with her with the concept in mind that you may learn something."

"But . . ." Brian said.

Santonio waved him away and turned his attention to the medical record in front of him. Brian turned and walked angrily out of the office.

Kristin Grey looked at the carbon copy of the incident report and tried to think what she would tell Dr. Tanner when she met him at two o'clock. She felt uneasy with the assignment, not knowing what kind of person he was. She was used to the often overbearing attitude of physicians but hadn't seen any of them resort to violence as Tanner had.

The report stated that Dr. Tanner had grabbed a man and slammed him against the wall because the man wouldn't allow his son to stay in the hospital. She looked at two other reports, one from the E.R. and one from the peds floor. Both were requests for follow-up on suspected child abuse on a Stevie Sanderson, the son of the man Dr. Tanner had assaulted. Kristin had immediately passed the information along to the State Department of Protective Services but as yet had gotten no results from them.

Dr. Santonio wanted his resident to understand how the system worked so that he would not involve himself so directly in these child abuse cases. She would use the Sanderson boy as an example to show Dr. Tanner what would happen if he handled things correctly. The intercom line on her phone interrupted her thoughts.

"Yes, Marian?" she said to her secretary.

"Mrs. Harper is here and wants to see you."

Kristin glanced over at her schedule. "Marian, I don't have her down. Was I supposed to see her?"

"No, she just stopped by to talk to you."

"All right. I'm expecting Dr. Tanner in fifteen minutes. If I'm not through with Mrs. Harper by then, please ask him to wait."

Shortly the door to her office opened and an attractive woman in her mid-twenties came in. When they had first met, Kristin was surprised to find that Joyce Harper was a woman not only living on welfare but also perched precariously on the edge of sanity. Joyce was bright, articulate and came from a privileged background but was so emotionally stressed that each day became an overwhelming struggle. If she didn't start show-ing more progress away from her suicidal thoughts, Kristin knew she would need to refer her to a psychiatrist for more intensive therapy. With her masters in social work, there was only so much she could do to help a patient.

Joyce had been adopted when her parents were in their fifties. Her father had been a judge and Joyce suspected that he had somehow paid big money and pulled some strings to get her on the baby black market. Her father had adored Joyce and she had felt the same in return but then he died of a heart attack when she was only fourteen. That left her at the mercy of a rich but domineering aging mother who hated her adopted daughter.

Some inner craving for failure had mated Joyce to a seldom employed, drug -dealing alcoholic who was currently doing time in Jackson Prison. Joyce lived on food stamps and public assistance in order to raise her two daughters, ages five and two. There had been a third child but she had given him away. She received no support from her mother, either money or emotional.

Kristin motioned for Joyce to have a seat in the chair beside her.

"How have you been, Joyce? I'm sorry you had to cancel our last session. It's good to see you." Kristin said.

"Ray's getting out," Joyce said without preamble.

"How do you feel about that?"

"I think that life will not be worth living for me and the girls. I thought sure they'd keep him in there longer. It would have given me a few more year's of peace anyway."

"Have you thought about moving away?"

"He'd find us. He said he'd kill me if I left him. He would too."

Joyce was looking inward and seeing mostly darkness.

"I went out with him to spite my mother, no not my *mother*, that bitch who raised me. Then he wouldn't let me leave and now I'm trapped until I die." She paused. "Is it hard to buy a gun?" she said.

"Killing him isn't the answer. Why don't you let me put you in touch with an attorney? He'll counsel you for free on your options."

Joyce looked further inward and all the light was gone. She stood up.

"There are no options, Miss Grey," she said and walked out.

"Wait, Joyce, let me help you!" Kristin said.

Joyce ignored her and left the office without a backward glance. Kristin knew that someone would likely die if Joyce couldn't find some reason to hope. She could potentially kill her husband, herself and the two girls. Kristin should call the police but they would probably not be any help. No "crime" had been committed yet.

There was a psychiatrist, Sarah Stewart, at the Medical Arts Center to whom she occasionally referred patients but first she had to get Joyce to agree to see the woman. Kristin looked at her schedule for the rest of the day and saw that she had the evening free. Since Joyce was without a phone, Kristin knew she'd have to go to her house in order to contact her. It would be better to see her in person anyway. Kristin wanted to see how the girls were. When Joyce had first been referred to Kristin, she had confessed to neglecting her daughters, often forgetting to fix their meals.

Kristin's heart went out to the children who were already victims. Sometimes Kristin cared too much, although most of her acquaintances thought of her as aloof. She was a thoroughly professional counselor who seldom mingled with fellow employees. The few people she allowed to get close found her to be a warm, gentle, fascinating woman. She presented a protective facade to most people because on the whole she didn't trust, or respect, much of humanity.

Her distrust was rooted in her childhood. When she was only fourteen, the father she adored walked out one day to live with another woman. All the years that she had known and loved her father had not prepared her for his betrayal. He was always there, then one day he wasn't. She thought he had loved her mother. Certainly, he must have loved his daughter too much to leave. But he moved out one Saturday and she understood from that day on that you couldn't possibly know what lurked behind another person's eyes. Smiles and lies, hand in hand.

Wisdom attained later in life told her that he had tried to make it up to her because in fact, he did love her. He spent most of his weekends with her, and sometimes during the week, but she never allowed herself to get close to him. She saw how it hurt him, and she was glad. Many years later she would forgive her father and love him again but they were wasted years caused by his perfidy and her stubbornness.

Kristin began to miss school at every opportunity and her grades dipped alarmingly close to failing. She played at drugs, drank and stayed out partying sometimes till dawn. She would come dragging home and her mother would be wide eyed in terror that something had happened to her daughter. Her mother was unable to help Kristin because she was struggling herself. She had been utterly dependent on her husband for everything. Now she was adrift, learning to deal with life on her own. There were fights, angry words and days when Kristin didn't come home at all.

By pure accident her mother did something that helped Kristin find a source of joy and self-fulfillment. She knew that her child was suffering and tried to find a diversion for her. She enrolled Kristin in a contemporary dance class at the YMCA. Kristin had resisted the idea but understood that her mother was trying to help and so she finally consented.

From the moment Kristin stepped into the studio, she knew she belonged there. She didn't know why, couldn't understand the feeling of comfort that came over her. From the first clumsy steps, dancing became her fever, her passion.

She allowed little else into her life after that. She became a protégée of the dancing instructor, practicing every day three to four hours after school. In the summer the sessions escalated to five and six hours. It was often agonizing drudgery. Muscles cried in agony. Blisters terrorized. Lungs burned. Sweat poured. She seldom minded. The results were totally fulfilling. When she was able to perform, she could, for a brief moment, be someone else.

The angry teen slowly became a young woman who took value from each moment. A tender person, Kristin would be depressed for days if she accidentally killed a bird when it flew into the windshield of her car. She could never bring herself to destroy anything on purpose, even insects. When she was eighteen, she decided to become a vegetarian so that she would not be responsible for the death of any animal.

In time she went to college. She continued with her dancing, but majored in sociology to have something to fall back on when she couldn't dance anymore. When that time came, she wanted a profession that would enable her to do something to help people.

Toward the end of college, she became exposed to higher and higher levels of dancing and suddenly realized that she would never be good enough to dance professionally. She knew she could have made it on the fringes but never as the star and she couldn't stand mediocrity. She worked with increased dedication, but the competition in beauty and athletic ability was just too great.

The feeling of failure and lost dreams left her devastated and rootless. The center of her existence for the past eight years was not going to be her future. Kristin realized she had squandered away much of her youth. She had isolated herself within the protective cocoon of the dancing mystique and never really experienced other things in life. She did not begrudge the time spent in dancing, however. The moments had been a joy, but she had done nothing else. She had no close friends, had never traveled, except to dance, never had a lover; so many things that she had missed. She was an incomplete person.

In the space of one short year, she made up for lost time. At first it was difficult coming out of her shell, but she worked at it. She made many acquaintances and a few close friends but it was in the area of sex that she had the greatest revelation. She discovered that she loved sex. After a crude, strained first attempt she found that it was incredibly exciting. She had always sublimated sexual stirrings partly because dancing required all her emotions, and partly a subconscious reaction to her father. In the midst of her sexual awakenings she discovered something disturbing. She did not trust men.

The first few times with a man were always the best. Lying skin to skin after exploring the newness of each other's bodies; discovering the nooks and crannies; finding the areas that made you arch your back and moan with pleasure; those were the moments to remember. Before she was done, many men had enjoyed her favors, each for only a brief time. The result was always the same. She quickly grew bored with them. She came to the conclusion that women were smarter, tougher and in general more complete than men. She enjoyed using men but didn't particularly want to know them.

There had been one brief flare when she thought she was in love. The wide receiver on the football team read poetry to her and seemed actually to have something intelligent to say. They walked hand-in-hand across the campus, made love at night in the arboretum under a pine tree or at the beach behind a sand dune. She would laugh later when she shook pine needles or sand out of her panties. His body was so beautiful; long and lean and it felt like he would crush her like a gnat when he had an orgasm.

She never knew what happened. One day it was a flame and the next it was an ash; joy one minute and then just sand in her crotch. He kept coming around like a lost puppy but she made more and more excuses not to see him. One day he stayed away and she was relieved.

Was it possible to really love someone? Was there some flaw in her that prevented her from honestly caring for one man forever? After the first excitement, was everyone going to be just another human who had bad breath in the morning and farted when he thought you weren't listening? She wanted so much to love someone, to want to always be near him, to just sit and talk with him by the hour. But that only happened in books, didn't it?

During her senior year in college, she completed her major in sociology. Then she became frightened by the prospects of survival in a world outside dancing. The fear led to the most inexplicable and disastrous event of her life. Her self-confidence left her and in a few short months she screwed up the following five years of her life. She often looked back on this series of decisions and screamed silently to herself.

Her dancing was gone. She had replaced it with a career in sociology. She couldn't make the transition in her head; thus she was afraid for her future. Could she handle life in the real world by herself?

At this low point she met Ted. She no longer believed in love, and he was a nice guy. After graduation she agreed to live with him while she looked for a job. She grinned wryly at her inconsistency, a woman believing in the superiority of females winding up depending on a man.

He kept saying, "Kristin, one of these days we're going to have to get married," and then one day they were. She looked around and didn't understand how it had happened.

It never worked from the beginning. He was still a nice guy but he was always out with his buddies, never with her. Eventually she got her Masters from the University of Michigan then a job with the State Department of Social Services. Her self-respect and independence returned very quickly. Strange, the more independent she became, the more Ted wanted to be around her. He consciously changed himself to be what he thought she wanted him to be. The more Ted changed, the less she respected him. It was a no-win situation for both of them.

Because she was a truly gentle person, it took Kristin four long years to be rid of Ted. Toward the end, she was seldom at home. She always had work to do, working with hookers in drug rehab or poor lost children caught in the foster care maze. She would come home late at night and he would be there waiting and wondering what he could do to make her care for him again.

A tear dribbled down his cheek the night she told him she was leaving.

"Do you really have to go, Kristin?"

"Yes, I can't spend a lifetime like this."

"But why? What can we do to fix things?"

"Nothing will change, Ted, and I just don't give a damn anymore."

She moved out a week later. She found an apartment where she could keep her two cats and begin to explore her new freedom. It felt wonderful! It was so good to have just herself again, answering to nobody, to come and go as she pleased without feeling guilty, to cook only for her own taste. For a long time, she would come back to her rooms and read and eat cheese and grapes and nuts and sip wine, then go to sleep, happily alone.

In the four years of marriage to Ted, she had let her body get out of shape. Her long beautiful dancer's legs had softened and her firm little buttocks and stomach sagged alarmingly. One day as she got out of the shower she looked at herself appraisingly and did not like at all what she saw.

That afternoon, she bought running shoes and appropriate apparel. Early the next morning she was on the streets. She ran a mile and thought she would die. The body, which had once worked out in dancing class for five and six hours a day, had gone away, and left behind an old woman's frame. She became obsessed with the need to find the old Kristin and bring her back. She wanted again to experience the joy of muscles responding in the old way, to feel the sweat gluing her hair to her forehead and to listen to her lungs grabbing great hunks of air without coughing or gasping. She ran early every morning and danced in her apartment every night. The music would take her on flights of ecstasy that often left her laughing and crying from the pure joy of it all. It was not too long before she looked in the mirror and saw Kristin smiling back at her. She took off her panties and bra and examined what she saw. She smiled and turned away. "Not bad, Kristin, not bad at all," she had told her reflection.

The people at work noticed her metamorphosis. Some of the women were concerned for her when they learned that she ran by herself through the city streets early in the morning.

"Any creep that wants to rape me better be darned fast," she retorted. "And by the time he catches me, he'll be so tired he won't be able to do anything about it."

Soon after her rejuvenation, she began looking for another job. She wanted to look at a different set of walls for a change and listen to some new people. And the foster children she worked with were tearing her heart from her chest. The courts were often incompetent and many of the foster parents greedy savages.

Reading the want ads one Sunday, she noticed that Genesis Medical Center was in need of a Director of Social Services. The position and the money would definitely be a step up. She sent them her resume`.

Kristin got the job with surprising ease. She received the distinct impression that the Vice President who talked to her was glad to get a qualified candidate so he would not have to interview anyone else. The first likely person was going to get the job. She just happened to be it.

Kristin sensed that the position became hers officially the first time she crossed her legs. The poor guy had a hard time keeping eye contact from that moment on. She was irritated. During her working career, she had gone to great lengths to downplay her sexual attractiveness. She wanted to be treated as a professional person, not just a sexy broad. She always wore suits with jackets that covered her bottom and blouses that buttoned at the neck and disguised the fullness of her breasts. Her long, luscious, dark-brown hair was always twisted up in a bun at the back of her neck.

The Vice President wasn't fooled. He liked what he saw. The face looking back at him was intriguing. You couldn't call it beautiful, but there was something about it. If you examined it feature by feature, you didn't come away with the right impression. The nose was too big, the upper lip curved up in a bow to reveal a little too much tooth and there was a scar marring the forehead. The eyes were gray-green, magnetic in their long lashed beauty. As a whole the face did something that the parts themselves did not. It was one of the most appealing faces he had ever seen and he could not explain why. There was absolutely no question about the legs. When she crossed them, his whole train of thought had been derailed.

Kristin walked out of the Vice President's office with the job. Two weeks later she came to work at the hospital.

CHAPTER 6

"Kristin, Dr. Tanner is here to see you," Marian informed her over the phone.

"Ask him to come in, will you?"

Brian entered the office, shook hands out of a sense of politeness and sat down. She could tell from the expression on his face and the way he slumped back in the chair that he didn't want to be there.

She had seen him only a few times since she had been at Genesis and that was from a distance. She had known his name because the nurses sitting at her table in the cafeteria had practically slobbered all over themselves when he walked by. He was wearing a Cincinnati Reds sweatshirt and jeans at the time, just as he was now in her office.

"Does Dr. Tanner have a nice ass or what?" one of the nurses had offered that day.

"What's the deal with him anyway?" a second woman had said. "There are women in this place who come on to him so hard their faces almost bleed. Any more overt and they'd have neon signs on their boobs flashing, "SCREW ME! SCREW ME!"

"He isn't gay is he? God, that'd be a serious waste of horse flesh," a third had commented.

Kristin had been just leaving so she hadn't heard any conclusions about Brian Tanner's sexual preferences.

She looked at him sitting across from her with his little pouty look and agreed that it would indeed be a serious waste of horseflesh if he was gay. At least to the female population it would be. Kristin made no judgments about people's sexual orientation.

She knew he was over six feet tall because she herself was fairly tall at five feet nine. He had shoulders that seemed all the broader because she could see that he hadn't succumbed to the paunchiness some men acquired after high school. His sandy blond hair was well past time for a haircut.

"Would you like to tell me about what happened the other morning with the father," she said, getting right to the reason for their meeting.

"Look, Mrs. Grey, . . .,"

"It's Miss Grey," Kristin informed him.

"Okay, Miss Grey, I don't want to waste your time and mine. Let's just assume I had a moment of bad judgment and that now I've seen the light. You tell Dr. Santonio that I'm a big boy now and that I won't do it again."

"You're not wasting my time, Doctor. If I can help you understand how we handle child abuse cases, maybe you'll feel more comfortable in taking care of parents like Sanderson in the proper way."

"Yeah, I know how effective the proper way is," Brian said with a look of disdain.

"And what makes you so knowledgeable?" Kristin said. "You've handled numerous child abuse cases in your many years as a resident?" She paused. "Wait, I apologize for how snotty that sounded."

Just then Brian's beeper went off and he reached under his sweatshirt to retrieve it from his belt. She noticed that he was definitely without a paunch. The voice pager spoke, "Dr. Tanner, please come to the E.R., please come to the E.R."

"Sorry, Miss Grey, I'm on call. Gotta go."

"I don't think we've accomplished much. When is a good time to reschedule?"

"I don't think I have any time in the foreseeable future. I'll let you know."

"What about Dr. Santonio?" she said.

"What about him?" Brian replied in challenge.

She stared at him for a few seconds then shrugged. "Never mind, Doctor Tanner, I see that it would be a waste of our time."

He nodded agreement and left the office.

Brian headed for the physicians' lounge in the lower level of the hospital. He wasn't really needed in the E.R. He had gotten one of the nurses to page him shortly after his session with the social worker lady was to begin. He didn't feel like being preached to, Santonio or not.

After checking his watch, he used his credit card to make a long distance call to Cincinnati. His mother wouldn't be home from work yet but he would be starting soon himself and he might not get a chance to call afterward. The phone buzzed four times and then his mother's voice came to life on the answering machine.

"Hi, this is the Tanner's residence. I can't come to the phone right now but please leave a message."

There was a beep and Brian spoke, "Hi, Mom, it's me. Just calling to say I love you. I have a couple of days off this weekend so I'm coming home to see you. One of your banana cream pies would make a great welcoming home present. Tell Grandpa Albert I'll bring some over to him. See ya."

He smiled as he headed for the cafeteria for a quick bite to eat before the mayhem in the E.R. would take over his day.

CHAPTER 7

Kristin's new Ford Mustang should have looked out of place in the seedy run down section of Lansing just off Kalamazoo Avenue, but it didn't. She was driving through an area where new cars were a sign of portable wealth and the run down houses the anchors that held the inhabitants captive. Dirt yards, windowless storm doors and broken eaves spoke of absentee landlords and renter indifference.

Kristin drove slowly down the street searching for the house number. At one point she was forced to stop because of a pedestrian, a black woman who's circumference equaled her height. The woman was working her way laboriously across the street by means of a walker; its tensile strength was being challenged with each faltering step. Her round head sprouted two reddish ponytails, one from each side of her skull. Upon reaching the curb, she leaned over her walker, visibly gasping and gathering strength for the next part of her journey. She looked at Kristin and gave her a wide genuine smile that seemed to belie the woman's obvious handicap. Just a smile and a nod. Sometimes the spirit of mankind surfaces at the most unexpected places. Kristin felt her throat tighten.

She had felt extremely troubled since Joyce Harper had left her office earlier that day. She knew the woman was crying out for help and that it was time for her to see a psychiatrist. It was nearly dark by the time she found Joyce's home, a green two story house with a broken sidewalk and dilapidated useless toys cluttering the front porch that covered the front of the building. A TV flickering in the front room told Kristin that Joyce was probably home.

She picked her way up the steps and pushed on the doorbell. Hearing no buzzer or bell from inside, she knocked on the aluminum storm door that still had the summer screens in it. She listened for sounds of movement within but heard only the muffled voices of the television. She opened the screen door to rap on the heavy inner door. She noticed one of the small panes of glass in the upper section was partially missing and covered with cardboard and duct tape.

Unexpectedly the door squeaked open a few inches as she began to tap it with her knuckles. She eased it open a little farther and was assaulted by smells unrelated to good housekeeping. She was used to those smells from her days of counseling hookers when she worked for the State. It had been an ugly but somehow intriguing period in her career. She knew now from the position of hindsight that most of the girls she had worked with were dead or in the process. So many lives caught up in a downward spiral from the moment they were born.

"Hello! Anybody home?" she said into the emptiness of the living room.

The light from the TV revealed trash and debris everywhere. There was no response from inside but instinct told her that someone was around. She felt tingles of fright work their way up her back.

"Hello! Joyce, are you there? It's Kristin Grey from the hospital," she said.

Still no answer.

She entered the house and went to the hall that led out to the kitchen area. The smells were worse from that direction. She called out again and this time she thought she heard something that sounded like a whimper. It was coming from upstairs. Cautiously she headed up toward the noise. She searched for a light but couldn't find a switch. In the dark she stepped on a plate and sent it clattering downward. The whimpering grew louder.

At the top of the stairs she found a bedroom where light was filtering in from the street lamp outside. Feeling the hackles on her neck vibrating in fear, Kristin saw vague shapes on the bed. She felt along the wall and found a switch. When she flicked it on, only one of the four bulbs in the ceiling fixture came on. It was enough for her to see Joyce Harper lying peacefully on her bed with two little girls huddled protectively on each side.

The two children were obviously terrified and cried out in alarm.

"Don't be frightened, honey, I won't hurt you," Kristin said to each girl. "Is your mama sleeping?" They shrank away from her as she approached. They looked gray and bony in the half light cast by the overhead bulb.

Kristin went up to Joyce and leaned over her. She was dead. She knew it instinctively. She had seen a few of her hookers after they had died and Joyce had that same cold empty look that said the spirit was gone to its new dimension. Someplace better it was certain. There was an empty pill container on the bedside stand. Kristin held it up to the light and saw that the contents had been sleeping pills.

She didn't know what to do. She knew Joyce didn't have a phone and her own cell phone was absentmindedly left back at the office. She needed to call the police. She hated to leave the girls alone while she found one but that was what she would have to do. There was no way she could get both of them in the car alone without traumatizing them even more.

She ran down the stairs and outside, then chose the house on the right. Beer breath and the smell of too many dogs wafted out of the door as a man in a v-neck tee shirt and boxer shorts answered her knock. He looked her over carefully and licked his lips without thinking.

"I'm sorry to bother you, sir, but I need to find a phone to call the police. Can I use yours?" she said hurriedly.

The sound of the word police seemed to deflate his amorous thoughts.

"What for?" he said generously.

"The lady next door is dead and I need help. Her girls are over there alone and I want to get back to them as soon as possible."

With a grunt of semi-indifference he pointed at a wall phone sitting on the floor of his living room. She hurried over and punched in numbers she had used before and would get the fastest results. The Department of Social Services would have to come out in addition to the police so that the girls could be taken care of properly. What must those little souls be thinking as they lay cuddled by the corpse that used to be their mother?

It took nearly two hours by the time the police and State Social Worker were able to take care of Joyce's body. Kristin held the five-year-old girl on her lap and the woman from the State had the two year old. She felt the undernourished body through the man's tee shirt that acted as a nightgown for the girl.

"What's your name, honey?" she said to the child. No answer other than a shrinking feeling from the little girl.

"I'm sorry about your mama. We'll try to find a nice place for you to live." The words felt inadequate. What could she possibly say to make things all right for them? She thought about calling the grandmother but hated the idea. The woman had been in large part responsible for Joyce's destructive life and would be too old anyway to take care of two toddlers.

Kristin heard a tiny voice from the girl on her lap.

"What did you say?" Kristin said. "I'm sorry, honey, but I didn't hear you."

"Will you be our new mommy 'till ours comes back?"

What could she say? Joyce wasn't coming back and Kristin wasn't in any position to take care of children.

"Please," the girl said timidly.

"Helen, where do you have for the girls to go tonight?" she asked the social worker.

"God only knows. I have a few people that I trust but they're already taking care of as many as they can handle. I hate to burden them with more. They will if I ask them, though. If there's a heaven these people are on a greased slide to the Promised Land as soon as they pass on."

"Can I take care of the girls for the night until you can find something more permanent for them? You might call the grandmother tomorrow to see if she's able to give them a home."

The social worker looked relieved. "Sure, be my guest. Really great of you to offer."

"It's for a selfish reason. I'm looking for a piece of that greased slide to the Promised Land you were talking about."

She knew she had no idea what she was getting herself into as the two of them carried the girls out of the squalor of their lives and placed them in her car. She drove off wondering what to feed two hungry, frightened little children.

CHAPTER 8

Hazel was almost giddy with excitement when she heard Brian's message on her answering machine. She wasn't sure if an old bird like her could get giddy but she was definitely excited. Because of Brian's residency, there were very few times when he could break away and come home. The night he had first left to move to Lansing was the worst of her life. She couldn't stand the emptiness of the house, the silence that called out to her from his bedroom. She cried and cried and walked the deserted streets of her neighborhood 'till dawn, her loneliness was so overwhelming.

At first light she had gone next door to see Albert, her best friend, after Brian. Brian called him "Grandpa" Albert although of course he was not. Albert had gotten her through that lonely time just as he had when they had first moved into the neighborhood almost twenty-five years before.

She thought of how impossibly far her Brian had come since those first days after she had stolen him . . . .

. . . . Brian looked up and saw the man standing in the doorway. He hadn't heard him coming and now he was trapped in the bedroom. The man was yelling as he pulled his belt from around his waist. "Hey, shit head, I told you you couldn't get away from me! I'm gonna punish you good this time. You think that woman's gonna save you again? Not very likely. I'll beat the hell outta her the next time she shows her face around here."

Too petrified to move, the boy watched the torturer come toward him. The belt lashed out and caught him across the shoulders. As he tried to dodge, the next blow caught him across the face. The end of the belt flicked his ear and drew blood. He screamed in agony. He dropped to the floor and tried to crawl beneath the bed, but the man caught him by the ankle and pulled him out, hitting him again and again.

The boy screamed. The pain was terrible. How could he make him stop? He screamed and screamed and - - -

"Brian! Brian! Oh, poor baby. Wake up, baby. Hazel's here. Hazel's got you. You're okay. Please wake up!"

Slowly Brian came back to the surface. His eyes opened and the man disappeared. The gentle woman was there again. He was sweating and tears were streaming down his cheeks. The cot where he had been sleeping was all torn up and wet with his perspiration. The relief he felt at seeing Hazel was indescribable. He knew he'd been dreaming and the man hadn't come back. He put his arms around her as she held him, and hugged her as hard as he could.

Hazel had never felt so complete. Her tears joined Brian's as she lay back down with the boy. At that moment she began putting together plans for making sure that she never lost him. She knew they would have to move from the apartment, mostly because she didn't want the boy's father to ever find them. If they stayed, how could she ever be sure he wouldn't return someday and try to take the boy back? Also, it would be hard for the boy to fully recover as long as he lived right next door to the place where all the terrible things had happened to him. He needed to start life over again. The less he remembered of his father the better. Lastly, if she was going to establish his identity as her son, she had to find a place where people would not ask too many questions. Everyone around there knew she was an old maid. They might wonder too much about how all of a sudden she was claiming to be a mother of a little boy.

She fretted about the need for deception, it was so against her nature.

She looked over at Brian and saw that he was sleeping again. Her arm was all prickly and dead feeling where his head was resting on it. She pulled it gently from under him, massaged it with her fingertips then got out of bed and went into the bathroom. As she washed her hands and face, she glanced at her mirrored reflection. She stood staring at herself for a long time, trying to understand what this stranger looking back at her was trying to do. The whole situation had an unfocused quality, not yet real or understandable.

The mirrored woman spoke to her. "Don't mess this up, Hazel. This will change your life. It's worth the risk. You can save that boy and finally make your own life worth living. You've got a son now, don't you dare lose him!"

After breakfast, Hazel got ready to leave for the day. She had called in sick for the first time since she had begun working at the hospital and she hated the feeling of being a liar. As she was putting her coat on, she remembered that Brian didn't have one. It was cold outside so she couldn't take him out with her in just his tee shirt, and especially not in his underwear. She put one of her oversized sweaters on him, then wrapped a blanket around him. She realized how odd she and her bundle looked as she hurried down the stairs. She checked to make sure the landlord was nowhere to be seen before hustling down the hall and outside.

Hazel headed resolutely toward the business district of Cincinnati two miles distant. She regretted not having a car of her own and knew she would have to get one if they moved farther away from her work.

Her blanket-wrapped cargo stared with wonder and uneasiness at the normal activities passing by him. The blanket wrapping had frightened him. He didn't know what the woman was going to do to him but he submitted without struggle, partly from fear, partly from curiosity. Coming outside had panicked him. He wanted to get loose and run but he was afraid to fight. The woman had her arms wrapped securely about him as she puffed down the walk.

Though the day was chilly, Hazel began to perspire. She had always sweated like a man and it irritated her. Her burden was light, but the accumulated weight and distance were making her arms ache and her breath short. She spoke to the boy as she walked, irrelevant comments just to speak, and to reassure them both.

Halfway to town, she parked herself on a bus stop bench, holding the boy on her lap and rocking him.

Brian was having a hard time coping with all the new sensations assaulting his senses. It was the first time he could remember being outside. If it weren't for the television, he would have been completely mystified by what he saw.

As they sat resting, one of the city busses hissed to a stop in front of them, exhaust fumes stenching the air. Hazel was taken aback when the door of the bus folded open and the driver sat expectantly watching them.

Why not? she thought. It was still some distance to the bank. She headed for the steps. She felt her bundle squirm, making fear sounds. The closer she came to the bus entrance, the more animated the boy became.

Sensitive to Brian's reactions, she realized he was afraid either of the bus or of the man who sat watching them. She backed quickly away and waved the driver on, his shoulders shrugged and eyebrows raised in question.

"No one will ever hurt you again, my Brian. Hazel will love you and take care of you," she said to the boy.

The rational Hazel watched from a distance as the middle-aged woman and her 'son' headed once again for town. She watched her reflection in store windows as she labored along. Cars honked and people ambled by just like it was an ordinary day. Only it wasn't.

Her arms were wailing nerve endings by the time she arrived at the bank. Using the revolving door, she entered the old gray sandstone building, high-vaulted ceiling soaring above them. Her bulky white nursing shoes made soft padding sounds on the marble floor. She watched the boy as he absorbed these new surroundings. The thoughts behind his eyes were unfathomable.

After waiting a short time in line, she approached the teller's window when the woman motioned her availability. Hazel sat Brian on the counter so she could make her transactions. The bank teller looked askance at Hazel while trying to act as if it were perfectly normal to have a blanket-shrouded child perched in front of her. Hazel put all but $250.00 of her $6,000 savings in her checking account. The two hundred and fifty she put in her purse. Her saving days were over for now.

Leaving the bank, her next stop was Harrison's Department Store three blocks to the north. She checked the directory as she entered: Boys Wear, Second Floor. The escalator deposited them in the Sporting Goods department. She searched the horizon and spotted the telltale children's mannequins.

Curiosity quickly brought a clerk to her side. The middle-aged saleswoman exuded a subtle air of condescension.

"May I be of help to you?" the woman asked.

"I need some boy's clothing," Hazel replied

"What did you have in mind?"

Hazel paused. "Everything. I need some of everything." She stopped again, trying to think of a plausible explanation for Brian's appearance. Up until then she had been operating on emotion and adrenaline. She needed to start thinking.

"This boy is a foster child," she began. "The authorities just took him from a dangerous home situation and left him with me. As you can see he needs all types of clothing. I'll pay for it now and they'll reimburse me later."

The clerk turned solicitous, all the while thinking that she'd never let a scraggly haired little beast like that into her home.

Hazel perched the boy on a glass display case, waiting for the woman to bring the proper sizes of clothing they had agreed on. They began at Brian's feet. New fluffy white cotton socks were a contrast to the dirty toes with cracked, broken nails. She saw the toes wiggle inside their unaccustomed, pleasant confinement.

She opened a package of underwear. The grayish homemade terry cloth ones he was wearing would have to go in the trash. When she attempted to pull them down, the clerk reddened and Brian refused to let her take them. Brian grabbed at the material and wouldn't let go.

"No! No off," he pleaded.

Years of work in the hospital had eliminated most of Hazel's modesty in handling others. Nudity in her patients was not something she thought about. She hadn't meant to be thoughtless with the boy. She set the new jockey shorts aside for when they got home. She pulled out a new, white tee shirt and held it up to Brian then touched his face gently with it.

"Let Hazel put this on you, Brian. Let's get rid of that old thing you have on."

Like an animal he smelled and felt the new material. At last he relented. He cried out when Hazel began to pull the old stained shirt over his head. It was too small and the neckband, though stretched, caught momentarily on his ears and pulled them. His father had once tied a pillowcase over his head and then beat him with a hanger. The subconscious comparison was too great. He began to fight the shirt.

Quickly Hazel pulled the shirt back down and comforted the boy. "There, there, Brian. Hazel isn't going to hurt you."

After he had calmed, she took the frayed cotton in her large, work-roughened hands and quietly tore the material apart and away from his body. She sucked in her breath in sorrow. Brian's back and chest were covered with welts and bruises.

Pity overcame the clerk's stuffiness. "Oh my!" she said inadequately.

Hazel stretched the neck of the new tee shirt and pulled it quickly over the greasy, tangled hair. Her fingers encircled the skinny arms as she pushed the claw-like hands through the sleeves. The eyes that looked up at her and the lips that couldn't smile wrenched her heart.

Next came a green, plaid, long-sleeved shirt and blue jeans. She set aside similar articles to take with them. She helped him down from the counter and led him across the department to the shoe section. Brian had never worn shoes. Hazel watched him try to adjust to their unfamiliar confinement as they snaked their way between clothing racks in search of a winter coat, sweaters, hat and mittens.

Brian nearly screamed several times. His emotions were in shock from all the new experiences. Each time he was about to lose control the gentle lady would hold him and croon words in his ear. He didn't understand much of what she said, but he sensed her feelings and the hysteria would slither back into its hiding place.

Hazel placed him in front of a full-length mirror to admire his new clothes. He stood, fascinated by the images staring back at him from the three-way mirrors. Myriad emotions vied for supremacy: astonishment, fear, puzzlement, excitement, fright, curiosity. He had never seen himself before. A wild little animal stared back at him. Long, matted hair that could be blond framed a cadaverous face. Blue-gray eyes were surrounded by sunken purple, the nose pinched. He touched the mirrored boy. The skin was translucent from hunger.

He screamed, a loud, keening wail of sadness and fear.

Hazel dropped to her knees in front of the boy and clutched him to her. "Don't be afraid, Brian. Hazel is here. Someday you'll forget all this and everything will be okay."

She continued to whisper in his ear until she could feel the trembling lessen. The clerk shooed away other clerks drawn by the scream.

By the time she was done totaling up the cost of everything, it came to well over $250.00 that she had in cash. Hazel was shocked. She also felt naive. She had not realized how expensive children's clothes were. Instead she wrote out a check for the entire amount.

Hazel left the store, a large shopping bag bulging with clothes and blanket in one hand and Brian's mittened paw held firmly in the other. She sniffed the air.

"Smell the river, Brian? Someday I'll take you for a boat ride on the Ohio. And we can go watch the Reds play ball. Cincinnati is a great place for a boy to grow up."

They continued on down the street looking for a place to eat. She didn't feel comfortable taking the boy into one of the larger restaurants so she picked a small hamburger joint. As they entered the Daybreak Cafe the smell of frying meat and potatoes put Brian's saliva glands in overdrive.

Hazel tucked a napkin in Brian's shirt and held him on her lap as he wolfed down a cheeseburger, French fries, and a milkshake. She laughed as the thick shake broke loose from the bottom of the glass and splatted on his upturned face. She quickly mopped the overflow as it headed down his cheeks.

"Moah, moah," he pleaded.

"You can have more later, honey. Hazel doesn't want you to get sick again."

Finished at last with their food, Hazel used the phone outside the restaurant to call a taxi. When it arrived, she gave him the address of one of the used car dealers she had picked out of the yellow pages.

The used car dealer watched her walking through the lot, a grandmother and grandson, looking lost. His carnivorous eyes squinted into a smile. He loved female buyers. Without a man along, they were easy pickings. Pasting on his best honest and sincere grin, he herded her toward a couple of jewels he had been unable to unload for a long time.

Hazel knew basically the kind of car she was looking for. She also remembered some of the things her father had told her about buying a used car. "The first thing you do," he had said, "is to insult the heck out of the first two cars they show you. By the third or fourth car, you're beginning to get what you want and maybe on the fifth car you'll start to get some quality. When you finally start up that fifth car, you should sneer a little and look questioningly at the dealer. Go ahead and test drive the sixth one and if it doesn't drop its guts on the ground when you put it into gear, you probably can make a deal."

By the time they got to the sixth car, the salesman's honest and sincere look was gone. He was pissed. His easy sale hadn't materialized and now he had to show one of his better cars, to a woman of all things.

Hazel had driven only a few times in the last twenty years. She renewed her license each time it was due as a matter of habit, just in case she ever needed it. She was embarrassed when they went out for a test drive. Barely off the lot she started attempting mayhem with the Ford. Twice she stomped on the brakes too quickly and had to grab Brian before he smashed his face on the dash. It was against the law but what could she do. She had tried to buckle him in before they started but the seat belt's confinement had frightened him, making him whimper. The presence of the salesman in the back seat had Brian hiding in the corner by the door, sucking his thumb. By the time she got back to the lot, she had the car pretty much under control.

As her father had instructed, Hazel ignored the first offer the man made and countered with a five percent reduction on his second one. They settled somewhere in between when he threw in the cost of the plates and helped her get insurance. Even with a small profit the man felt a failure.

By the time they got home with the car, Hazel and Brian were physically and emotionally drained. He had sat huddled on the seat beside Hazel, watching the tops of the buildings and trees go by and wondering about all the new things he had experienced.

They hurried up the stairs to her apartment and sat slumped together in a chair until she could work up enough energy to begin calling the rental locations she had listed from the newspaper. When she had finished, her list showed seven of the ten places were still unrented. She had told each of the people she would be by the next day to look at them.

That night Hazel was so exhausted that Brian was deep into his nightmare before it registered in her sleep-clogged mind. The man had inflicted a lot of pain by the time Hazel pulled Brian away.

Early the next day, Brian and Hazel began their search for a new home. She had asked for a week's vacation to take care of a family emergency. At a gas station, she bought a map of the city and they drove to the first place on the list. The hunting was discouraging. Everything they looked at was either too expensive, too crummy looking or just not what she wanted. Bone tired, she and Brian returned home to search for more possibilities in that day's newspaper.

The search went on for two more days. Hazel was beginning to feel desperate. On the fourth day of her quest she saw what she wanted. At first she was unhappy with the place, it was obvious that it had been poorly cared for. It was a small Cape Cod style house surrounded by a patchy looking lawn out north of the city on Route Four, fifteen miles from her work at St. Thomas Memorial Hospital. The place was located near the end of a dead-end gravel road. None of the houses were new, but all were fairly tidy, with the exception of the one they were looking at. It hadn't been cleaned, the grass cut nor the windows washed in a long time.

Hazel got reluctantly from her car, looking skeptically at the white frame structure. She walked around it, inventorying the abuse. In the fenced back yard bare earth and dog leavings were everywhere. The smell could almost be seen. Weeds grew at the fringes of the fence and choked off what had once been a flower garden. Leaves from a huge old maple had been blown into a corner. A small cement slab led up to a back door with a broken storm door.

Already disgusted with the place, Hazel was guiding Brian back to the car when she noticed a little old man coming toward them from next door. As he approached she saw that he wasn't as small or as old as he first appeared. He was canted forward and in obvious distress. From what she observed, Hazel assumed that he probably had arthritis of the spine. She had seen similar postures at the hospital. He looked up at her with a pain-etched smile.

"Are you here to look at the house?" he asked hopefully.

"I was, but I'm afraid it's not what I'm looking for," Hazel said.

"Please don't be put off by the looks of it. It's really a very nice place under all the dirt. I rented it out a year ago to a young couple and they just turned it into an awful mess. They only paid the rent the first six months and never did anything to keep the place up. They had four German Shepherds that ran around the back yard and tore it all up. By the time I was able to have them evicted, they had almost ruined my place. I'm willing to rent it out quite reasonably if I can get someone to help me clean it up. And keep it that way, of course. Is your husband good with his hands, ma'am?"

"My husband's dead," Hazel answered quickly.

"I'm sorry to hear that. You're probably not interested then. There's a lot of work to be done. Probably too much for a woman to handle."

Even though his manner was kindly, it irritated Hazel.

"I don't need a man to do any work you might have around here. If you don't mind, I'd like to see the inside."

She urged Brian from behind her where he had been hiding as she started toward the front door.

The man came slowly up the walk after her and unlocked the door for her. She stepped inside. What a mess! The two-legged animals that had dwelt in the house had been less civilized than the four legged ones that had lived out back. The carpet stank, the walls were filthy, the tubs and sinks uncleaned and there was crud everywhere. Hazel could not comprehend people living like that.

Back outside, breathing fresh air, Hazel looked around the general area. There was a big empty field behind all the houses across the road. Long, tan grass waved in the breeze. On the other side of the field she could see what looked like a high school. At the end of the gravel road was a small woods. The area was just what she had been seeking.

The rent the man was asking was so reasonable that she had to accept. It was what she could afford. He signed an agreement stipulating that he would not raise the rent for five years if the place was cleaned to his satisfaction and kept that way. The old man even agreed to furnish new carpeting for the living room and to make his lawn mower available to her.

Both knew the agreement had a lot of holes in it, that they were going to have to trust each other. Hazel wrote out a check for the first month's rent, which would begin in ten days. In the meantime, she would spend as much time there as she could, getting the place ready to live in. The first thing she did was borrow a claw hammer from the man to tear up the living room carpet. Fortunately the room was small. Because of accumulated filth, she was barely able to roll the carpet up and pull it out the front door. The weather was in the high forties so she was able to leave all the windows open when she left for the evening. She'd be back the next day with a mop, broom and an armload of cleansers.

Brian didn't have the slightest idea what was going on, but he didn't care. All of his days were turning into treasures. Whatever the gentle lady was doing must be all right.

CHAPTER 9

The moon was so full and intense that Brian hardly needed his headlights even though it was nearly four in the morning. The cornfields of Ohio, south of Lima, were visible as they lay stripped and naked from the fall harvest. The moon softened the edges and made the nearly vacant Interstate 75 not so lonely as Brian aimed the Ghia toward home.

He had left the Genesis Emergency Room at a dead run shortly after midnight and was on Interstate 96 within fifteen minutes, headed for I-75 where it slipped around Ann Arbor, Toledo and Lima on its way south. The nightglow of Dayton and Cincinnati beyond blended with the moonlight and beckoned Brian onward.

The Ghia puttered along like there was indeed a God, and He was a friend of the mechanic who had only charged Brian for a fuel filter and a carburetor adjustment. The elderly mechanic also had suggested that Brian begin checking the classifieds for a new, or at least newer, vehicle.

His mother would still be asleep when he got home but he knew she would be at the back door by the time he silenced the Ghia's motor. He smiled at the thought. If he ever loved a wife as much as he did his mother, he would surely die of ecstasy. He would give his mom a great hug and then sit in her kitchen while she made them both a warm breakfast and for a while the demons that chased him would be silent.

After they ate, he would take a tray of food next door to Grandpa Albert, just as he had every morning since he was a little kid, up until the time he had needed to leave for his residency in Michigan. Grandpa Albert was nearly ninety by now and the arthritis of the spine that had forced an early retirement was now an incredibly painful, debilitating handicap. Next to his mom, Albert was the kindest, most gentle person Brian had ever known.

He frowned slightly at the thought that the pain he had once known had been more than worth the two "parents" he had gotten in return. But there was still the debt to repay. Thinking of Stevie Sanderson and his father, his fists clenched involuntarily on the steering wheel.

His thoughts carried him through Dayton and soon he was in the northern suburbs of Cincinnati, headed for home. He could still remember when the area was more farm than city but slowly shopping malls and condos and apartment complexes had consumed the open spaces.

The road he lived on had been gravel when he was in high school but now it was covered with asphalt. It seemed somehow to have lost much of its personality in the process. The front porch light came on before Brian even pulled in the drive and he laughed aloud. The light over the garage came on next, illuminating the old basketball hoop where he and his best friend Kevin used to shoot hoops until all hours of the night.

Hazel lumbered out of the back door and was swept up in a giant bear hug. Neither spoke for a long time. There was no need.

At last she said, "All right, you big oaf, put me down before you get a hernia."

"Like lifting balloon filled with helium, Ma," Brian said.

Hazel snorted happily. "Filled with concrete would be more like it. I see that German thing made it all the way," she said, pointing at the Ghia. "I couldn't get to sleep knowing that it was probably going to conk out somewhere in the middle of nowhere and leave you stranded."

"It's got more miles left on it than you do, Mom, and you're good for another hundred thousand."

"Don't I wish. Some days I feel like all my tires are flat. You hungry by the way?"

"Starved. I'll just sit here and watch you since I wouldn't want to get in the way."

Hazel laughed. "It's a deal and I'll get out of your way afterward while you do the dishes."

Brian groaned in mock dismay. He hated dishes, especially greasy skillets with leftover egg and cheese from the best omelets in the history of the universe. His mother refused to bend to modern science and the non-stick benefits of the Teflon covered pan. Hers' were the old cast iron kind that "kept the taste in the food."

"Okay, it's a deal," Brian said. "Will it be too early to take Grandpa Albert's to him?"

"He'll be awake. He doesn't sleep very well these days with the arthritis and his prostate kicking up. Besides I told him you were coming so he'll have been awake as soon as that machine of yours turned in the driveway. I'll bet if you look out the back door, you'll see the light is on in his bedroom."

Brian stuck his head out the back door and came back in smiling. "Yup," he said.

"By the way, I called Kevin. He was excited to hear you would be home. He said he would make dinner reservations for us at Mike Fink's Riverboat for eight o'clock tonight. He wants us to meet his new girl friend."

"Another one?" Brian said and laughed.

Hazel grinned in response. "Kevin said this one's the 'real deal'." Hazel giggled at the phrase. "He says he's positive she loves him for his personality not for his future earnings potential as an orthopedic surgeon."

"Did you tell him that the money would be a better reason?"

"No, I thought I'd let you do that."

Kevin had been Brian's best friend since they were in elementary school together. Brian could still remember him moving in across the street one hot August day. A little redheaded boy with a three-inch sole on his left shoe had limped out of the front door while the movers were unloading the truck.

Brian's other friend in the neighborhood, Chad Peterson, had diplomatically opened the conversation with, "Boy, I bet you can't run too fast with that shoe on your foot like that."

Kevin had been born with the congenital anomaly of one leg being shorter than the other and the foot malformed. The "shoe" was a physical and emotional handicap that Kevin battled for years.

Brian sat back and watched his mother at work around the stove. For the first time in months he felt the tension leave his shoulders because for at least a couple of days he was home. He frowned as he noticed all the grey in his mother's hair. One of the worse things about being away was that changes were more noticeable. She was nearly ready to retire from the hospital. When he got home for Christmas vacation, he'd start scouting the area for a good place for an office. Her job would be a lot easier then. He never ceased to admire how she continued working year after year on the cancer ward. Soon she'd help him with the kids instead.

"I'll be gone to work by the time you get back from Albert's," Hazel interrupted Brian's thoughts. "I'm sorry I couldn't get the day off but they're shorthanded with this flu that's knocking everyone for a loop."

"Duty calls, Ma. We'll have a great time tonight with Kevin, listening to all his latest surgery war stories and things. I'll grab a quick nap until you get home."

They finished breakfast together and then Hazel made fresh bacon and eggs for Albert while Brian poured the juice and coffee he would take next door. Balancing the tray, Brian headed out the back door and across the adjoining lawns to his grandfather's house.

He entered the back door that led through the kitchen, living room and hall toward the bedroom area. When Brian was young, his adopted grandfather would sit with him in the kitchen and talk while he ate the breakfast Hazel had fixed. Over the recent years, however, he was confined more and more to his bed.

Brian saw his grandfather propped up against the headboard but curled forward painfully from his arthritic spine. Brian was shocked at how frail the old man looked. But then again he *was* old, just over ninety. His white hair was thinner and the ears and nose seemed to dominate his features. His hands lay twisted and aching in his lap.

"It's good to see you, Brian," Albert said with a smile. His voice had lost much of its strength.

"It's good to see you too, Grandpa. How about some early breakfast?" He put the bed tray down in front of Albert.

"I'm ready. Soon as I heard your car pull in I started for the bathroom. Just got back," he said and laughed. "Getting so I have to plan about an hour ahead of time when I think I might have to go. The way I have it figured, when I finally can't get there on my own, it will be time to wrap things up."

Brian started to protest but Albert stopped him.

"Happens to all of us sooner or later, Brian. Doesn't seem scary at all at this end of life. I'm looking forward to moving around again without this old body attached to it. You just remember when I'm gone that this life is just a phase leading on to something better. If it's half as good as your mother's cooking, it will be worth getting there, that's for sure."

Brian watched as Albert struggled to make his fingers cooperate as he brought a fork full of scrambled eggs to his mouth. Brian knew how much the arthritis hurt him but Albert had always made a point of hiding the pain from others.

"Almost done up there in Michigan?" Albert said between bites. "Cold place. Never liked it. Especially a place like Lansing that's full of politicians."

"End of June and I'm all finished, Grandpa. It's been a long haul."

"But worth it. I know you, Brian; you'll be a great doctor. Hard to believe how far you've come since that first morning.

. . . .The alarm went off beside the bed and Hazel reached out groggily for the button to stifle the irritating sound. The little body nestled at her side stirred. Brian didn't sleep in his own bed. The nightmares had brought him to Hazel's bed so often that she just put him in with her each night. She loved having him near her. Her large, warm body communicated affection and calmed Brian's damaged psyche. It would take a long time for him to get over the abuse he had received but he was lucky; hidden within the tiny frightened boy was a fighter, a survivor who would rise in time from the ashes of his horrible beginnings.

Still tacky with sleep, Hazel left the comfort of the bed to shower and get dressed. It was five-thirty in the morning, an ugly time of day. It was earlier than she usually arose, but today she was beginning to cook breakfast for Mr. Bricker. She couldn't believe the old man was willing to get up that early but apparently he did every day. He had mentioned to her that he didn't want to miss life. When he was sleeping, he was already partly dead.

The days preceding had been packed with work and activity getting the house ready to be lived in. Hazel had used some of her hoard of money to replace much of the furniture in the house, finding bargains at used furniture stores closer to town. The house still had a lingering odor of rot and mold so she burned scented candles or opened doors and windows when the weather permitted.

The closer she had come to going back to work the more desperate she became to find a baby sitter for Brian. His emotional handicaps were so extreme that she couldn't trust just anyone to take care of him. It was unthinkable to leave him home alone while she was at gone.

She didn't know anyone in the neighborhood yet, except for Mr. Bricker and she had no friends she could ask to help her find a baby-sitter. She decided to go next door and talk to the old man. He might know of someone trustworthy in the area that she might hire to care for the boy.

Bricker had been a schoolteacher until five years ago when the arthritis had caused his early retirement. Hazel had talked with him several times in the last week and had learned to like him. When she approached him with the problem, he thought about it for some time before offering a solution.

"I have a question to ask and then perhaps I'll make you a proposition," Albert said. "Is your boy well-behaved? He seems pretty quiet to me, from what I've seen."

"He's very, very shy, Mr. Bricker. That's part of the problem. I can't leave him with just anyone. He'll behave, but he has to be treated very, very gently."

"Well, in that case," Albert replied, "I'd like to offer you a trade. As you can see, my arthritis keeps me somewhat immobile, so I have a hard time taking care of my own place. I'll watch your boy for you if you will do three things for me: clean my house, do my laundry and fix me one good meal every day that you go to work. It can be breakfast or supper, whichever is easiest for you. You and the boy are welcome to share it with me if you like. It's been ten years since my wife died and I can't stand my own cooking. What do you think? We could try it for a week or two and see if it works out all right for both of us."

Hazel thought about it for a few moments. The offer was a Godsend. It would save her a lot of money and there wouldn't be all that much more work for her to do. Being right next door would certainly make it handy for her.

And so they had begun.

Hazel knocked at the back door of the Bricker house that first morning. The pre-dawn air was cold, making streams of vapor in the air as she waited. Brian looked out on the blackness of the morning and was afraid. He held tightly to the gentle lady so that she couldn't leave him. Inside this house was a man and men hurt him.

Mr. Bricker came to the door and let them in.

"Good morning, Mrs. Tanner. How are you?"

"Fine. Call me Hazel, will you?"

"Sure, if you'll call me Albert."

"Okay. What would you like for breakfast?"

"Two eggs, over easy, bacon, toast, orange juice and coffee. Lord, I can hardly wait. I woke up early just thinking about it. I always eat cold cereal."

Hazel tried to put Brian on one of the kitchen chairs but he clung to her like a burr. When she put him on the counter beside the stove, he finally let go but only after she convinced him that she was just going to cook breakfast for them. He never took his eyes off her as she walked away to go to the refrigerator or to the table. While Albert ate at the table, Hazel fed Brian and herself at the counter.

"I have to go to work now, Brian," Hazel began worriedly. "I'll be back in a little while. Okay? Mr. Bricker will take good care of you."

She gave him a hug and a kiss then pried his arms from around her neck. Brian's sobs tore at her heart, but she had to leave. He held his arms out to her, crying for her to come back. She turned and hastened from the kitchen and out the back door.

Brian jumped down from the counter and tried to run after her. Albert had anticipated his leap and had inserted himself in the doorway. He hoped he wouldn't have to wrestle with the boy. The arthritis in his spine would hurt like a son-of-a-gun if he did.

Brian saw the old man looming above him. With a cry of terror he turned and scuttled back through the house. In the living room he hid in a corner, curled into a whimpering little ball.

He shook with fear. Already he missed her terribly. The gentle lady had left him. Why had she gone away? Was this crooked old man going to beat him? He was too petrified to move.

Albert entered the room carrying Brian's clothes; belt and pants in one hand, shirt and shoes in the other. He felt sorry for the boy and was going to try to coax him out of the corner. Maybe he'd watch cartoons. He was perplexed by the boy's intense fright. Something was terribly wrong here.

He heard a strange little cry from across the room. The whites of the boy's gray-blue eyes showed and Albert saw that he was plainly terrified.

Brian whimpered as he watched the man coming toward him. The belt hung forgotten from Albert's hand as his mind searched for the source of the little boy's terror.

"What's the matter, Brian? What are you afraid of?" He slowly crossed the room.

Before Albert could reach him, Brian screamed and dashed past him and out of the back door before he could react. By the time he got to the back door, the child was nowhere in sight. Albert called out, but not expecting any response.

He grabbed his coat hanging by the back door and went outside. He labored around the house in search of the boy. Shuffling across the lawn to Hazel's house, he tested all the doors and found them locked.

As he rounded the back corner he saw that the side door of the garage was ajar. He approached quietly and peered inside. He heard a slight rustling in the darkened interior. The stale smell of dog feces assaulted his nose. He was saddened anew by what the last renters had done to his place. Although he had scraped and hosed the floor, some of the stench remained.

He pushed the door open a bit. In the gloom, he heard the whimpering begin. He moved inside. The whimpering grew. He didn't know what to do. This was no normal fear. He had no inkling why the boy was so afraid, but he didn't want to make things worse.

"Brian? Come on out. I won't hurt you. I promise you. I'm just an old duffer. It smells in here. Let me take you back to my place," he pleaded.

It was no use. No amount of pleading would persuade the little boy to show himself. Albert knew he must be hidden back under the workbench where he couldn't get at him.

Brian was numb with fear. The cold and smell and darkness of the garage added oppression to his fright. He realized he had urinated in his pants when the man first appeared in the doorway. A couple of times he almost wavered and left his hiding place. The voice calling to him didn't sound like the man who used to beat him. But he wouldn't dare take the chance. It might be a trick.

Albert didn't know how to proceed further with his dilemma. He didn't want to frighten the boy more, and yet he couldn't go back home and risk having him run away and get lost. He was not strong enough, because of his arthritis, to take the boy by force. Besides, he had no heart for drastic action. He was stymied.

He was no closer to a solution when Hazel pulled into the driveway later that afternoon. She saw Albert sitting in a lawn chair by the garage, hunched miserably into his coat, trying to stay warm. As she stopped he slowly unfolded from the chair, looking like a pain-filled comma.

She rushed up to the old man, her eyes darting about him for her boy.

"Where's Brian?"

The disgusted gesture of a bone-chilled thumb sent her rushing into the garage.

He heard the woman's pleading voice from inside. It continued for a long time before she at last reappeared clutching the trembling child. "How long has he been in there?"

"Since you left. Mrs. Tanner, Hazel, this is not the normal reaction of a child who is unhappy at being left at the baby-sitter's. I think we need to have a talk before tomorrow. This sunbathing is all right on a fairly warm day like today, but what happens when it gets cold?"

She saw his attempt at humor and liked him for it. It had been a bad day for him as well as for Brian.

"I'm terribly, terribly sorry, Albert. I'll be over after I feed him and get him calmed down."

The wave of his hand was meant to dismiss the discomfort he had suffered, but it was painful and he was hungry and exhausted. He headed slowly for his house and some warm coffee.

Brian was shaking uncontrollably. The cold cement floor would have made the wait unbearable but fortunately there had been an old tire in which he could curl up on, close enough to escape back under the workbench if necessary. The damp, fall day had seeped through his pajamas and he was miserable. It used to be normal to feel so bad, but not lately. He felt worse because of the comparison. Though he was incredibly glad to see the gentle woman it took a while before he would let himself come out of hiding.

Hazel wrapped him in a big, fluffy comforter and rocked him. Time passed. Nothing mattered but the boy. The trembling gradually ceased. After awhile she fed him warm soup and hot chocolate. Then she dressed him.

"Brian. We have to go talk to Mr. Bricker."

"No go."

"Yes. We must. He's a nice man. He watched over you all day even though it hurt him a lot. He deserves an explanation."

"No go."

"We are going," she replied firmly, bending forward to look him full in the eyes. "Did he hurt you?"

No answer.

"Of course he didn't. Not every man is like the one who hurt you. You must learn that, so that you can be alive. Learn to be happy so we can have a loving life together. You have to trust him, like you trust me. Do you understand?"

Brian shook his head slowly, but Hazel thought she detected a spark of comprehension.

She gave Albert the foster-child story she had given the sales clerk when she bought Brian's clothes. She couldn't afford to completely trust anyone.

Albert looked skeptically at her. "So he's not your son?"

"No."

"Why the subterfuge?"

"What do you mean?"

"I mean, why not tell me that he's a foster child to begin with? I would have been more perceptive of his needs if I had known."

She didn't reply immediately, hunting for a plausible excuse. "I wanted to let him start fresh with no one treating him like a cripple." It sounded lame.

"He is a cripple. There's more to it than you're telling, isn't there?"

A reluctant, "Yes."

"Well, you can tell it to me some day when you know you can trust me. Is the basic story true?"

"Yes."

"Do you still want me to take care of him?"

"Oh, yes, I'll work with him so he doesn't run away again."

"Don't worry about it. The fresh air was good for me."

Hazel was beginning to like Albert a great deal.

She called in sick the next day to reassure Brian that he had nothing to be afraid of. They spent the day with Albert in an effort to acclimate Brian to his new surroundings. She embarrassed the old man when she gave him an occasional friendly hug to prove to Brian that Mr. Bricker was not a threat.

The combination of Albert's semi-immobility and genuine kindness eventually brought Brian out from behind the couch to play quietly around the house. Hazel had bought him his first toys, cars, trucks and little farm animals and people. She had to show him how to play with them. He sat quietly by the hour amusing himself while Albert watched from his easy chair. Still timid, the boy seldom spoke.

Hazel worked constantly with Brian, quietly but firmly changing the habits forced on him in his short lifetime.

He was a little animal really; one who had lived at a subsistence, survival level. The miracle was that he could communicate at all.

The green scum on his teeth showed the absence of a toothbrush. The cavities she was sure were hidden inside would have to be repaired someday when the boy could survive the mental stress. She would try to find a female dentist to make the experience less frightening.

She stopped at the county library near the hospital. She checked out a half dozen books about child abuse. She needed to understand better Brian's problems and his needs. She also brought home a stack of children's books, big words and lots of pictures, so she could read to him. The more he heard the words and associated them with objects and concepts, the faster he would learn.

Whenever she wasn't cooking or cleaning, she had Brian on her lap. He was inundated with affection. He couldn't get enough of it. Nor could Hazel.

Mealtime brought problems. Knives, forks, and spoons were alien objects to the boy and she had to softly force their use upon him. She learned quickly the first time she made oatmeal and let him feed himself. His first handful was halfway to his mouth before she caught his wrist and forced the goo back into the bowl. The scared look he gave her as she pried open his fingers wrenched her heart.

She fed Brian each morning and left sandwiches for lunch so Albert wouldn't have to struggle with the problem. Each evening she taught her son table manners.

She had finally gotten him clean. He shied away from the isolated feeling of the shower, but when she made a giant, frothy bubble bath and enticed him into its warm, feathery confines, his laughter and splashing flooded the bathroom. Hazel sat on the floor getting soaked and laughed with him until she cried, great gasping sobs of happiness.

One afternoon after Albert had been baby-sitting for about a month, he succeeded in coaxing Brian onto his lap. He had one of the little books Hazel had brought along for Brian. Albert pointed to the pictures and read aloud the words that went with them.

After he finished the book, Brian leafed back through it to the front and looked up at Albert. "Do 'gin?"

Albert obliged him. At the last page Brian asked again.

"Okay. I'll read it one more time just because you're such a nice boy." The third time through, Brian began to tell in his halting way what was on the pages before Albert could read them. He didn't read the words, but he remembered the substance of the things Albert had said the first two times through.

"Very interesting," he said to Brian. "You learn very quickly." An encouraging intellect was surfacing.

As the weeks turned into months, Brian grew in many ways. All the love and attention Hazel lavished on him was healing some of the emotional scars. He absorbed her almost smothering care like a sponge. Both of them were making up for the loveless years of their earlier existence.

Hazel was happier than she ever dreamed of being. She knew that no man would ever make love to her, but the fact no longer held any importance.

CHAPTER 10

While Brian was next door at Albert's, Hazel showered and got ready for work. Standing by the tub, toweling herself dry, she spotted herself in the full-length mirror on the bathroom door. She laughed ruefully at the image there. Not a very pretty picture, she thought. Gray hair, wrinkles, drooping breasts, bulges, cellulite on her buttocks and legs; not an attractive feature anywhere to be seen. Hard to believe we're created in God's image, she mused. God must really have a sense of humor, she thought as she smiled to herself.

She finished drying her hair, got dressed, did the dishes for Brian and left for work. She took a couple of aspirins to douse the headache that had been nagging at her for the last couple of days. She wanted to avoid the flu that had been going around lately.

As she drove toward the hospital, she remembered she had never once been late in the thirty-one years she had been working there. "You're an incredible broad, Hazel," she said aloud to the interior of the car.

When she got to the hospital, she drove around the block long enough to make sure that she would be fifteen minutes late.

She dawdled a bit, putting her jacket and her purse in her locker, then went to the nursing station for her patient assignments for the day.

The RN in charge of the area looked at her quizzically. "Your car break down or something, Hazel?"

Hazel smiled back at her. "Nope, I just had a hard time getting around this morning."

The nurse stood there, somewhat unsure of herself. She kept expecting an apology but there was none forthcoming. At last she shrugged and turned to the assignment sheet for the day.

"You're in luck, Hazel. You get Ruby Sheppard today. She's in great form already."

Hazel laughed aloud. She didn't mind taking care of the old lady even though Ruby was hopelessly senile. The real Ruby was long gone. Hazel often wondered where the real personality went as it waited for the body to die. Hazel wouldn't mind dying, but she hated the thought of someone having to take care of her like some giant, wrinkled old baby before she finally went.

As she made her way down the hall, she heard Ruby hollering in her raspy plaintive wail. "Betty! Betty! Goddammit, where are you? I have to go real bad!"

Betty was the old woman's daughter, who had died eleven years before, presumably to avoid her mother's senility.

"Somebody come and help me to the bathroom!" Ruby shrieked. "I can't wait much longer! Somebody help me! Help me, help me, help me! Oh, I have to go so bad! Somebody, please! Oh, I can't wait!"

Hazel came into the room in time to see Ruby shouting into the device used to raise and lower the electric bed. Ruby evidently thought it was a microphone attached to the P.A. system.

"Hi, Ruby. Do you really have to go to the bathroom this time?" Hazel laughed.

"Hell yes! Dintcha hear me just say so? Now you better get me to that bathroom before I pee all over this bed!"

"Now, Ruby, we had seven false alarms the last time I took care of you. Are you really sure this time?"

"You'd better get me in there right now! I can feel it coming any second!"

Hazel knew it would be another false alarm but why not humor the old girl? While Ruby was sitting through her imaginary urination, Hazel got a basin of warm water ready to give her a small bath.

Ruby sputtered and fumed but Hazel finally got the bath completed. The next item on the agenda was really going to whiz ol' Ruby, Hazel knew. The doctor had left standing orders that Ruby was to be gotten out of bed and put in a wheelchair to insure that she wouldn't be lying down all day. The wheelchair had a tray that attached over the lap so the patient wouldn't fall out. Ruby hated the thing. The moment she was in the chair, she began to wail like a hound baying on the scent of its quarry.

"They're killing me, Betty! Help, Betty! Where is that damn girl?"

"Now, Ruby, just relax. I'll be back in a while to put you back in bed," Hazel promised.

"Help me, help me, help! Betty! Come get me!"

Hazel left Ruby to her inner struggles. As she entered the hall, she met one of the porters from Nuclear Medicine.

"Hi, Norma."

"Hi, Hazel. That must be old Ruby howling away in there. I'd recognize that voice anywhere. That old broad pulled a sneak attack on me the other day."

"What do you mean?"

"Well, I had her down in Nuclear Med and I was bringin' her back from her treatment. Just as we get on the elevator and the door closed, Ruby Baby cuts a big one. I mean this fart would curl your hair. It was so bad, the thing completely grossed out the entire elevator. We were going to the fifth floor and I knew I couldn't hold my breath that long, so I real quick punched the first floor button and wheeled her off as fast as I could go. While I was getting off, a bunch of visitors got on. I spotted the looks on their faces and laughed so hard I nearly passed out."

Hazel chuckled at the image. "You really have to be on your toes with these old folks, that's for sure."

Hazel spent the rest of her morning going through the same basic routine she had performed for years. She still enjoyed taking care of the cancer patients. It was something that provided continued meaning to her life. She knew she was unusual, in that she had lasted for so many years on the cancer floor without it getting to her. She had occasional moments that caused her heartache, especially when someone young died. Still she continued to stay there.

Things would be different next summer, though. She was old enough to retire but she was going to help Brian get his pediatric office started instead. They'd have to go into debt but that was no big deal. Brian would be a success. She'd make sure they got a good biller and receptionist and for a while she'd do the nursing for him. In a year or so she'd really retire and just enjoy working on her quilts and in her garden.

She would really miss the hospital tremendously, though. The people there had been a part of her extended family since before Brian came to her. She laughed aloud. The hospital had even provided a place for Brian to be born . . . .

. . . Hazel wasn't sure how old Brian was. Somewhere between five and seven, probably. Frankly, she hadn't given the matter much thought. He was, in fact, almost six years old the summer day Albert casually remarked that Brian must be about ready for kindergarten.

"I know this sounds pretty dumb," Hazel said, "but what do I need to do to get him started? How do I find which school he'll go to and that sort of thing?"

"If I were you, Hazel," Albert replied, "I'd call the district school administration office and get the details. I would guess that he'll probably go to Washington Elementary. Before you can enroll him, you'll need to make sure that he's had all his shots." He paused. "I just thought of a small problem. What are we going to do about a birth certificate?"

By this time Albert knew the whole story about how Brian had come to Hazel.

Hazel was startled. "What do I need his birth certificate for?" she blurted. "Won't they just take my word for when he was born?"

"I'm sure they won't. We'd better figure out something. He's going to need one eventually for other reasons anyway such as getting him a social security number when he goes to work."

"Yes, I guess you're right."

Hazel knew she had a problem. Brian Tanner had been born two years ago. The little boy who had given birth to Brian no longer existed. How was she going to come up with a birth certificate? She worried over the problem for several days with no solution in sight.

While at work one day she began to come up with a plan. During her lunch break, she wandered up to the newborn nursery and looked in at the babies. Moments later she sauntered over and got into a casual conversation with the ward clerk.

"Jean, who does the birth certificates for the babies in the hospital? I have a friend who had a baby here about five years ago and she lost the birth certificate. Whom should she write to in order to get another one?"

"They come out of the Medical Records Department, Hazel. I think old Mrs. Feldstein takes care of them. You know who she is, don't you? The blue haired lady with the big wen on her chin. Doesn't matter who does them, though, just tell your friend to write to Medical Records and they'll tell her how she can get another one."

"Okay. Thanks, Jean. See you around."

Hazel had occasionally run errands to the Medical Records area. Once in awhile the ward clerk at Hazel's nursing station needed someone to retrieve a patient's old chart. Hazel occasionally volunteered just for a chance to get a respite from the suffering surrounding her.

The Medical Records Department was a zoo. The flow of paperwork in the 650-bed acute care hospital reached avalanche proportions every day. Unfortunately the place was not staffed adequately and a barely controlled disaster was the result. In fact it seemed to Hazel that utter chaos might be a step in the right direction for them. Normally she cornered the first available person and asked for the chart she needed. However, this particular day, she went directly to Mrs. Feldstein with her request.

Blue Hair looked up in obvious irritation. "What do you want?" she snapped.

"I need a chart pulled. Here's the patient's name and number. Can you get it for me?"

"Damn. I just get started on something and then another interruption. Maybe I should quit and go to work in a mental institution where things make more sense. Okay, gimme the slip. Sit down and wait. I'll be back sometime today."

Blue Hair grumped off in the direction of the rows of shelving where patient charts were buried. While Hazel sat waiting, she scanned Mrs. Feldstein's desk. Her eyes widened. On the other side of the desk was a small pile of blank birth certificates. A partially completed form was in the typewriter. Hazel began to think about the possibilities. She had to have a birth certificate for Brian, but the thought of stealing really distressed her. The very idea of stealing was repugnant to her. While she sat wrestling with her conscience, Blue Hair unexpectedly returned.

"We're in luck. The damn thing was where it was supposed to be. I guess I can still believe in miracles."

"Thanks, Mrs. Feldstein. You're a dear."

"Take your bullshit with you and let me get back to work."

Hazel worried about having to steal a birth certificate form for the rest of the week but eventually she subdued her conscience. The crime itself would be insignificant; a mere piece of paper. If she got caught, though, she could foresee unpleasant consequences, like unemployment, but she didn't allow herself to dwell on them. She was already scared. If she thought about it very long, she wouldn't be able to go through with it.

Hazel knew how she was going to get the birth certificate; she just had to work up the nerve. Late the next week, she got her opportunity. The ward clerk again asked her to get an old chart that Medical Records had forgotten to deliver for a recent re-admission.

Prior to leaving the area, Hazel went into the back room and picked up a manila folder full of papers she had stashed in one of the cupboards earlier in the week. She again sought out Mrs. Feldstein.

"Hi, Mrs. Feldstein. I need a chart. Can you get it for me?"

"What the hell is this? Am I suddenly your favorite go-fer? Why don't you spread the fun around with the rest of the girls?"

"Well, you found it so fast the last time, I thought maybe you knew more about what was going on in here that some of the rest of them."

"Look honey, that was just dumb luck. You give someone else a chance next time. Okay?"

Hazel was glad Feldstein was being bitchy about the request. It would make it easier for her to go through with the theft. Her heart had been pounding and her stomach fluttering from the moment she had left the nursing station. What she was about to do was completely alien to her and she was a nervous wreck. She sat down beside Feldstein's desk as the old lady disappeared muttering into the labyrinth of shelving.

Hurriedly Hazel scanned the area. The stack of blank certificates she had seen the previous week was gone. Only two or three lay in the middle of the desk; just enough that a missing one might be noticed.

Hazel didn't want to have to work up her nerve again. She had to get one now. She needed an excuse to bend over the desk.

Across the desk was a box of Kleenex. Just the thing. Trying to look casual, she slowly stood up. Hazel placed her manila folder on top of the birth certificates, then reached for a tissue. She blew her nose and dropped the Kleenex in the wastebasket. Carefully, she leaned over and retrieved her folder, sliding one of the blank certificates underneath it. She was positive that every eye in the place was on her. In truth, no one was paying the slightest attention.

When Mrs. Feldstein finally returned, Hazel placed the chart under her folder and quickly escaped, the form safely tucked between them. She went to the basement and put the folder and certificate in her locker, then returned to the nurse's station. She felt weak and washed out the rest of the day.

That night, she got the paper out and scanned it. There was information she would have to fill in to make the thing look complete. She would borrow Albert's portable typewriter and peck out the words. There was the baby's name, of course, as well as those of the parents. The rubber-stamped name of the hospital administrator added authenticity to the document.

Apparently old Blue Hair made an assembly line process of the certificates. The hospital seal was already on the blank ahead of time. Hazel would only have to forge the name of an obstetric doctor on the second line. She scrawled it as illegibly as possible to make it look authentic.

When she turned the paper over, she discovered her first real problem. Along with the thumbprints of the mother, it required the footprints of the baby. Where am I going to get a baby's footprints, she wondered. Brian's feet were much too big. It had to be a newborn's footprints. She grinned wryly, picturing herself walking casually into the hospital nursery with an inkpad, and getting a newborn infant's prints. As she mulled over the problem, she suddenly remembered a trick she had seen on one of Brian's kiddy shows on TV. The woman on the program had been using finger paint and was showing the audience how to make little footprints using the side of the hand and fingertips.

Hazel filled in as much of the certificate as possible and the next day she brought home an inkpad from the nurse's station and practiced making footprints. The first thing she did was to get Brian to take off one of his shoes and socks and to ink the bottom of his bare foot.

"Whatcha doin', Mom?" he said.

"It's, `What are you doing, Mom?' There's no such word as whatcha. I'm just having a little fun. I'm trying to make footprints, like we saw on TV one day."

"Why?"

"I don't know. I just thought it would be fun."

Brian didn't ask any more questions. It didn't make any sense to him, but whatever his mother wanted was fine with him. After she applied the ink, he stepped dutifully onto the manila folder and left a footprint. She cleaned the ink off Brian's foot then studied his print on the folder.

Hazel then made a fist and put the bottom edge on the inkpad. By rolling the edge of the hand, including the curled up little finger, onto a piece of scrap paper, she was able to make a miniature footprint similar to Brian's real one. She created the toes with the tips of her fingers. After practicing numerous times, she felt uneasy, but confident enough to try the real thing. She went into the bedroom. There she made what she hoped were passable fakes on the birth certificate. She sighed. The prints would not bear close scrutiny but they would have to do.

Hazel got her hands cleaned up and then sat down to read Brian a story. He was a little puzzled. It didn't seem like his mom had had that much fun with the footprints.

The birth certificate did the job. When she enrolled Brian at the nearby elementary school, the clerk barely glanced at it, except to record the birthday and the name.

The first day of school was going to be traumatic for both Brian and Hazel. They were content with life as it was and neither wanted anything to intrude.

Hazel had known that the change would be more difficult for Brian than for herself. She realized she had insulated him from the world since she had taken him. She had tried to act as a buffer against sadness or unhappiness while she worked to repair as much of the damage as possible. She knew she had been successful in helping him forget much of the terror of his first four years. He seldom had his nightmares anymore. All the same, the isolation had built-in drawbacks. She feared it would be difficult for him to learn to play with other children, since no other kids his age lived in the neighborhood.

In the few weeks left in the summer, Hazel tried to prepare Brian for the first day of school. She spoke excitedly of the fun he would have playing with all the kids and of the new things he would learn.

When Hazel first mentioned school, he said simply, "I'm not going," and then went in his bedroom to play with his toys. His fragile psyche rebelled at the idea of school. Hazel wisely didn't press the issue but casually brought the subject up more often each day.

They spent several evenings at the school playground trying out all the equipment.

"After we get done swinging, let's go peek in some of the windows and see what the rooms look like, Brian," Hazel said as they walked around to the back of the school.

She sat on one of the swing seats, making short, heavy arcs in the air. The fat of her bottom rolled over the edge of the wood. Brian swooped high above her, pumping his legs at the sky.

The late summer sun cast long shadows across the playground. She swatted an occasional mosquito. A gentle eddy of air pushed a puff of dust along the ground. She wanted nothing else from life. It seemed perfect. She reflected on its perfection. There was, after all, one thing left incomplete. She wanted Brian to feel the same pleasure in living that she did. That would come in time.

A gust of wind billowed her dress. When she grabbed at the material she almost fell out of the swing. She whooped and brought the rebellious swing to a standstill.

"Brian. Did you know that I went to a school almost like this when I was little? It wasn't out in the suburbs like this and there wasn't as much grass, but it was fun. I used to jump rope with my friends."

"Did you really jump rope, Mom?"

Brian tried to translate his heavy, gray-flecked mother into a little girl, skipping rope. He couldn't. His concentration brought the swing back to earth.

"I know it's hard to believe this old, tubby body used to be a little giggly girl chasing boys around the playground, isn't it?"

Brian nodded vigorously.

Hazel smiled. "Don't be so agreeable, sonny. C'mon let's go look at the school."

Brian grabbed her outstretched hand and they ambled around the one story elementary building.

By the time school was ready to start, Brian realized he would have to go. He didn't like it, but his mom said it would be okay. So it would be. Mom didn't lie. Not never.

The first day, Hazel drove Brian to school rather than have him ride the bus. She wanted to meet his teacher and make sure he got started right so they arrived early. When they got to his classroom, only the teacher was there. Hazel introduced herself and stood talking with the woman while Brian hid behind her. Hazel knew she should not prolong leaving so she knelt down and helped Brian off with his jacket.

"Mrs. Lucas is your teacher, Brian. She's a very nice lady. She's going to show you where to hang your coat and where you can sit. She's also going to show you which bus to get on to go home after school. It only lasts until lunchtime, so you must go to Albert's when you get home. Okay?"

Mrs. Lucas leaned over to him. "I'm sure we'll have a good time, Brian. We'll play games, color and learn lots of interesting things. Let me show you where you'll sit."

Tears were brimming in Brian's eyes as he looked at his mother and then at the teacher. He was going to have to go through with it. As his resolution was gaining strength, the herds of kids began arriving from the buses. As the room began to fill Brian grew more frightened.

"Please, Mom, don't make me stay. I wanna go home." The tears were rolling down his cheeks.

"You have to stay, honey. It will be all right."

She gave him a kiss and a hug and turned to go, fighting her own tears. Part way down the hall, Brian's drumming footfalls turned her around. He flew at her, grabbed her by the leg and held on for dear life.

"Please, Mom, I'm scared. I can't stay."

Hazel bent down and hugged him to her. She was crying too as the stream of kids parted around them, flowing up and down the hall.

"I love you, Brian. I would never make you stay if I thought anything would hurt you. Ever. You know that, don't you?"

"Yes," Brian sobbed.

"You must trust me then. I promise you that it will be all right. In awhile, maybe not today, but soon, you'll be glad you're here. You'll make lots of friends and you'll learn things and forget all about being scared. Will you be brave for me now, and go back to your classroom?"

Brian stepped back and looked at his mother. He knew she was telling the truth. He'd have to do it. He gave her a hug and then walked back down the hall. The lump in her throat was so big that she couldn't keep from crying even harder as she watched his retreating figure. She was so proud of him. What might seem like such a small thing to most people was a triumph.

Brian had come a long way.

CHAPTER 11

After leaving his grandfather's, Brian slept for a few hours but felt restless and decided to go for a run to burn off the uneasiness gnawing at him. The run had been a temporary remedy for him for as long as he could remember. After a hard run, the hidden anxieties that oppressed him would lay dormant for a while. His mother would be back soon and they'd have a great evening with Kevin down on the river.

He dug out some old sweats and aged Nike cross trainers from his closet and headed for the door. He was just starting to get loose by the time he got to the main road a half-mile from his house. It was the corner where the elementary school bus had once picked him up. The bus was the first place he had realized the intensity of the anger that lay hidden within him . . . .

. . . . Brian waited in the early morning chill for the school bus. He saw it turn from the highway and rumble toward him. It came to a halt in front of him and the doors folded open. He spotted an empty seat at the back of the bus. He skirted carefully past Bill Kilgore, who was leaning over talking to someone. Kilgore was the bus bully. The bus carried only elementary children, but Kilgore was one of those kids whose body had outgrown his brains, so he looked much older. His size made him feel superior and he loved to make sure everyone knew it.

Brian had been sitting at the back of the bus for a couple of minutes when Kilgore looked up and saw him.

"Hey, you little punk! Get outta my seat," he sneered at Brian.

Brian didn't move. He was undecided what to do. Kilgore scared him but he didn't like to be pushed around. He didn't want to look like a chicken in front of the other kids.

"Did you hear me? I said get the hell outta my seat. I was sittin' there. I'm givin' you to the count of three to move or I'm gonna smack you in the mouth."

Kilgore came toward him, counting. At the count of two Brian was on his feet looking for another seat. Kilgore smirked in triumph as Brian tried to pass. As he was going by, Kilgore reached out a foot to trip him and gave a vicious shove at the same time. Brian went sprawling and hit his mouth on the edge of a seat. He lay on the floor of the bus. He covered his mouth with his hand and felt a wet, sticky mess. He pulled away the hand and saw blood on his fingers.

Kilgore's laughter was joined by some of the other kids. "Clumsy little shit, ain't he?" he said.

Brian remembered very little of what came next. In sudden fury, he came roaring off the floor clawing and punching at Kilgore. His swift attack took the bigger boy by surprise. Brian's rush drove the startled Kilgore backward, where he fell and hit his head on the rear door. Stars sparkled before Kilgore's eyes as Brian tore at his face, hardly realizing what he was doing, his anger was so intense.

The bus driver stopped the vehicle when she saw what was happening in the back of the bus. She waded through the yelling spectators and tried to pull Brian off his prostrate opponent. He turned on her, fists pummeling away in blind anger. After a short struggle, she got him under control. She turned him around, pinioned his arms to his side and held him against her until he stopped fighting her.

Slowly he came back to reality. After he calmed down, the woman marched him up to the front of the bus and sat him in a seat behind her. The whole thing embarrassed him. He also knew he was in big trouble.

When they got to the school, the bus driver took him immediately to the principal's office. Brian tried to explain what had happened but all the man heard was that he had been fighting and had struck the bus driver. The principal gave him three whacks. The pain and humiliation wakened other barely dormant emotions. Hazel was called at work and had to take time off to bring him home. Brian was expelled for three days and denied the privilege of riding the bus for two weeks.

At home, Brian looked up at Hazel defiantly. "It wasn't my fault, Mom. They're punishing me, but I didn't start it."

His anger had been so consuming that he remembered little of what had happened. He did know that Kilgore had hurt him and he was just protecting himself. He explained as best he could what he recalled of the incident.

Hazel didn't punish him. She didn't know what to say. She hadn't been aware that the temper existed. It was going to be a problem if she could not find a way to help him.

Brian didn't forget the punishment the principal had meted out. His pride was so hurt by what he saw as the unfairness of it, that he never rode that school bus again. He went back to school at the end of the three days, but from then on he walked the two miles from his home. Rain or shine, fall, winter and spring, he walked to and from school until he went to junior high. Kilgore never bothered him again - nor did anyone else.

Hazel never said anything about his not riding the bus. In her heart she was proud of him for the way he had stood up for himself.

CHAPTER 12

Brian's run led him through subdivisions and streets that had not existed even on a drawing board when he was young. Many of his memories were paved over and forgotten. Eventually he came full circle back to the junior high school and high school near his home. He jogged to the back of the high school to the small stadium where he ran the steps to strengthen the quads in his thighs as he had done almost daily when he had been on the wrestling team.

His first love had been basketball but his career had been aborted in junior high when he had gotten into a fight with one of his teammates during practice. The pushing and shoving had escalated to mayhem on several occasions when the coach wasn't watching and when Randy Bostic had brought blood from Brian's nose with a well-timed elbow, Brian had gone for him. By the time they pulled him off Bostic, the boy had a severe concussion and as a result Brian had quit the team.

His fuse had blown so badly he could hardly remember anything of the fight except the feeling of dismay as they carried Bostic off to the hospital. Brian had been pounding the boy's head on the floor as the coach returned from the locker room to pull him off Bostic. Brian was terrified that his father's evil was lurking somewhere in the back of his mind to erupt and maim innocent people.

His reputation as a tough guy grew with the telling so he was never challenged again until one afternoon when he was a sophomore . . . .

. . . . It was crisis time. Like a dummy, Brian had put off going to the bathroom before coming into that hour's study hall so he couldn't concentrate on his books. The discomfort was growing by the minute. He had a mental image of his bladder expanding and exploding urine all through his insides. The image brought him to his feet and up to the teacher for a hall pass. He hated asking the old biddy Mrs. Nusbaum for permission because she always made a case of it any time someone asked for a bathroom pass. It was as if administration docked her pay for every student she let free into the hall.

"Well, Mr. Tanner. I see we haven't learned to pay heed to nature's call at the proper time, have we? Are you sure it can't wait?"

Several of the girls in the front grinned at Brian.

"No, Mrs. Nusbaum, 'it' can't wait. I'm about thirty seconds away from using your wastebasket right now."

Mrs. Nusbaum wrinkled her nose and handed the pass to him without another word. With a brief "Thanks" he hurried from the room and down the hall into the boys' john.

With a sigh of relief, Brian finished his business, flushed the urinal and turned to go. As he was zipping his pants, he noticed someone sitting on one of the stools, smoking a cigarette. Gary Wilson was smirking up at him. He knew Wilson only by reputation. His friend Kevin had said that "Wilson is the diction-ary's definition of an asshole. Look it up and you'll see Wilson's picture beside the word."

"Hey, Tanner," Wilson said. "That is your name, ain't it? I'm amazed that a guy with such a tough reputation as you would have such a small cock. I always thought he-men were well hung."

"There you go thinking again, Wilson."

"What d'ya mean by that, you little piss-ant?"

Brian had already said more than he wanted. He wasn't afraid of Wilson; he just didn't feel like lending dignity to anything the guy had to say. He couldn't stand the constant irrationality of people. It was best to just leave them alone when they started becoming unreasonable. Ignoring Wilson, Brian turned to leave.

"You better answer me quick or I'm gonna kick your ass!" Wilson shouted as he was pulling his pants up and heading toward Brian's retreating figure. Brian was out the door already and into the hall before Wilson could get his pants buttoned up.

"We'll maybe have to talk some more, chicken shit." Wilson's voice floated down the hall, after him. Brian paid little heed.

Ill chance brought them together again that same week. On Thursday, Brian stayed late to finish a chemistry experiment. As he cut across behind the school to head for home, Wilson came out of the locker room exit. Brian angled off toward the football field to avoid the contact. It was obvious that Wilson had seen him and was changing direction to intercept him.

"Hey, chicken shit! I see you're trying to run away again."

Brian stopped by the bleachers and waited for Wilson to catch up to him. "What's your problem, Wilson?"

"I don't like the way you tried to insult me the other day, that's what."

"Why don't you just leave me alone, Wilson? You've got nothing to prove. You're big and tough and twice as smart as a goal post, so why don't we pretend fate never allowed us to meet?"

"Look, you lousy piece of shit, I can't stand to have people going around saying 'Don't mess with Tanner. He is one mean son-of-a- bitch.' That irritates me a lot for some reason."

Brian knew his self-control couldn't stand this kind of test. He turned and started walking away.

"Hey, chicken shit! I'm not through talking with you yet." Wilson reached out, grabbed him by the coat and yanked him back.

Instantly, Brian lashed out and slapped Wilson's hand away from his jacket.

"Don't you ever touch me again! Leave me alone! There's nothing in it for you, so just get away from me!"

"Not only am I gonna touch you again, Tanner, I'm gonna rearrange your face!"

He swung a fist as he spoke, catching Brian on the side of the chin.

Brian staggered back, any hope of avoiding the fight gone. Instinctive rage was back, and he gave no heed to the fact that he was outsized. He threw himself at Wilson. Wilson had never fought anyone who was impervious to pain. No matter what he did, Brian kept coming at him, kneeing him in the groin, kicking him in the shins, biting him on the hand and clawing him like a wild animal. When Brian blasted Wilson's head against the side of the bleachers, the boy's vision was reduced to starbursts as consciousness fled momentarily. Wilson was overwhelmed by the onslaught. Vaguely he realized that Tanner was sitting on his chest pounding away at his face with both fists, but he was helpless. He tried to roll over, to rid himself of the demon mauling him when he sensed that Tanner wasn't going to stop. He grew desperate.

Brian hissed through clenched teeth, "You'll never beat me again! Do you hear me?"

Shouting began at the periphery of the melee. The cross-country coach, Jess Hammond, happened by, as the fight was raging. At five feet, six inches, and weighing only a hundred thirty-five pounds, he knew he was no match for Tanner's frenzy. Though he suspected that Wilson had mouthed off once too often, the kid was in deep trouble and needed rescuing, if only to save Tanner from committing murder.

He grabbed a large hose, coiled and ready for use in watering the football field, turned it on and blasted both boys with a torrent of icy water. The water's impact shoved them apart. Brian struggled to his feet and turned to face a new adversary. The cold, gushing stream pounded him in the face. He couldn't see and fought to catch his breath. He put his arms in front of his face to protect himself from the relentless cataract of water.

He was coming to his senses. He heard himself gasping, "Okay! I give! I give! Stop it, you're drowning me!"

The coach dropped the hose. Wilson lay groaning on the ground. Brian stared, stunned at what he had done to the bigger boy. Wilson's face was becoming a mass of bruises. One eye was swelling shut, blood was trickling from his nose, down across his cheek and puddling in the mud under his head. The boy was rolled into a fetal position, clutching his groin.

Brian felt no sense of victory, just overwhelming anguish, for himself and for his victim.

"I didn't mean to hurt him like that, Coach. Please believe me. I didn't mean to do that."

Brian's very real agony of conscience softened the teacher's fury.

"That's a terrible thing to do to someone, kid. When were you going to stop anyway?"

"You won't believe this, sir, but I didn't realize how much I was hurting him."

The excuse sounded hollow.

Hammond walked over to the prostrate Wilson and knelt down to examine him. He was beginning to recover, trying to sit up. The coach helped him, checking him over carefully. The entire faculty knew Wilson's reputation as a bully. Whatever reluctant sympathy Hammond had for the bigger boy was tempered by a subtle admiration for the destruction wrought by the smaller Tanner kid. Although he didn't condone the violence, he was amazed at how completely Wilson had been dominated.

"The son-of-a-bitch was killing me," Wilson moaned.

"Are you going to be all right, Wilson? Let's go in and clean you up."

He helped the boy to his feet. Once standing, Wilson shook the coach off.

"Just let me be. I don't want any more help."

"Look, Wilson, I can't let you go home like that. Your parents will skin me alive if I do."

"Don't worry yourself, Coach. No one at home gives a shit about me anyway. Just leave me alone."

He turned and began to limp off, then stopped. He looked back at Brian.

"I guess those stories about you were true. You are one tough bastard."

Brian didn't respond. He just stared miserably at the ground as Wilson limped away.

Hammond returned his attention to Brian.

"I think we'd better go to my office and talk about this awhile," he said.

They walked back into the school without speaking. Their footsteps echoed through the silent building. Brian trailed water along the polished tile floors. Together they went down into the basement to the coach's tiny office, located near the boys' locker room.

As they entered the little cubicle, the man nodded at the metal folding chair in front of his desk. Brian sat down, soggy and miserable.

"How do you explain what you just did out there, Tanner?"

Brian remained silent, staring at his lap.

"You're something of an enigma, Tanner. Obviously, I don't know you very well, since I've never had you in class, but I know something about you. For instance, Coach Hirshon told me what you did to a teammate several years ago in basketball practice. Before he stopped you, you broke the kid's nose and gave him a concussion by pounding his head on the floor.

"But I've also talked to other people about you. Most kids say you are one tough sucker, but I've never, until today, seen you fighting. The teachers all say you are a super student, quiet and intelligent. I have more than a passing interest in you, Tanner. I see you out running every once in awhile and any kid who runs just for fun interests me. How do I reconcile that quiet serious person I've heard about with the little savage I just saw in action? I had a feeling you could have killed Wilson if I hadn't stopped you. If I report what you were doing, it could have serious implications on your status in this school."

Brian looked up, tears brimming his eyelids.

"I don't know what I'm doing when someone tries to hurt me, Coach Hammond. I lose control of myself."

"Any idea why?"

"Yes, sir."

"Well?"

"I'm not sure I can tell you, sir."

"I think you have to tell me, Tanner. If it's privileged information, it won't go any further. I think it's important that you tell me."

He could see the boy struggling with himself.

Finally Brian spoke. "When I was a very little boy, my father beat me all the time. I hardly knew a time without fear, or pain, or hunger. He barely fed me or clothed me, or even liked me. My mother took me away from him but the mark he left on me is still there. I can't stand for anyone to hurt me. It's as though that man is still out there and I'm trying to get at him. I would kill him, I think, if I could find him."

The fury and the tears mingling in Brian's eyes startled Hammond.

"You can never get even, Brian. The world doesn't work like that, you know. You'll only turn into an animal like your father, and then he wins."

"I can't help it. I hate him with everything that's in me. I want to just once do to him the things he did to me. I want to beat him until he begs me for mercy. God, it would feel so good!"

"No it wouldn't, Brian. It would be an empty victory. You'd be the loser in the long run."

Brian looked at the coach. Hammond could see that the youngster was not convinced. Brian knew he had little chance of his getting vengeance anyway. He didn't even know who his father was. Not even his name.

They sat looking at each other, the silence growing. Finally the coach asked, "Well, Brian. Do you spend your life looking for a ghost in your past? What's the answer to all this?"

"I don't know if there is any answer, Coach," Brian replied sadly. "Can I go now?"

"Yes. Go on home. If you ever want to talk more about it, come see me. Okay?"

"Sure." Brian got up and walked slowly out of the office.

Many of the scars on his soul were not healed. Some were still festering virulently inside, eating their way into his subconscious mind.

The fight and the subsequent conversation with Coach Hammond had a beneficial result for Brian though. Coach Hammond, recognizing Brian's need for a constructive way of venting his anger put him in touch with the wrestling coach. Reluctantly Brian agreed to work with the man and found to his surprise that the harsh discipline and sometimes exhausting workouts and matches helped him gain better control of his emotions. By the time he was a senior he was a pretty good wrestler, losing only six times that year. Because of his late start in the sport, he was never great but he took intense pride in the fact that no one had ever pinned him.

CHAPTER 13

Dressed in an old sports coat and slacks he had found in his closet, Brian pulled Hazel's five-year-old Chevy Impala out of the garage. It was a good half hour's trip to the spot on the Ohio River where Mike Fink's Riverboat Restaurant was moored.

The Saturday night traffic they found on I-75 was fairly heavy as they followed it toward the heart of Cincinnati. It was a trip he had made many times during his undergraduate work. Brian looked past Hazel in the passenger set and spotted a sign advertising Xavier University. He thought of Lani and the evening darkened for him. Even that many years removed from her and he couldn't shake the feeling that he still loved her. . . .

. . . . Brian sat, engrossed in his chemistry book. The school year was beginning only that day but he was already several chapters into the text. He was in the cafeteria of the University Union, munching on a tuna salad sandwich and waiting to go to the first class of his senior year. The days since high school had flown by before he had known it.

By this time, Brian had matured into an attractive young man. A shade over six feet tall, he weighed a hundred and eighty-five pounds. Straight, sandy hair often fell across his forehead. Blue-gray eyes were the dominant feature of a face accentuated by high cheekbones and a nose that was a large enough make him look ruggedly handsome. On the few occasions when he laughed, his lips would draw back to reveal a straight set of teeth with a small chip out of the corner of the left central incisor, the result of falling off a bike and using his face as a landing strip when he was in grade school.

To his classmates and acquaintances, he seemed a humorless person with an extremely limited social life. An introspective young man, he spent a good deal of time staring out at the world with dismay because of the cruelties and injustices he observed. Brian had little use for humans as a whole. It was his feeling that the human animal had not been long out of the trees. It was fascinating to him that a race could produce such completely opposite people as Hazel and his father; gentle love and unspeakable depravity. Brian could never quite reconcile the existence of both in the Creator's plan.

He closed the chem book and turned his attention to the rest of his sandwich. He noticed with disgust that he had dropped a glob of mayonnaise on the fly of his jeans. He dipped a napkin into his water glass and began rubbing at the spot. He was suddenly aware of movement across from him that became a lovely pair of thighs. They moved around the table and stopped beside him. His eyes followed them to where they disappeared into a pair of white shorts. Higher still his eyes traveled, stopping at nipples straining to find a way out of the blue cotton halter-top. He couldn't seem to raise his sights any higher. The face attached to the body apparently was staring down at him since the body was not moving.

The face cleared its throat to get his attention. He looked up even though he knew his own face was flushed with embarrassment. Ah, she was beautiful! Like the thighs, her face was tanned a golden brown. A pale-blond cascade of hair framed it. White teeth and bright blue eyes highlighted the tan. The lips were over-generous, but the nose was perfect. He had never seen a perfect nose until this one.

"Hi," the lips said. "Would you mind if I share your table? This place is a zoo today and I can't find a place to sit down. I promise not to bother you."

Brian, embarrassed to be found rubbing the front of his crotch with the wet napkin, hurriedly withdrew his hand.

"Sit-sit down," he said, red-faced.

"My name's Lani Kelly."

"Hi, I'm Brian Tanner."

The girl took a few moments to arrange her food, during which time Brian checked her out further. She was awesome! He felt intimidated by her presence. It was a large university and he had seen her only from a distance.

The girl looked up from her food and smiled. Brian searched his mind for something to say but instead could only grin idiotically back at her. She looked down at his chemistry textbook.

"What are you doing with a bookmark a quarter of the way through a schoolbook on the first day of classes?" She continued with feigned disgust, "And a chem book at that. I'd be lucky to be that far along by the end of the year."

"Well," Brian began defensively, "I like to stay ahead a little if I can. I need the grades so I can get into a good med school."

"Are you going to be a doctor? I think that's terrific! I'm glad there are people like you. I couldn't stand to touch sick people." She gave a slight shudder. "And actually operating on a person, and all that blood and stuff. No way."

Brian felt warmed by the praise. He relaxed slightly. He found that talking with Lani was easy because she did most of it. Everything he said triggered a whole long sequence of comments from her. She was a complete extrovert. Not the loud-mouthed, overbearing kind, but rather a vivacious outgoing girl who saw nearly everything as terrific, or neat, or great, or wonderful. She was refreshing.

They sat and talked for a long time. Brian saw some of the looks of envy he was getting from other guys as they passed by. Too bad he didn't deserve them. He looked at his watch. His lunchtime had disappeared. He hadn't been aware of the time passing. He needed to leave for class. Reluctantly, he began to clear his tray.

"It was nice talking to you, Lani, but I have to get to class. It wouldn't be good to be late the first day."

"Which way are you headed? I have to go too."

"I'm going to the Science Building."

"Terrific! I have to stop at Hardy Hall. That's right on the way. Can I walk with you?"

Brian couldn't believe his luck. "Sure. It's bound to help my social standing, being seen with a beautiful girl like you."

Brian wasn't sure where that sentence had come from. What a cheese-ball come-on!

"You're nutty, Brian. You probably kick better looking girls than me out of your bed every day."

She laughed at her own comment. She didn't believe it for a minute. She was confident of her own beauty, aware that not many girls on campus could outshine her. Anywhere for that matter.

They carried their trays to the stacking area, then headed through the main lobby and out to the front walk. It was a perfect September day and the campus was alive with the subtle tension that the first day of school brings. Freshmen were bustling about in confusion, their expressions telegraphing satisfaction at finally being away from their mothers, or, conversely wishing fervently that they were back home.

As they crossed the campus Lani was constantly greeting someone, most of them guys. Brian only saw three people he knew by name, while Lani said hello to dozens of people, without making him feel neglected. She gave attention to everything he said, as if it were important.

They cut across a tree-shaded section of lawn and came to the Science Building.

"Well, I guess this is where I get off," said Brian. "It was a pleasure talking with you." He tried to think of something more to say to prolong the moment.

"I enjoyed it too. Why don't you give me a call at the Delta Chi House sometime? Maybe we could go study or something."

"I'd really like that." He was surprised by her offer.

They were interrupted before he could say more. "Hey, Lani."

She looked around. "Oh, hi, Gary."

"Mike's waiting over in front of the library. He said he was expecting you fifteen minutes ago. He was getting a little tense."

"That's his problem," Lani replied with a touch of anger. "He must have forgotten that I have a class. I'll call him later."

She turned back to Brian. The momentary hardening of her face disappeared instantly. "I have to get to class, Brian, so I'll see you sometime, okay?"

She headed toward Hardy Hall, turning to give him a little wave. Brian watched the strain of the breast on her halter-top as her torso twisted around toward him. He waved back sadly. She was too beautiful, he said to himself. There's no way she'd ever go out with me. He ran up the steps into the Science Building. The essence of her bothered him for several days until he finally drove her out of his head.

A week later he was walking across the campus when he heard someone calling his name. Turning, he searched for the source of the voice. Lani floated out of the stream of students and ran across the grass toward him. She had on a gray jock shirt and blue running shorts. She looked delicious.

He wondered if she realized that she was so incredibly sensual. She had an air of naive innocence and provocative sexuality surrounding her.

"Hey, you, I'm kind of mad at you," she began.

Brian was surprised. "What do you mean?"

"I mean I thought you might call me. You said you would, if I remember correctly."

"I thought you were just being nice. Why would a beautiful girl like you want me to call her after only just meeting me?"

She looked at him quizzically, cocking her head to the side like some gorgeous tropical bird. "Come on now, Brian. I don't tell just anyone to call me. I liked you right away. Besides, you have a nice butt." She laughed aloud, her white teeth flashing. "Pick me up tonight at seven o'clock. We'll study for a while and then you can spring for a pizza or something. Okay?"

"Sure. That'd be great."

"Terrific! See you then." She was off and running back to rejoin her companion who was waiting for her, a frown on his face as he stared across at Brian.

They "studied" that night for fifteen minutes before Lani got bored and they went to one of the pizza places at the edge of the campus. She took his hand as they walked. Brian felt almost exalted. They talked and laughed and ate pizza and the night flew by.

As he walked her back to the sorority house, she guided him into the shadows of one of the buildings. She turned to embrace him. Brian felt like a rookie. He really had no experience with women. Oh, he had kissed a few, and wrestled around occasionally in the back of his car, but he was still inexperienced. The taste of pizza on her lips and tongue was exhilarating. The breasts and stomach shoving against him were creating a swelling sensation in his groin. It was like feeding tequila to someone only used to beer.

Lani felt the growing erection pushing against Brian's jeans, trying to get at her. She loved being able to do that to men. That little critter down there wanted her the worst way. Maybe next time. She wasn't that easy. Well, she was that easy, but she usually faked as if she wasn't.

With a little giggle she pulled away and led him the rest of the way to the house. Embarrassed, Brian laughed when she asked him why he was walking so stiffly. She was so natural and outgoing and fun. She was wonderful!

Brian fell helplessly in love with the golden vision. He couldn't wait to be with her. He took her to movies and football games, and concerts and anywhere she wanted to go. She took away his virginity in the back of her Lincoln. She was, or rather her daddy was, very rich. His grades went all to hell, but he didn't worry too much. He had never felt so alive. He told her he loved her and she said that she liked him a lot, too.

They came close to arguing only once and that was when Brian became incensed about an article he had read in the paper about a father raping his daughter. He was talking angrily about it when she interrupted him.

"Let's don't think about things like that, Brian. Those kinds of things are too unpleasant and there's nothing we can do about them anyway."

When he tried to protest, she put her finger to his lips and with a laugh changed the subject. His subconscious mind registered the fact that they never discussed anything unpleasant nor of any consequence. The conscious part of his brain inhaled her perfume and plotted the curve of her breast.

"I won't see you 'till after Thanksgiving, Brian. My mom and dad are coming in late tonight and then we're flying to Colorado sometime tomorrow. I don't know when we're leaving. Dad made the reservations."

"I hope you have fun skiing, but I'll miss you, Lani. Will you call me once in awhile?" Brian said.

"Sure I will. You don't think I could be away from you that long and not call, do you?"

Brian smiled happily. "Can I come tomorrow and say goodbye to you?"

Lani hesitated. "Probably you'd better not. I'm not sure when we're going and it'll be really hectic around the house with all the girls leaving for the holiday. It just wouldn't be romantic. Let's just say goodbye tonight."

Brian was disappointed. He would really miss her.

Hazel was still up when he got home near midnight. She missed having her son around all the time the way he used to be.

She was glad for him though. It was good to be in love. She could see how it brightened his life.

Brian came quietly in the back door expecting her to be asleep.

"Oh, hi, Mom. You still up?"

"Just getting ready for bed. I just had to finish up a few chores first. How's Lani?"

"She's wonderful, Mom. She's going to Colorado to ski over the Thanksgiving break."

"Sounds pretty nifty."

Hazel didn't know what else to say. For some reason, she didn't really like the girl and didn't know why. She didn't think it was jealousy. Who knew? She shrugged. She would never tell Brian anyway.

"I miss her already," he continued. "I think I'll run down in the morning and say goodbye."

The next morning Brian rolled over and looked at the clock. It said seven o'clock. He had been awake since six, waiting for the time to pass before he could get up. He knew that Lani wouldn't be up for awhile, so he had to kill some more time. Finally, too restless to lie in bed any longer, he got up, showered and shaved.

He dressed, then got out one of his books. He planned to use the Thanksgiving vacation to shore up his sagging grades. He sat for a while staring at the writing in his anatomy textbook, but nothing filtered through to his brain. He found himself reading the same paragraph over and over again. His mind kept wandering to Lani's anatomy. He was going to miss her. He couldn't let her go without one last goodbye.

The clock said eight-thirty. By the time he got through town to the campus it would be after nine-o'clock. She'd be up and around by then. He put on his winter jacket and raced for the back door. Thirty-four minutes later he turned the Ghia down Sorority Row, a block of large, once private residences, inhabited now by many of the sororities.

The aura of snobbishness emanating from the block always turned Brian off. The attitudes of many of the girls who lived there irritated him. If you weren't in a sorority or a fraternity you were considered a lesser human being. Lani once laughingly told him that he was a special case. As a rule she never dated a boy who wasn't in a fraternity. She couldn't understand why he had never joined. When he tried to explain, she had told him "never mind." The discussion was getting too serious. It was good that he was going to be a doctor and someday he would probably be rich.

The street was full of activity as he drove down it. The Row was lined with cars whose trunks and doors were hanging open, being stuffed with suitcases and boxes of the departing girls.

As Brian eased slowly up the street he spotted a car pulling away from the curb. He quickly accepted this offering from the god of parking and pulled into the vacant space, a few buildings down from Lani's sorority house. As he got out of his car, dead maple leaves crackled underfoot. He paused to inhale the autumn with its own subtle mingling of scents and emotions.

He passed several of Lani's sorority sisters as he headed through the front door. They gave him tentative waves as they were leaving. Parents and daughters were scattered through the lounge and on the stairway of the large two-story house. The polished mahogany banister and woodwork spoke of more opulent days, and of workmen who once had pride in their craft.

Brian followed somebody's father up to the second floor. The man was puffing mightily from a third trip up the stairs to fetch his daughter's luggage and appeared to be working on a first class cardiac arrest. Brian headed for the back of the building to Lani's room. He had been there once, during one of the sorority's open houses. He hoped she was still there so he could surprise her.

Her door was open and conversation floated into the hall. Thick pile carpet absorbed much of the sound, making the words indistinct. As he drew close, they took on an unfortunate clarity. ". . . . long before you have to be back at school?" It was Lani's voice.

Brian grinned but then paused when he heard a male voice respond.

"A week," the voice said.

"I think it's just sensational that we can use your father's condo. We can just play house and ski and forget about everybody and everything for seven whole days. Are sure you can afford it?"

"Sure, my father's paying for everything, even the plane tickets. I told him I had a buddy at school I was taking with me. He likes you all right, but I'm not sure he's ready for us to spend a week living together. He doesn't want me to screw up my career as a future Supreme Court justice."

Lani laughed. "I might screw you, but not your career, Richard, Honey. You can marry me after you graduate from law school."

"I've really missed you, Lani. It's been a long three months. Your body looks fantastic. I can hardly wait to get off that plane."

"Well, let me give you a little appetizer to tide you over."

Lani came to close her door as Brian walked through the opening. A flicker of embarrassment and irritation passed across her face.

"Hi, Brian. What are you doing here? I thought you agreed not to come down today." She tried to block his way.

Brian didn't speak. He thought he had known Lani. He hadn't. Only the surface had been visible, not the person beneath it. He stared at her; anger, pain and sadness all taking their turns with him.

"I think you should go," Lani said.

He continued to look at her.

"Who is this guy, anyway, Lani?" Richard asked, plainly irritated.

"Just someone I study with once in awhile."

"Well, why doesn't he get the hell outta here? What's he doing just standing there?" He came toward Brian,

Brian switched his attention to Richard. The face and clothing spoke of money, self-confidence, culture and Ivy League. He topped Brian by a couple of inches, but seemed to be looking down from a greater height. Although he outweighed Brian, the seeds of a corporate paunch appeared to be taking root around his waist. Brian looked the man up and down. He wanted very badly to leave but he felt rooted, incapable of movement.

Richard became uncomfortable under Brian's unwavering stare.

"Well, what's your problem, buddy? Didn't you just hear her ask you to leave?"

He grasped Brian by the arm and shoved him toward the hallway. Brian felt the tension and anger escalate alarmingly.

"Keep your hands off me," he said between clenched jaws.

Richard felt the age-old mating challenge. If the two of them had been big horn sheep, the valleys would already be echoing with the sound of their crashing, head-on collisions.

"Who's going to make me?" he challenged. It sounded like a scene from a grade school playground.

Brian laughed suddenly and tried to shake his arm loose.

Richard tightened his grip. "I said who's going to make me?" The punk was giving up the battleground and he was going to enjoy his victory.

White-hot anger flared in Brian's eyes. He shoved Richard away. Taken by surprise, Richard stumbled back and fell across Lani's bed. Brian turned and left. Before he had taken more than a few steps, he heard Richard in pursuit. He turned to meet the man. Richard's rush carried them both to the floor. Brian felt the carpet burn his cheek as he slid along it. Richard punched him in the kidneys with one hand as he tried to get Brian in a headlock. Vaguely Brian's brain registered Lani's voice screaming at them to stop. Richard's forearm was tightening across his throat.

Brian's temper finally blew. He had made such strides over the years to keep it under control that he had become confident it could not get out of hand again. He was wrong. He grabbed the little finger on the fist that was pushing painfully against the side of his head. He pried it away from the hand, forcing leverage until the finger broke with an audible crack. Richard shrieked in agony as he pulled away. Brian turned his body in Richard's loosened embrace. He grabbed the man by the hair on each side of his head and smashed his own forehead into his opponent's face. Richard's nose broke and the blood came gushing forth over the two of them.

Brian was astride him now, punching wildly. Suddenly he felt stinging sensations on his cheeks and a screaming in his ears. He lashed out blindly. A cry of pain brought him rudely back to reality. He looked over to where Lani lay slumped against the wall. She was holding her face. He had struck her when she had raked his cheek with her nails to make him stop.

"I hate you! I hate you!" she spat at him.

He didn't even recognize her.

He looked down at Richard. The man was staining the blue carpet red. Brian got unsteadily to his feet. He stumbled down the hall, descended the stairs and out the door. The bright sunlight surprised him. It should have been cold and raining. There was no one you could trust. No one except Hazel. He would have to remember that.

CHAPTER 14

Brian followed I-75 to where it crossed the Ohio River in the middle of downtown Cincinnati. Once across the bridge he cut left and wandered the back streets of Covington, Kentucky until the came to the access road that headed back down to the river. Brian knew the restaurant would be packed and that parking would be at a premium in the narrow area between the bluff and the riverboat. Brian eased down the ramp, let Hazel off at the gangplank, then maneuvered his way back up the hill to find an open parking spot several blocks away.

Brian jogged back toward the restaurant and as he approached he spotted Kevin's red hair and slightly rolling gait. A body that even from a distance was enough to make Brian's eyes widen in appreciation accompanied him. If there was a brain attached to those legs and lungs, it would be a serious bonus, Brian thought.

Kevin and the woman were already up the gangway and inside the boat near the hostess stand by the time Brian caught up to them. Kevin was just about to introduce his guest to Hazel as Brian approached. Kevin spotted him and without a pause he came and grabbed him in a big bear hug. The affection of a lifelong friendship flowed between them.

"It's good to see you, son," Kevin said.

"You too, Kev."

"Let me introduce you to my friend. Brian, Mrs. Tanner, this gorgeous young lady is Katey Doll. Katey, this is my best friend Brian and his mother, Mrs. Tanner."

"Just Hazel," Hazel amended the introduction. "Hello, Katey, what's your last name?"

"It's Doll, Mrs. Tanner," Katey giggled. "Everybody asks that. My name's Katey Doll. Kevin says it's lucky my parents didn't have a sick sense of humor and call me Barbie."

"Kevin and Barbie Doll would have been too close for comfort," Kevin added as they all chuckled.

Kevin still looked like he had back in high school despite a slight thickening in his body and thinning of his red hair. Brian always thought Kevin looked like a taller version of a young Dustin Hoffman. He wasn't handsome but he was appealing. Katey seemed to think so as she hung on his every word. She was a striking young woman who exuded a certain gentle obtuseness. Brian found himself liking her.

The multi-deck riverboat was packed with the murmur of diners grazing contentedly on expensive steak and seafood, amid the subtle clatter of silverware attacking plates. There was an aura of comfortable anticipation from the small crowd waiting in the lobby for a table.

In a short time Brian and the rest were seated on the second deck by a window overlooking the river. Riverfront Stadium dominated the shoreline across the way. Office buildings and the modest skyscrapers of Cincinnati loomed above the stadium. The occasional office light punctuated the darker silhouette of buildings and reflected irregularly off the river, giving it a dark oily look as boats plowed the waters back and forth. It was the kind of scene that Brian had missed while living in Lansing.

"Must have been a real shocker for the pioneers to come paddling around the bend and see all this sitting here, I bet," Kevin said into a lull in the conversation.

"This wasn't here . . .," Katey began, then giggled to a halt. "Oh, Kevin, you're such a silly guy."

"Yeah, a real stitch. Speaking of stitches, there was this surgery resident the other day who went into Recovery to see one of his patients just coming out of anesthesia from a complicated hernia operation. He says to the guy, 'I've got good news for you and I've got bad news.' The patient, kind of out of it, opts to hear the good news first, so the resident says, 'Well the good news is that we were able to save your testicles,' The patient breathes a sigh of relief and asks, 'What's the bad news then, Doc?' 'The bad news,' the resident says, 'is they're in a jar under your pillow.'"

Brian and Hazel laughed appreciatively while Katey sat there sorting out the good news from the bad until the bulb clicked on.

"How goes your fellowship, Kevin?" Brian asked as the four of them sat watching the scene before them and perusing menus the size of road maps.

Kevin was a year older than Brian and was specializing in orthopedic surgery beyond his regular surgery residency.

"Pretty intense," Kevin said. "I had to bribe everyone but the mayor to get off call tonight when I knew you were going to be home. I'm looking forward to getting out and starting my own practice. I hope I can get it going here in Cincy but you know how clannish and territorial physicians can be. If there's enough business to go around I probably won't have too much trouble getting referrals. After all I'm a local boy not some 'outsider'. How's the kid business going for you?"

"Almost there. Mom and I will start looking for an office location over Christmas. I don't see any trouble getting on the staffs of all the hospitals in the area."

"Shouldn't be problem. People aren't exactly beating down the doors to become pediatricians. Not enough money in it."

"There'll be enough," Brian said simply.

"For you, maybe but not for normal greed. I'll tell you something funny, I can remember the first time you said you were going to be a doctor and 'take care of kids.' . . . .

. . . . Because of his background and his view of life, Brian tended to mature mentally much faster than most of his high school classmates. While his peers were worrying about their acne and their next date, Brian was more concerned with where the future would take him. He thought briefly about being a minister, but he had grown skeptical about God's interest in the world. Where was God when the babies were being beaten? Brian wondered. There was a need in him to counteract the evil his father had created but he didn't know how.

His compulsion had grown more demanding as a result of a sophomore social studies project. Not surprisingly, Brian had chosen child abuse as his topic. Unfortunately, he found a wealth of information on the subject.

He sat in the library making sporadic attempts at a beginning. Everything he wrote sounded so trite. He felt impotent at the extent of the disease. A disease without a cure.

He leafed through a newspaper article. As he read he felt the icy sweat of revulsion and pity bead up on his face. His body tried to shrink away from the words in front of him.

A three-year-old girl had been imprisoned in the bottom of an outdoor toilet in a state park. She had been missing for three days before she was found. The park was closed for the fall and winter so the toilets were seldom used.

Cold, hungry and covered in human excrement, the child had endured. The man who found her said she had looked up at him and asked for a glass of Kool Aid.

The little girl was in the hospital suffering from shock, exposure and infection in her feet and legs. The kidnapper, a man, was unknown.

In one fierce movement Brian crumpled the newspaper in both hands. For a moment he had been at the bottom of that pool of filth with the child.

The librarian, aghast at Brian's destructiveness, was coming toward him. He left library books, magazines and papers behind as he ran from the library, not from the woman's anger but from a need to move, to flee the feeling of hopeless rage.

Sweat was soaking into his notebook as he slowed to a walk near his house. Chad and Kevin were throwing a football in Kevin's front yard. Kevin turned and rifled a pass at Brian's head. His notebook went flying so he could free both hands to protect himself. In one swift motion he snagged the ball and threw it over the house and into the back yard.

They laughed together as Chad went to retrieve the ball. The run had calmed Brian but his eyes betrayed his anxiety.

"You got problems, son?" Kevin always read him well.

Brian needed to talk. He described the newspaper article, then repeated it when Chad returned with the football.

"If I was that little girl's dad," interjected Chad, "I'd beat the livin' shit out of the guy who did it! If they ever find him, that is."

Brian had a better solution. "I'd take the guy and dump him in the toilet and leave him there for a couple of days. I'll bet he'd think twice before he did it again. I'd love to see him beg just before they dropped him through the hole."

Kevin chuckled at the idea. "Instead of an eye for an eye, you'd have a shit for a shit. It's almost biblical."

Brian smiled as he headed for home. It wasn't that ridiculous an idea.

Later that night he was sitting on the front porch steps watching the evening sky darken. The sun had disappeared but the fall air hadn't cooled. Kevin was outside shooting baskets by the light over his garage. The tap tapping of the ball on cement and "clung" sound of the rim after a missed shot wafted down the road to Brian. Kevin's football career had ended two years before when he tore the ligaments in his good leg. But he still loved sports, even just shooting baskets late at night by himself.

Without a trace of self-consciousness Kevin wore shorts, revealing the prosthesis that substituted for his missing foot. Many years ago he had personally made the decision to replace his malformed foot with an artificial one so that he could walk without the hated club shoe. With long pants it was almost impossible to tell that he wore a prosthesis, except for the slight roll to his stride.

Kevin took a final shot and kicked the basketball into the garage. He stopped at his back door. He saw Brian's silhouette outlined against the living room light. He detoured across the gravel street to his friend's.

"What's happening, Brian?" Kevin inquired as he sat down on the steps.

"Nothing much, Kev. Just out here getting some fresh air."

"And thinking about a little girl trapped in an outdoor shitter?"

"Yes."

Neither spoke for a while. Brian looked up at the sky. The crystal clear night was covered by emerging pinpricks of light.

"Did you ever wonder how many stars are up there?" Brian asked.

"There are thirteen million, one hundred fifty-five thousand, thirty-five and a half."

"What's the half?"

"One of them just exploded but we won't know about it for a million years."

"Seriously, there are so many. We're just a speck of sand. Meaningless."

"Probably."

"What are we anyway?" Brian continued. "Up inside our skulls is this gray blob of flesh full of electrical currents. That blob is us. It's trapped up there, connected to a body that carries us around, feeds us, excites us, hurts us. What are all those electrical currents? How can electricity be a person? Is there a soul or something that's in control? . . . Why do some gray blobs throw little girls into a pit full of shit and piss? If you try to figure it out, you could lose your mind."

"Don't then. There isn't an answer, so don't mess yourself up by searching."

"There has to be a meaning, Kevin."

Silence engulfed them.

"I think I'm going to be a doctor, Kevin."

"Yeah?"

"I need to do something worthwhile in life. Maybe I'll just take care of little kids."

"Why only kids?"

"I don't know; just appeals to me." But he knew. Knew there were countless children out there who needed to be saved. By a fluke of luck, a miracle, he had survived, and risen from the ashes. He had a debt to repay. His life was incomplete until he paid it.

Pointedly he changed the subject. "I went out with Brenda Kruger the other night."

"You asked Brenda out? I don't believe it."

"No, she asked me. I didn't know how to turn her down."

"Why would you want to? She has an incredible body. And those legs. Two of them." He laughed.

Brian smiled. "Yeah, but her mind is made of silly putty. You have to be spacey to be a cheerleader."

"True, cheerleaders are a whole different breed. They stand out there jumping and yelling and the only ones cheering with them are their six-year-old sisters. Most of the time I don't think they even know the score."

"You're telling me. Last Friday they were yelling something like 'Look out Westcott, we got the ball. There's no doubt you're gonna fall.' Not only did we not have the ball but Westcott was blowing us away thirty-two to nothing in the fourth quarter. I about puked."

A note of amusement came into Kevin's voice. "I guess some gray blobs didn't get their full quota of electrical currents."

"No doubt, Kevin. No doubt."

The more Brian thought about medicine, the stronger became its appeal. The goal rapidly became an obsession to him.

Hazel warned him it would be a long, costly process, but together they could do it. Hazel started to save any extra money she could set aside and they began searching for scholarships.

Life was, in general, fairly enjoyable for Brian, but he could never quite shake the feeling that he was out of synch with the people around him. But Hazel was always there, to help him maintain his mental balance. Without her, he wasn't sure he could cope with life. There had been many times when he had awakened in the middle of the night just on the edge of the nightmares. The knowledge that Hazel was always there to love him would calm him and allow him to go back to a peaceful sleep.

As he got older, though, he became more aware of how fragile life was and he worried that he might lose his mother. Each night he would stare at the ceiling of the darkened bedroom and send a plea toward Heaven.

"Please don't let anything happen to Mom, God. I really need her."

She was always there each day, so he knew that God had heard.

CHAPTER 15

The day after their excursion to the riverboat restaurant Hazel traded one of the other nurses on her floor so she could get Sunday off to be with Brian. They spent time together shopping, planning for their new office, and talking about all the interesting things that had occurred in their similar professions.

Hazel had gone back to school so that she could get her LPN license. She knew that, had she been born into different circumstances, she would have made a good physician. She had lost the awe with which most people hold doctors, realizing that few of them were geniuses and were simply people who had the courage and financial resources to stay the course through the eleven to sixteen years of college, med school and residency training. She had seen some gifted physicians and some that must have been in partnership with a mortuary.

Toward evening Hazel startled Brian when she said, "So, when are you going to get around to telling me what's bothering you, Brian?"

"Bothering me?" he said.

"Something's eating away at you. This is your mom speaking. I know you better than you do yourself."

Brian sat back in the couch across from his mother and thought, knowing she was right but that he hadn't realized it until she had asked.

"Just my temper again. Not a big thing but I hate it when I lose control, you know?"

"What happened?" she asked.

"A little boy, maybe four or five, came through the E.R. the other night. He had been beaten by his parents, at least that's my opinion. I had him admitted but the next day this slimy creep masquerading as a father took the boy out of the hospital without my permission. When I saw him in the hall, things kind of got out of hand and I slammed him up against the wall."

"Did you hurt him?" Hazel asked.

"Not much, but I wanted to. It was right there at the edge but fortunately one of the RN's was around to talk some sense into me. That would have looked pretty good in the old Lansing State Journal. **PATIENT'S FATHER BEATEN BY DOCTOR!** They'd probably have suspended me."

"You have a natural hatred for those people, Brian. Forgive yourself for those feelings."

"Yeah, I suppose so. You know, when I was young, I had such fear that there was some genetic flaw in me that would make me be like my father, that someday I'd turn mean and start beating on helpless children for no other reason than there was some evilness I had inherited." Brian looked pleadingly at Hazel. "How could he do that to me, Mom? How could a man be so full of ugliness that he could beat and starve a little child that was his son?"

"There's no easy answer to that. There are no excuses but there are many reasons. Evilness does exist, but certainly there isn't an ounce of it in you. You're the most caring, lovely person I have ever known, Brian. In some perverse way, I thank him every night of my life for what he did to you."

Brian smiled ruefully. "Yeah, me too. I'd like to find him and thank him personally."

"Now, Brian," Hazel said.

"Just kidding. Whoever he is, he probably died of cirrhosis of the liver, lying in some gutter years ago. It's a strange feeling, not knowing who your genetic parents are, though, you know?"

"Of course I do. You have no beginning, no roots that you can relate to and somehow deep within your subconscious you still feel there must have been some reason for them to reject you. There isn't, Brian. The flaw was entirely within their damaged minds."

"I'll never understand how minds can work like that. My biological mother left me and never came back. And that man ran away from his own child without a backward glance."

"Well, not quite," Hazel said hesitatingly.

"What do you mean, 'Not quite?'" Brian said.

"He tried to steal you back," Hazel said.

Brian felt a surge of irrational fear rush through him. His hackles rose and a feeling of having nearly walked off a cliff in the dark, only to be saved by a flash of lightning, surged across his mind.

"What do you mean by that?" he said.

"He found us some time after we moved out here and threatened me."

"You're serious! Why didn't you ever tell me before?"

"It would have been too frightening for you when you were young. You would always have wondered if he was out there waiting. When you got older, it just seemed like something better left buried."

"Why are you telling me now?"

"To help fill in as many of the missing pieces as possible so there won't be anything left unsaid between us."

"How did you get rid of him?" Brian said.

Hazel looked back through the years and said, "Ah, that was an interesting experience. . . .

. . . . Hazel pulled the car into the garage. She was exhausted. Some days working on the cancer ward got to her. She had lost a young girl today, dead at twenty-three with never a chance to live. For a brief second she allowed a flicker of doubt about God's mercy to pass across her consciousness. She shook it away.

She hauled herself wearily out of the car and headed across the snow-covered yard to get Brian. Albert had been baby-sitting for her for over six months and everything was working out fine. The thought of her little boy made her smile. She tapped on the back door of his house and went inside. Brian came running into the kitchen and she picked him up and gave him a hug. The gauntness was almost gone from his face. His appetite had only recently slowed nearly to child-normal.

She said "Hello" to Albert then retrieved Brian's coat from the hall closet and put it on him. Together they put toys and color books away and went on home. Unlocking the back door, she paused, fear clutching at her throat. She had spotted foot-prints in the patchy spring snow. They made a single path away from the back steps, across the back yard and around the end of the house. A tremor of despair tugged at her heart.

"Go on in and hang up your coat and put away your toys, Brian. I'll be right there."

"Where you goin'?"

"Just out to the car for a sec. Go ahead, I'll be right back.

"'Kay."

Hazel closed the door behind the boy and went to look at the footprints. They were a man's. She followed the tracks around the corner. They approached closer to the house. Soon she saw why. The basement window was broken and the latch ajar. The tracks didn't lead away from the house. Someone could be in there . . . and Brian was in there too!

Hazel lumbered back around the house, raced up the porch steps and in the back door.

"Brian! Brian, where are you?" she cried.

No answer.

She hastened across the kitchen and into the living room.

"Brian!" she screamed, near hysteria.

"In here, Mom. What wrong?"

"Where's 'In here'?"

"In the bathroom."

She flew down the hall and banged open the bathroom door. Brian was just zipping up his pants. She went to him and hugged him fiercely.

"What wrong, Mom?"

"Nothing, Brian. Nothing at all."

She had to search the rest of the house. She couldn't leave Brian alone so she carried him along as she began to search all the rooms and closets. She was terrified that at any minute someone would jump out at her but she needed to assure herself that no one was in her house.

In the basement she stopped at the open window. Cold air poured in. She covered the broken pane of glass with cardboard and tape. She was perplexed. No one was in the house and nothing appeared to be missing. It might be just a prank, but in her heart she didn't think so. As she passed the phone she saw the note perched on it.

The writer of the note was miles away by the time Hazel got home from work. The note had ended a weeklong quest, begun the day the man realized that he was almost out of money and had nothing left to hock for more booze. He kept searching his bleary mind for a way to get some cash. He had almost reached the desperation point when he thought about the kid. The old bitch who'd taken his kid should be good for a whole lotta money or he'd call the cops on her for kidnapin'. She'd be good for five hundred, maybe a thousand bucks.

He took the bus back to his old apartment and went inside. Careful to avoid the landlord, he went up the stairs to the apartment where the old lady lived. Only she didn't live there anymore. Some greasy son-of-a-bitch slammed the door in his face when he asked for the old woman.

He was stumped. His alcohol-riddled brain wasn't handling the problem very well. He knew he couldn't ask the landlord where she'd gone. The fucker would try to get his back rent.

He searched the vacant corridors of his mind for an answer. He couldn't figure it out. He spent some of his dwindling hoard of money on a fifth to help him think.

As he came out of the liquor store an ambulance went by with its siren wailing. A couple of cells came together and an idea began painstakingly to form in his head. He strained at it and after awhile it became a full thought. The old broad had worn a pink nurse's aide uniform and those weird white shoes that people wore when they were on their feet a lot. He had seen her on different occasions walking down the street, coming home from work. If she was a nurses-aide and she walked to and from work, then there was a good chance that she worked at that big hospital near by; he couldn't remember the name of it.

Pushed by the need for money and a newly born desire to get even with the bitch, he hurried over to the hospital. Just the few blocks of walking wore him out and the cold numbed him to the bone. His body had no resistance to the spring chill. His unshaven face was gray with fatigue.

Once he got to his destination, he wasn't sure what to do. He didn't know the old broad's name so he couldn't go askin' around to see if she worked there.

He tried going in the front door, but the security guard at the desk wouldn't let him into the hospital since he couldn't give the name of a patient he wanted to visit. Calling the guy an asshole hadn't done him any good either. He wandered around outside the hospital complex, feeling nervous and out of place. After a time he spotted one of the maintenance men going in a back door. He waited a few minutes, then followed the man inside. He had no idea where he was, nor how to look for the old broad, so he just started wandering up and down hallways. He hated the smell of hospitals. He had spent too much time in them as a child to ever forget that they stood for pain and fear. Days of broken bones and fear slithered and crawled through the alcoholic haze of his mind.

He went up a stairway and through a door into a long hall and came to one of the patient care areas. He saw nurses going up and down the hall and into patients' rooms. An occasional pink uniform revealed the presence of several nurses aides.

Along the corridor toward a central artery of the floor, he rounded a corner and spotted the security guard who had kicked him out before. He was about to turn and beat a hasty retreat when the guard looked up and saw him. The guard jumped to his feet and headed for him. The man turned and scurried back down the hall, through the door and down the steps he had climbed moments before. He heard the pursuit above him and kept running until he found an exit sign. Panting and worn out, he stood outside and looked up at the massive building. He was angry and frustrated. It was an impossible task. Furious and in need of a drink, he turned to go.

The building was beginning to disgorge its load of first shift employees. Most of them were coming out a side door. He stood behind a sign and kept watch as the gush of people soon slowed to a trickle, then dried up completely.

The man was pissed. Maybe the old woman didn't even work there. His vision of easy bucks was dying. He trekked back toward his one-room dump, pausing long enough at a supermarket to shoplift a bottle of wine and a package of hot dogs for his supper.

The wine and food revitalized his greed. He'd go back again the next day at shift change. Maybe he had just missed seeing her leave.

He didn't spot her the next day or the next but he kept coming back each afternoon. What the hell, he didn't have anything else to do and besides, that supermarket was an easy mark.

On the sixth day he spotted the fat old toad waddling toward him. He couldn't believe his bleary eyes. He ducked behind a sign, an ugly smile spreading across his beard-stubbled face. He followed her as she ambled across the street and into the parking lot. The bitch had a car! He'd never seen her other than on foot. So she did have money. He watched her through bloodshot eyes as she got in her car and drove away. He noted carefully the make of the car, an older model Ford Escort. He'd be back tomorrow.

It slowly occurred to his alcohol-sotted mind that just stopping her in the parking lot wouldn't be enough to scare her into giving him money. She had to know for sure he could get his hands on the kid anytime he wanted to. He paused for a second. How did he know for sure she had the kid? He had always assumed that she did, but for all he knew she coulda taken the boy to the cops. If so, she could get him in trouble with the law.

He would have to find out where the old lady lived. He didn't own a car anymore. The sons-of-bitches at the bank had repossessed it. Everybody was against him. He hated the goddamn world. There were some days he could hardly wait to die. He wished he had enough guts to kill himself, but he didn't. He shrugged the thought away. He knew a guy who would loan him his car if he promised him some of the money he was gonna get.

The next day, he was parked at the curb, watching her car when the broad was supposed to get off work. He was glad that it was almost shift change. The damn heap he was in didn't have any heat.

In a short time the employees came hurrying out of the building, beating a welcome retreat for their homes. He watched the herd divide into individual people and disappear into their cars. Most of them had driven away by the time the old lady came into sight. He had begun to get a little worried about missing her. He watched her get into her car, back out and start to leave. He turned the ignition key and the old clunker coughed to life in a cloud of conspicuous blue smoke. He cursed aloud. Grinding the gears into first, the car lurched off in pursuit.

He followed at a safe distance through the rush hour traffic, sweating with the mental effort it required. He thought he had lost sight of her half a dozen times, but he stayed on her tail as she finally pulled off the freeway onto a side street and finally onto a gravel road. He slowed to a crawl but kept her in sight. Up ahead he saw her car turn into a driveway. He drove slowly past and saw the woman plodding through the snow, away from her garage, toward the neighbor's house. He drove farther up the street, turned around, parked the car in neutral and waited. In a little while he saw something that gladdened his heart. He watched as the woman and the brat came walking hand-in-hand back across the yard. They were deep in conversation.

"Ain't that just fuckin' tender," he said aloud as he put the car in gear and drove away.

The next day he returned to the same street and parked in front of a vacant lot. He walked cautiously the rest of the way to the old woman's house, trying to look inconspicuous. He checked for nosy neighbors then slipped up the driveway and headed for the back of the house. The garage was empty. A deadbolt lock secured the back door. The front door was the same. He cursed quietly.

He skirted the house, leaving unwelcome footprints in the crunchy old snow. The cold seeped in through the holes in the bottom of his shoes. The basement window looked big enough to squeeze through, but he felt vulnerable at the thought of lowering his body through the small opening.

He needed all his nerve to kick in the pane of glass. He reached inside and unlatched the window, tugging at the seldom-used hinges. It squawked and protested but slowly came open. Gingerly he lowered himself to the cold, wet ground. His gloveless hands clutched at snow and dead grass as he backed carefully into the opening. He tried to turn his head and see into the velvety darkness but his pupils were still adapting to sunlight. He hung briefly and then fell clumsily into the basement, landing on the water pump and banging his shins.

"God damn son-of-a-bitch!" he cried out in pain.

He moved cautiously through the dark as he felt his way toward the stairway, vaguely illuminated by the light from the window. The silence and darkness were frightening. He stumbled up the stairs and opened the door into the kitchen, not pausing to consider that anyone might be there.

He wandered through the house growing more and more angry at the cleanliness and the feeling of comfort. Originally he had intended asking for a thousand bucks but now he was going to soak the bag for five thousand instead. He searched for something to write on in all the tidiness. At last he spotted a grocery sack sticking out of a wastebasket. He tore off a piece and picked a crayon out of a pack on the kitchen table. Laboriously, he wrote, "You got my kid. For $5,000 I won't take him back and you can keep him. I'll call you to git the money."

He tore another piece from the sack and wrote the number from the front of the telephone. He stuffed the number in his pocket. He placed the note on the phone, then unlocked the front door and ran clumsily back to the borrowed car.

With trembling hands, Hazel laid the note on the table. So he'd found them after all. She had almost begun to believe that the man was gone for good. She looked down at Brian, who was hungrily annihilating a stack of Oreo cookies. She would run away again if she had to, out of the city if necessary. She would never give up her son. Her life would be worth nothing now if she lost him.

The ringing telephone startled her. It would be him. She crossed the room and lifted the receiver.

"Hello," she said sadly.

"You see my note?"

She remembered that despised voice. "Yes," she replied simply.

"You got 'till the end of the week to get the money."

"But I don't have that much," she protested.

"Bullshit! You got a car and a nice place. An old broad like you don't need to spend money no place anyhow. You probably got a ton saved up."

Even over the phone, she felt his contempt, his venom.

"I'm sorry but I don't have it. I might be able to get five hundred dollars, but that's all."

"Look, lady, you better scare it up someplace," the man screamed into the phone, "or the cops are gonna be on your ass for kidnappin'. I'll call you tomorrow night."

The line went dead.

She had to leave. Even if she could talk the man into taking the four hundred and some dollars she had saved up, Hazel knew he'd keep coming back, again and again. She would have no peace.

Come on, Brian, we need to go back over to Mr. Bricker's"

"Why?"

"I have to talk to him about something. It won't take long, then I'll fix some supper."

"Okay."

Reluctantly she went across the yard to her landlord. He came to the back door.

"Hello again. Did you forget something?" he said.

"No. Something has come up. I'm afraid I'm going to have to move."

Albert could see the pain in Hazel's eyes, the barely suppressed tears. "Will you come in and tell me about it?" he asked calmly. "Something's wrong isn't it? Maybe I can help."

"I don't think anybody can help me," Hazel's voice echoed hopelessness.

"Maybe not, but I'd like to try. I've become rather fond of … of having those good meals every day."

"There's nothing that can be done, Albert. I just have to move. I appreciate everything you've done for me. I'm going to miss …" her voice caught in her throat and her eyes filled with tears.

"Come inside, Hazel. Let's talk about it."

So she told him the rest of Brian's story. She had learned to trust him almost from the beginning but she had not wanted to discuss Brian's true history. There was nothing he could do now but she needed to talk to someone.

When she finished, Albert reached across the couch where they were seated and took her hand. Anger was in his voice as he spoke.

"Let's not give up so easily. Maybe we should fight before you run."

"How can I? If he reports me to the police, the very best that could happen is that they'd put Brian in a foster home. They could even arrest me for kidnapping. They'll never let someone my age keep a little boy, especially one with emotional problems."

"I wish I could argue with you, but the authorities do strange things sometimes."

"I can't let him go, Albert! I love him and I need him. And he needs me! We're good for each other. His life will be worthwhile because of me, and mine will be worth living because of him. I finally have a reason to exist. I will never risk losing him. Never!"

Albert sat silently absorbed in thought. "If you run," he said finally, "you're letting this animal win. You can't let that happen. Here's what we're going to do." He hunched forward and began to explain a plan.

The next evening Hazel's phone rang. It had to be the man. Her hands shook as she picked up the receiver.

"Hello."

"You got the money?" The harsh, raspy voice sounded confident.

"Yes."

"I thought so," came the smug drunken reply.

"Do you promise you'll go away and leave us alone if I give you the money?"

"Sure. What the hell do I want the little shit for? You gimme the money and you seen the last of me. He was always a pain in the ass anyway."

Hazel had never hated anyone until she had met this man. Why was he alive anyway? Certainly God would never care if this creature was blotted from the face of the earth. No one would mourn his passing and the world would be so much better off without him.

A tiny film of sweat beaded the fuzz over her upper lip as she continued, "When are you coming out to pick the money up?"

"Oh, no you don't, lady. I ain't comin' out there. Not that I don't trust you, y'understand, but let's pick someplace safe and quiet."

Hazel hesitated a moment. "All right. Where?"

"You know where the corner of Genesee and Harrison is downtown? I wantcha to be there at eleven o'clock tonight."

"You want me to be on the street at that time of night? I might get attacked!" Hazel argued.

"You should be so lucky, lady. A blind goat wouldn't touch an ugly old bird like you."

She could imagine the sneering, loose lips, savoring the insult, getting even for her having humiliated him. "I'll be there," she said and hung up the phone.

She smiled.

At five minutes before eleven Hazel drove past the corner where she was to meet the man. The streets were empty, other than an occasional car. Except for the puddles of light from the street lamps the streets were frighteningly dark. The large buildings surrounding her blended into the blackened sky. Piles of gray, crunchy snow were scattered around, waiting to melt.

She parked a short way down the street from the intersection. She checked her watch, then got out of the car and walked back up the street to the corner. She watched warily as a young black came out of the darkness, eyeing her as he passed. The streetlight illuminated his face briefly and then he was gone.

Down the block, Hazel saw the door of a place called The Olympia Bar ease open. Her heart began to pound almost uncontrollably as she recognized the man. She was panting, little gasps of breath. Would the plan work? She had so much to lose. A lifetime.

There were no preliminaries. The man stumbled up to her and asked, "You got the money?" His drunken slur savored the last word. She smelled his boozy breath on the night air.

"Yes," she said.

"Well, give it the fuck here so's I can get goin'." Gray-speckled whiskers surrounded the sneer, days old.

Hazel reached inside her purse and withdrew a wallet, cheap, smooth vinyl, one she had bought for this purpose. She tossed it toward the man. He snatched at it greedily, fumbled it, then tore it open with eager anticipation. He pulled out the money and threw the wallet on the ground. He began to count the bills. A look of anger formed on the man's sleazy face.

"Hey, you goddamn bitch, there's only fifty bucks here! What do you take me for, some kinda fool?" he yelled and advanced menacingly, stuffing the money in his pants pocket.

Hazel met him, head on, consumed by hatred. "No, I don't take you for a fool. I take you for a piece of scum that shouldn't even be alive." She leaned forward and spat in the man's face with all the force and disgust she could summon.

Shock rendered the man temporarily still, the spittle running down his face. With a sudden yell of rage he lashed out with his fist. The knuckles caught her flush on the cheekbone, snapping her head back and knocking her to the pavement. She hadn't dodged. She had known that he would strike her but naively hadn't anticipated being knocked out. Her vision was reduced to a little white speck as he began kicking her. The added pain brought her to consciousness. She huddled into a ball to protect herself. Her heavy, padded winter coat protected her from some of the force of the blows.

"Hey, you! Hey, stop that!" came a voice out of the night. The beating ceased for a second as the man sought its source. It had come from a darkened car, parked unnoticed a short distance away. The door opened and a little, hunch-shouldered old man got painfully out. A flash camera went off in his hand.

"I saw him, ma'am. I saw that man steal your money and now he's attempting to rape you. I can make a positive identification on him. He'll rot in jail for years."

Hazel reached out and snaked up the billfold covered with the man's fingerprints.

He stood there blinking at them for a long moment. Then a dim light clicked on in his brain. "You set me up, you fuckin' old piece of shit!"

Hazel lay on the ground staring up at him. He made a move toward Albert, who pulled out an aged old revolver he'd had since he was a kid. He pointed it at the man and nodded.

"Listen you," Hazel said, "the boy is long gone so you can't take him away from me. If you even try, we'll have you put in jail for a long time for stealing my money and beating me, and trying to rape me. You would have destroyed that child if I hadn't taken him and now he's mine. If you ever try to take him again, I tell you from the bottom of my heart, I will find a way to kill you! And I'll have help. You'd better get out of here or I'll start screaming bloody murder!"

The man knew he was beaten. He lacked the mental capacity to think the problem through. But first he was going to get even. He headed back toward Hazel's prostrate form. From Albert's lips came the shrill call of a police whistle. The sound reverberated off the buildings.

"Rape!" screamed Albert at the top of his lungs and blew the whistle again.

Hazel reached inside her coat. She withdrew another whistle and blew it with all her might. Patrons began to stream out of the bar, avid for excitement but wary of involvement.

The man was done; he could do nothing. Turning away he fled into the night. Albert went to Hazel. She looked up at him and gave a tremulous, watery smile. In the dim street light Albert could see the swelling distorting the left side of her jaw. She reached up, touched it gingerly and winced.

"Well, is he gone for good, Albert?" Her voice had a desperate hopefulness.

"I don't know, Hazel. Only time will tell. Let's go home."

Albert helped her to her feet. She leaned over to him and gave him a kiss on the cheek.

She turned and hurried toward her car. Hopefully Brian was still asleep at home with the hastily recruited baby sitter, oblivious to the events that had set him free.

CHAPTER 16

Brian had been back in Lansing only a day when he got a page from Dr. Santonio, his program director. He ignored it for the time being. The social worker woman from Genesis would have complained to Santonio that Brian had not participated in the "learning" sessions after pushing the Sanderson creep against the wall. The chewing out could wait. He had just started a new rotation, an elective in peds oncology with one of the East Lansing physicians, and he was involved with a young boy who was giving him a problem during the examination.

Fourteen-year-old Chad Hoover struck a chord with Brian since he was being raised at the St. Vincent's Home in Lansing. The boy was hiding an overweight body within baggy outsized clothes. He was back for an annual checkup after having been cured of cancer several years previously.

"I need for you to take your sweatshirt off, Chad," Brian repeated. "It's important to the examination."

"Nah, that's okay. I'm all right. I didn't ask to come here."

"I'm sure you're fine, Chad, but I need to check you out thoroughly."

"Why, so if I have it again I can have more chemo and puke my guts out and lose my hair?"

"The 'it' he was referring to was the cancer that had invaded his body years before.

"I won't lie to you, Chad. That's why we have the checkup. But the sooner we spot things the faster we can take care of them."

"So I can maybe live longer?" He shrugged his chubby shoulders. "It's not that big a deal. Life isn't that fucking enjoyable." He looked up furtively at Brian to see if his language had bothered him.

"You want to talk about it, Chad? Most of the time that helps. I always go running to my mom when I get low."

Brian cringed, realizing that Chad didn't have a mother.

Chad looked over at him with pain-filled eyes. A tear dribbled out of the corner of his eye. Angrily he wiped it away.

"I'm sorry, Chad." Brian paused. "I know how you feel."

"You don't have any damn idea how I feel! At least you got a mom," Chad said.

"Well, you're right, I'm lucky, but I didn't always have one."

The boy looked at Brian suspiciously. "You got adopted?"

"You could say that."

"I ain't never gonna get adopted. I'm too old. And besides who wants a kid with . ." He stopped.

"With what?" Brian prompted.

The boy paused then pointed angrily pointed at his chest. "With tits!" he said.

Brian understood what Chad was referring to. He knew that the chemotherapy the boy had undergone had enlarged his breasts.

"So that bothers you a lot?" Brian said.

"Hell, yes! Wouldn't it you? The kids call me Chad Boober. I even put on weight in my stomach so my boobs don't show so much. The other night somebody left a bra under my pillow."

Brian watched the boy clench and unclench his fists.

"What if I could find you a solution, would that help?" Brian said.

Chad looked up instantly, eyes wide in hope.

"Not some diet? That doesn't work," he said skeptically.

"A friend of mine is a plastic surgeon. If I ask him, he might do a simple cosmetic surgery called a breast reduction on you.

He can take out the extra tissue and flatten you out pretty good."
Brian raised his hand in caution. "I'll have to make sure everything's all right with Dr. Nichols here, but my friend's done it
before with some of his other patients. Doesn't hurt much and
leaves only tiny little scars."

"I don't care how much it hurts. I'd do it anyway," Chad
said. "If you could get that guy to do it, man, I'd . . ." he said,
unable to voice the joy he would feel at losing his physical and
mental burdens.

"I'll give you a call about it some time this week, okay? In
the meantime I still need you to take off your shirt so we can get
on with the examination."

Brian's next patient was a no show so he found a phone in
the doctor's dictation room and called Santonio's office. In a few
moments Brian's program director came on the line.

"Brian, just wanted to let you know I appreciate you keeping your appointment with that Grey woman, the social worker
at Genesis."

Brian wasn't sure if the man was being sarcastic so he replied
with a non-committal, "Uh huh."

"She said you picked things up so fast it was unnecessary
for any further sessions. Just remember what I said, though, if
you want to stay in business, keep your hands off the civilians.
Understand?"

"Perfectly," Brian said. "Thanks for your concern,
Dr. Santonio."

"Okay," Santonio said and hung up without any sign-off
pleasantries.

Brian put the phone down and sat back in his chair.
Apparently the social worker woman hadn't told Santonio about
his lack of cooperation. If he saw her again, he would have to
thank her.

At the moment Kristin was busy with her on-going baby-
sitting saga. She was now "Aunt" Kristin to Joyce Harper's two

daughters since Helen, the State social worker, was unable to find a suitable foster care situation for them and Kristin didn't want them to be placed in one of the juvenile care facilities. According to Helen, the grandmother didn't want "anything to do with those brats," and the father wasn't due to be paroled for a couple of months. Kristin shuddered at the thought of Heather and Holly being at the mercy of their father. If he was as bad as Joyce had described him, the girls would have a very tough life ahead of them. Probably a lot worse than it had been with their mother.

From her days as a State social worker, Kristin knew the power she had possessed within the court system. Either through overload or indifference the judges would frequently defer to a social workers' assessment of where a child should be placed, either with foster parents or back with the natural mother or father. She would begin work with Helen to check on Joyce's husband's worthiness to act as a caretaker for his own daughters. If he was a slime, they'd get them away from him immediately. It would be interesting to see how much he wanted them.

Kristin knew the foster care system to be inhabited by both saints and sinners. There were many wonderful people who gave of their lives to help kids and were a godsend to the system. There were also people involved who had their own agenda, most often money from the State, but frequently it was about sex and other forms of abuse.

After caring for the girls over the weekend, she understood that they both had serious emotional deficits. She wasn't about to let them be placed improperly if she could help it. She had already rejected one couple after visiting with them for a short time. Helen had spoken highly of how immaculate their home was but Kristin understood that cleanliness was not always next to godliness.

She had been in the couple's suburban home for only a short time before the vibrations given off by the two people took on an atonal quality. The wife was an obese slug of a woman who was perched on the sofa and seemed unlikely to be the good house cleaner that the home seemed to indicate. The husband was a dark, whippet-like man who seemed an even more unlikely candidate for housekeeper of the year. He seldom made eye contact mainly because he was always surreptitiously staring at Kristin's breasts. He actually licked his lips once when Kristin carefully crossed her legs. She felt like a piece of meat.

They would not allow her to speak privately with the two teenage girls who were industriously cleaning away in the kitchen when the man gave her a brief tour of the house. Kristin beat a hasty retreat and wiped herself emotionally clean as she drove away. On Monday she planned to ask Helen to go talk privately to those girls in the "clean" house.

In the meantime she needed to look after Joyce's daughters. From an experience standpoint, she was ill equipped to care for a five and a two year old. She found, however, that the experience was growing on her. She discovered moments of unaccustomed contentment as she sat watching "The Littlest Mermaid" on the DVD player while Holly, the two year old, lay huddled in her arms, tiny thumb being sucked intently. There was the same feeling that came from watching the two of them wolf down grilled cheese sandwiches and tomato soup.

Or when they called her Aunt Kristin.

CHAPTER 17

Hazel leaned over and rested her weight on the snow shovel. Sweat glistened on her face and she felt her heart thudding away energetically in her chest. She stretched the tightened muscles of her back as she surveyed her work. A premature cold front from the north had brought several inches of snow to the southern part of Ohio and she had been hard at work removing some of it. Even at her age Hazel still enjoyed shoveling her own walk and driveway. Snow blowers were for lazy people or ones with large driveways or clogged arteries. She pulled crisp cool air into her lungs and smiled contentedly.

The sun wasn't up yet and the light over the garage intensified the darkness surrounding her. She enjoyed winter but then again she enjoyed what each season had to give. She guessed that spring was still her favorite though. Hazel loved being in her garden. She could never get over the joy of working in the earth. The birth of green from brown and the new life all around always gave her a sense of peace, of the continuity of God's world.

Unlike Brian, she was not troubled that she could not figure God out. The cycle of life she observed, its ebb and flow, was miraculous. The constant birth, death and re-birth of things only made her feel more strongly that the Creator was good and marvelous.

Even death did not disturb her. It was a simply a natural culmination to life, not a thing to be feared, as Brian did. The blackness and finality of death terrified him and Hazel could never make him feel otherwise. Hazel saw death almost daily on the cancer ward. In its final stages it was often beautiful to see. When people finally quit fighting and were ready for the end of pain and trouble, she could see a peacefulness slip across their faces. Death was just the beginning of something somehow better.

She was in no hurry to leave, of course, for her life was a treat. She had much to do to help Brian with his new office when he got home for good in the summer. The love she had for him was beyond description. She was so proud of him. What a tremendous life Brian had brought with him. Out of the pain and heartache Brian's father had created came a pleasure of the opposite extreme.

Hazel went inside and sat at her kitchen table to rest and relax for a few moments before getting ready for work and taking Albert's breakfast to him. She was more tired than usual and her headache was back. In a few minutes she would go get up and take some aspirin and grab a good hot shower.

She thought of Brian. It had been wonderful to have him home for a couple of days, but she had that aching sadness that always came when he had to go back. Shaking away her small depression she strained to her feet and headed for the bathroom. In mid-stride, she caught her toe on the threshold of the kitchen and went sprawling comically into the living room. More irritated than hurt, she picked herself up, went into the bathroom to wash her hands and get the aspirin from the medicine cabinet for her headache. Her reflection laughed back at her as she pictured how she had fallen all over her ample bosom. With any luck she hadn't broken any floor joists, she kidded herself.

She still felt lightheaded and disoriented when she got to Albert's with his food. Her eyebrows were knotted in pain and she nearly stumbled as she entered his bedroom.

"Are you okay, Hazel?" Albert asked.

"Yeah, I'm just getting old, I guess. I've been having these headaches for the last couple of weeks. I think I'll go see an optometrist one of these days. I probably need glasses."

"How do you feel otherwise," Albert said.

"I feel great, especially for an old bird who should be retiring pretty soon."

"When was the last physical you've had?" Albert asked.

"I can't remember the last one. I feel fine. No need to waste my money."

"Hazel, you work in a hospital and you have an attitude like that? Do me a favor and go in for a checkup. Please?"

She looked at the aged face of the only real friend she had ever had other than Brian. In a strange, platonic way they had been husband and wife for almost a quarter of a century. Albert was everything she had ever wanted in a man if she ignored the sex drive, which she had found easy to do. Shortly after meeting Albert she had ceased to have the dreams about having someone to care for her.

She understood that he wouldn't live many years longer and her heart ceased beating momentarily at the thought. She would see him later though; she truly believed that. The more of death she had observed, the more she understood that it was just an interim step to something so overwhelming as to be incomprehensible. There was another dimension they would evolve to and then things would finally make more sense.

"Okay, Albert," she said to her friend. "I'll go see Dr. Dodds as soon as he can squeeze me in. All right?"

He nodded agreement as he aimed a hot cinnamon roll toward his mouth while Hazel headed off for work.

Hazel spent the rest of her morning going through the same basic routine she had performed for years. She still enjoyed taking care of the cancer patients. It was something that provided continued meaning to her life.

About lunchtime, Hazel noticed the headache coming back. The fact that it had returned scared her. The two aspirins she took at lunch made only a small impact on the pain. As she was taking the elevator back to her floor for the afternoon, a slight feeling of vertigo struck her. When the elevator doors opened, she had difficulty exiting.

She entered the hall and passed one of the oncology specialists who was leaving after making his rounds. Hazel teetered unsteadily as she went by him.

"What's the matter, Hazel? You don't look very well," he said.

"Oh, it's nothing, Dr. Helcher. I just have a bad headache and it's made me dizzy."

"Well, you'd better go sit down awhile until you feel better." He was about to continue on down the hall when Hazel fell. He helped her to her feet and escorted her to the nurses' report room across the hall.

"Have you had these headaches before, Hazel?"

"Yes. Off and on for about three weeks. At first they were just light ones but lately they've been getting worse. Any idea what might be causing them?"

"Not without examining you, I don't. I could only guess that it might be caused by sinuses or nerves, or who knows what. You'd better go see your doctor as soon as you can."

"All right."

Hazel got through the rest of the day with the aid of double doses of aspirin that made the pain manageable.

She made an appointment to see her doctor the next day. In the meantime, she could only take things as easy as possible.

The next day was a repeat of the prior one. She awoke in the morning without the headache, but it returned shortly afterward.

By the time she got to the doctor's office after work she was in almost unbearable distress. The examination showed nothing.

"I can't really say what's causing the pain and dizziness, Miss Tanner. I'm going to have a C.A.T. scan done on you tomorrow morning at the hospital."

"Are you trying to say that there might be a tumor, Doctor?"

"I'm not saying anything of the kind. I just want to touch all the bases. Something's causing the pressure and maybe the scan will tell us what it is."

The C.A.T. scan showed a small mass at the base of the brain. At that point it became necessary to do a craniotomy to biopsy the mass.

Hazel lay in her hospital bed. She watched with a feeling of foreboding as the doctor entered her room. From the expression on his face, she could tell that the news was bad.

"Don't go beating around the bush on me, Doctor. This old lady's been around you guys too long to buy any song and dance. What exactly did the biopsy show?"

"Astrocytoma," the doctor said bluntly.

The word was a death knell reverberating around the room. Hazel moaned aloud. She had been around cancer patients long enough to know all types and phases of cancer. What a terrible way to die, she thought as she looked up at the doctor. She knew perfectly well what the next two to three months would be like. Astrocytoma moved like lightning and within that time she would be dead. Of course, they would try to save her, chemotherapy, radiation therapy, but it wouldn't do any good. The headaches would get worse until the pain was beyond bearing. She would become more and more disoriented, confused. She would have nausea and vomiting, paralysis, probably blindness. The few lucid moments left at the end, and they would be there, would find her praying to die.

Hazel turned her head toward the window at the sun shining into the room. A tear trickled down her cheek onto the pillow.

It really doesn't seem fair somehow, she thought. My poor Brian.

CHAPTER 18

A soft wind blew oak leaves gently along the ground. The color and life were gone from them and they rattled as they passed. The sky was gray with clouds ambling along in search of another place. The newly dug earth at Brian's feet was an obscenity in the midst of the new green of the spring grasses. Row after row of gravestones served as silent reminders of the brevity of life.

Off to his right, Brian saw a second, healing gash in the soil. The gravestone at its head spoke briefly of the ninety-two years of Albert Bricker. Heartache had taken Albert to be with Hazel. Brian had no more tears left in him. He had cried until he ached. All that was left was a sadness so great that he knew he would never be happy again. There was a vast emptiness within, leaving him without motivation to function. He looked forlornly up at the sky.

"Why did you let her die that way, God?"

There was no answer, only the wind, blowing through the empty branches of the trees.

"It's a shitty world, Old Man. Are you satisfied?"

Alone he turned and walked slowly back through gravestones to where his Kharmen Ghia was parked on the gravel road that meandered through the small country cemetery. Almost painfully he got into the car and drove the ten miles to the silent house awaiting him.

Brian wandered through the empty rooms, trying to remember the sounds and smells that had been Hazel. It was like a nightmare from which he must awaken but couldn't. He sat down at the kitchen table and took out the wrinkled letter, which had been Hazel's last contact with him. The paper had been crumpled in his first anguish as he had read it.

My Lovely Brian,

How do I begin? I need to share with you what you have meant to my life. Because of you, life has been worth living for me. You have made each day a thing of joy and wonder and I have no adequate words to tell you how my heart soars whenever I think of you. You gave something special to a fat, dumpy old lady, something that few people ever experience. Between the two of us we made a miracle, didn't we? I don't know how to say it, Brian. The word love just cannot express how I feel; but you know, don't you?

I would do anything in my power to keep you from ever having any pain or sorrow, but what has happened to me is beyond anyone's control. My time to die has come just as it does for everyone. How can I say that gently? I have a cancer that is so swift that I will be gone very quickly. There is no way I can spare you the final sadness, but I could not bear to have you grieve for the few months that I had left. You would have left your training for those months and that would have been a waste. What you are doing is so very important. You must promise me that you won't let it be interrupted for anything. I pray that you will forgive me for my deception, but I truly couldn't bear to tell you sooner.

You must promise me that you will go ahead with your dream. There are lots of kids out there waiting for you to take care of. And don't you go moping around the house and wasting your time feeling bad. Remember, when you see me again we'll be in a place where they don't allow fat and gray hair and wrinkles. And certainly not cellulite. I'll see you again some beautiful day after you get done with all the great things that are in store for you. **I promise!** Be happy, my Brian.

Love, Mom

Brian had not found out about his mother's illness until toward the end. He had finally been contacted by Hazel's doctor when she was in the final stages of dying. Up until then she had spent enormous physical and mental resources deceiving Brian so that he would continue his training. At first she had hoped that she could hold out until his graduation but the cancer refused to cooperate.

When Brian had first heard from the doctor, he could not, would not comprehend what the man was telling him. When he finally let the reality in, an emptiness beyond description swept through him. Grief stricken sobs wracked his body and he sank to the floor. Hours later he got slowly to his feet, packed his clothes, and began the infinitely long drive back to Hazel.

When Brian was finally able to talk with Hazel's doctor, he was livid with rage.

"You should have called me when you first found out that she was dying! You had no right to keep it from me! You let my mom die a terrible death by herself."

"She wouldn't allow it, Brian. I pleaded with her to let me get in touch with you but she wouldn't have it. She insisted that you not be permitted to watch her as she got worse. At the end, she wouldn't have known you and she couldn't stand the thought of having you suffer. What a selfless person she must have been."

"How could I keep getting letters and phone calls from her if she was as bad off as you say?"

"She wrote all those letters before she deteriorated and became disoriented. She made me promise to mail two each week while they lasted. I still have one left over that I must give you. As to those few phone calls, they were made in the midst of great pain. Whenever she would have one of her lucid moments, she would try to call you."

"That's the reason that I could never reach her at home," Brian said sadly. "I thought she was finally getting out and socializing after all these years."

Brian sat in the darkened house trying to make his mind go blank so the pain would go away. He hadn't been to bed in almost forty-eight hours. Eventually he slept.

In a very short time, his father began to beat him.

CHAPTER 19

Without Hazel's last, loving letter, Brian would have had no direction left in life. He returned to his residency program only because of what it had meant to Hazel. Her last request of him required a contract between them, a promise that he would continue. How could he break faith with her? He owed his life to her.

All the same, he went through each day like an automaton. He took care of patients but derived no pleasure or satisfaction from the work. Loneliness overwhelmed him any time he was alone so he filled every waking hour with his pediatric training or moonlighting at E.R.'s and urgent care offices around the area.

It was at this low point that Stevie Sanderson came back into Brian's life. Brian had made a point of checking the records of each facility where he worked for any evidence that Stevie had been treated for any further abuse. Brian knew it was the pattern of abusers to go different places each time they were forced to seek medical treatment for a child.

Brian had already queried the State Department of Social Services and found that the parents had moved soon after Brian had confronted the father in the hospital discharge area. The case was on hold, waiting further information concerning their whereabouts. Brian knew the case would die from lack of attention and limited resources. The boy didn't stand a chance.

At the end of one arduous night in a Readi-Med center on the west side of Lansing, Brian found Stevie again. Brian had not been there in several weeks so he was checking the billing computer system when he paused by the name, *Sanderson, Stevie* on the screen. The date of the entry was the week previous. The child had a dislocated arm and assorted bruises from a fall.

Angrily Brian found the medical record in the files and glanced at the injury description. The bastards had not let the arm heal properly! Brian screamed silently. Furious and feeling impotent he wrote down the address given on the medical record.

An early season warming pattern went unnoticed as Brian left for the evening shortly after nine o'clock. He stopped at a 7-11 store and purchased a city map so he could find the location of 325 Fulton Street.

He found the street and the Landover Apartment buildings without difficulty. The place was part of an urban renewal complex. From the looks of it, Brian thought, urban rearrangement would have been a better title. All that had been accomplished was to take single and double story wrecks and pile them up into apartments. A mere two years after completion, the inhabitants had turned the buildings into four story pustules on the face of the city. The genetic failures of the area accumulated there like human excrescence.

Brian parked his car. Broken glass sparkled, reflecting Brian's headlights, looking deceptively attractive in the weed- bordered lot behind one of the buildings. A Mexican girl stood on the corner, bare flesh advertising her services. She looked expectantly at Brian who ignored her. The graffiti spray-painted walls and the dirt were oppressive.

He was feeling less sure of himself now and his mission began to seem futile. But he wasn't going to be deterred. Not now. He went into the building and climbed the stairs to the fourth floor. He started to use the elevator but someone had recently taken a leak in the corner and Brian wasn't about to ride the enclosed box surrounded by the sickening-sweet ammonia odor from some mental deviate's bladder.

On the fourth floor, Brian searched for apartment 418. When he found it, he paused momentarily, then knocked on the door. No answer. Again he knocked, this time louder. Still no answer. His anger grew and he gave the door a savage kick. The sound reverberated down the empty hall. As he turned to go the door opened behind him.

"Hey asshole! What the hell ya doin', poundin' my door like that?" a man's voice spoke angrily.

Brian turned back. It was Sanderson. Apparently he hadn't yet recognized Brian because of the unlighted hallway.

"Sanderson," Brian said simply.

A note of caution crept into the man's voice. "So what? I still want to know what you're doin', kickin' my door like that."

"I was wondering which one of you cretins has been beating up on your son this time?" Brian said, advancing toward the man. "I want it to stop, right now, whichever one of you it is."

Sanderson recognized him at last, a look of astonishment crossing his face. "You! The mother fucker from the hospital!"

He started to slam the door but Brian shoved it open, sending Sanderson stumbling back into the apartment. At the back of his mind, Brian knew what he was doing was crazy. He didn't particularly care at the moment.

The apartment was dimly lit with only the glow of a TV set to illuminate it. The man stood uncertainly, his back against the wall.

"What the hell are you doing, mister?" Sanderson said. His anger was right near the surface. The only thing keeping it in check, Brian was sure, was the man's innate cowardice; the kind that would let him beat on a child again and again.

Brian ignored the man and began searching the room for Stevie, shoving aside moldy clutter in his path. No sign of the boy. He began to explore the other rooms.

"Hey, you son-of-a-bitch! What you think you're doin'?" Sanderson said, trailing along behind.

Brian flicked on the light in the bedroom. He spotted the boy in the far corner. Stevie blinked his eyes at the sudden brightness. From a bare mattress he looked up at Brian with a tear streaked face. A clavicle strap was dangling uselessly from the boy's neck. He was clutching his arm to keep it from hurting.

Brian bent over the crib to examine Stevie and to refit the shoulder brace. The boy had a fresh bruise on his cheek. Hatred for the parents came surging through Brian.

Sanderson finally came to grips with his indecision, anger overcoming his caution. He had already grabbed his motorcycle helmet from the couch as he followed Brian into the bedroom. As Brian was about to stand up Sanderson aimed the helmet viscously at Brian's head. Off balance, Brian was still able to get an arm up just enough to keep from taking the full force of the blow. A crashing pain erupted on the back of his head.

The weapon did little real damage despite the pain it created. Brian turned on the man, rage and joy forming a strange mixture of emotions in his mind. He was glad the man had hit him. Before Sanderson could swing the helmet again, Brian was on him, driving him to the floor, pent up tensions and frustrations experiencing a welcome outlet. Brian hit Sanderson again and again, fist against flesh, until his arms were tired and his breath labored. The man lay barely conscious beneath Brian. Brian sat on his victim's chest, catching his breath.

The fight had carried them back out into the living room. Chairs were overturned, lamps broken and beer cans strewn around the floor. Brian looked down at the groaning man. With one last swing, he brought the side of his fist down on the man's chest and broke his collarbone. The man screamed in agony. Brian brought the man's pitted face up close to his.

"If you ever hit that child again, I'll find out about it and I'll be back. Only next time it will be worse! Do you understand me?" Brian yelled.

The man turned his head and spit blood on the floor. Some of it ran down the side of his cheek. He nodded.

"Yeah, I won't touch him again. Lemme alone." A barely conscious whisper. He licked more blood from his torn lip.

"You tell your wife what I just told you. If she hurts Stevie, I'll do the same thing to her. I don't care if she's a woman or not. Don't ever touch that baby again," Brian repeated as he got up and moved toward the door.

He walked unsteadily down the hall, down the steps and out to his car. He was shaking hard from the adrenaline pumping through his body. When he calmed enough to be in control, he started the car and headed for his apartment.

Driving home, he tried to analyze his emotions. He knew what he had done was irrational and could ruin his career. Somehow he didn't care at the moment. He was glad he had done it. After all these years, he had finally gotten back at his own father, repaid some of the debt.

That night, Brian had a bizarre dream. In it he recalled vividly the beating of Stevie's father, but it was followed by Stevie screaming for help. Suddenly Stevie was joined by another little boy begging for help, then a battered little girl, imploring him to save her, then another child, and another until his mind was filled with a giant chorus of voices all calling out to him. He awoke, crying for the lost children in his dream. It had been so real! They were out there by the thousands with no one to protect them.

He couldn't get back to sleep. The children haunted him. He knew their helpless terror. Knew they had no way to escape. Knew they had no Hazel.

Brian tossed and turned, courting sleep that would not come. He kept thinking about the children who would never stand a chance in life, children who would be battered, sexually assaulted and emotionally shattered by their parents. Poor, tiny lost children whose only crime was to be born to people who would destroy them.

Brian could not conceive how an adult could abuse a child, but he knew that an incredible number did. The methods they used to harm their sons and daughters were limitless. Tens of thousands of children each year were hammered, torn, slugged, suffocated, cut, burned, boiled, disfigured, raped, kicked, starved and tortured in countless ways. The devices used in these crimes were limited only by the parents' imagination. Bile would rise like acid when Brian thought of parents attacking babies with fists, belts, ropes, baseball bats, shoes, pipes, scissors, bottles, sticks, fire - the list was endless. It could not possibly happen.

But it happened all the time.

The greatest crime of all was that these people got away with it. Time after time it happened, with no punishment. You could batter your child almost to death but you sure as hell better not hit your neighbor, Brian reflected.

The more he thought about it, the more infuriated Brian became. He grew so restless he couldn't lie in bed any longer. He arose, dressed and went for a run through the dark, silent back streets of the neighborhood to calm his nerves and anger. The night was cold as he ran. A steady wind was blowing through the trees, causing the bare branches to dance attendance to his passing figure. There was no traffic at that time of night so he ran down the center of the street into each pool of lamp light and then into the darkness between, chased by the voices of helpless children calling out for help.

CHAPTER 20

It had been over five months since Kristin had seen Brian in her office for the ill-fated learning session with him. She had spotted him on occasion after that but never approached him. She hadn't thought much more about him until she saw him sitting in the cafeteria one April evening. She had worked late that afternoon and decided to eat supper at the hospital. Holly and Heather would be okay. Kristin had found an elderly lady who was working with the Foster Grandparent's program in Lansing and was a wonderful lady for the girls to stay with until she got home. Kristin was sure that they were certainly getting better tasting meals than she could fix.

The two girls' father had been released from prison two months before but had not come back to Lansing. Kristin prayed every night that he never would. Heather and Holly were part of her life now and she would fight like a tigress if necessary in order to keep them.

She saw Brian sitting by himself, staring down into his plate without touching the food. He looked so absolutely forlorn. She couldn't explain the feeling that came over her as she sat watching him from across the room. The place was fairly empty at that time of the evening but she picked up her tray and made her way toward him.

"The food's not that bad, Doctor," she said as she stopped in front of him.

Brian looked up. "I beg your pardon?"

"Nothing, Doctor. Do you mind if I sit down?"

Brian looked up at her and then around the room at all the empty tables. The gesture made her furious and she almost walked away. She felt like giving him the finger, but checked the impulse.

"How's the peds business going?" she asked as she sat down. "You're a pediatric resident as I recall."

"You're the lady from the social services department aren't you?" he said without answering her questions. "I'm sorry, I forgot your name from when I was in your office."

"I can sense from the excitement in your voice that it was one of the high points of your life," Kristin said sarcastically.

Brian didn't know how to respond to her jibe. He just looked down at his plate and moved some of the food around with his fork.

Holy Smokes, thought Kristin, the guy really is a jerk. She pushed her chair back and stood up. Brian was startled by her abrupt move.

He looked up at her. "Please, don't go," he said quickly. "I'm sorry if I offended you."

Something in the pained look on his face changed her mind. For a brief instant she looked into his eyes and saw herself. She saw herself as she sometimes did when she gazed into a mirror and wondered just what the hell it was all about. She had never found an answer. The eyes looking up at her were asking the same question. She sat back down.

"I'm sorry too. Sometimes my tongue runs when I haven't put my mind in gear." She looked over at him expectantly. He tried a tentative smile. She was intrigued by the attempt. The fire was gone from him for some reason. He wasn't the same guy who had been in her office. Maybe he'd had a long day or something but it seemed deeper than that. She extended her right hand across the table.

"Maybe we should start out fresh. My name's Kristin Grey."

Brian took the hand. "Mine's Brian. I guess you already know the last name."

"May I call you Brian, or do you prefer Dr. Tanner?"

"Brian is fine."

"Do you always have this much trouble picking up beautiful women?" She couldn't help being ornery. It was her nature.

"No, Brian said, with no expression on his face.

They stared at each other for a few seconds, then both averted their eyes. The silence grew awkward as each searched for something to say.

"So, what year of your residency are you in?" she asked finally.

"Third."

"In June then you become a real doctor, eh?" she needled him, looking for some sort of response.

"I guess," he replied.

"What will you do then?" she said.

He shrugged.

"No plans?"

"No."

"Really? You just finished off what, eleven years of education, and you have no plans?"

Irritation flickered across his face. "Not yet. Maybe one of these days. I was going to start a peds office in Cincinnati but now . . . I just can't afford it. I can pick up work around here for now."

He didn't know what else to say. He had never been much of a conversationalist, except with Hazel . . . and with Lani. He flushed the old love quickly from his mind. The thought of never sitting and talking with his mom again brought his grief back to the surface.

Kristin looked up in time to see Brian bow his head and squeeze his eyelids together as though he were in pain.

"Is there anything wrong?" she asked gently.

"No." His voice was quiet.

It was apparent that he didn't want to talk about whatever was bothering him so she didn't ask again.

Through the rest of the meal the conversation went in short, inane bursts. Kristin usually had no trouble talking with people, but this man was a challenge. She couldn't figure out what the problem was, and things just weren't flowing right. The guy wasn't a jerk, as she had hastily concluded at first, but she couldn't get him to talk. She was curious how someone so apparently introverted would want to be a doctor, a profession normally requiring people- oriented individuals.

"Do you enjoy taking care of people?" she asked.

Brian did not answer for a short time. She thought he wasn't going to. He was staring down at the gravy congealing on his plate, moving his fork slowly around in it. He raised his eyes and looked at her. "Not entirely."

Kristin thought about the answer. "You mean, you're dedicating your life to being a doctor and you don't really like it? I don't understand."

"I meant that I only like treating some people . . ."

"How will you handle that problem when you go into practice for yourself?" She interrupted. "How do you decide if you like someone before you take care of them? Maybe you could give them a personality test when they fill out their insurance information. You're not going to make much money that way, though."

"I don't care about money. I meant that I only want to take care of children. There are a lot of them out there who need my help."

It was a strange way of putting the phrase and the intensity in his voice was interesting. "That's an unconventional motivation, Brian. All people need your help, not just kids.

"The adults aren't important. There's still some hope for the children."

"Are we talking about the same thing? If an adult comes to you for medical attention, how can you say it's too late?"

As Brian looked at Kristin, he suddenly understood what he had been saying. Kristin could sense a change as he spoke. "I guess I didn't say it very clearly. It's just more meaningful for me to work with little children. When they come to me, they're usually all scared and trying to understand what sickness is all about. I like taking away their sadness and apprehension if I can."

Kristin knew he hadn't meant that originally, but she liked the fake answer.

He looked up at the clock. He was overdue back in PICU.

"Well, I have to get back to work. I've got a little guy going bad on me. The nurses haven't beeped me yet so apparently he's still stable." He pushed his chair back, then paused, remembering something. "Would you do me a favor, Miss Grey, I mean, Kristin?"

"Sure, if I can."

"You remember the reason I was in your office some months back was about a little boy named Stevie Sanderson?"

"Of course. You suspected the parents of child abuse. Why?"

"Well, I heard that no one followed up on his case because no one bothered to find out where they had moved to. Typical bureaucratic indifference," he said angrily.

"That's not entirely a fair statement," Kristin responded. "The Department of Protective Services tries hard to help these children as much as they can. It's not always easy."

"They don't try hard enough," Brian interrupted. "Do you have any idea of the number of children our police, bureaucrats and judges throw back to the wolves every year? These children are looking for just one person to save them. Time and time again we fail them! Countless babies and children who will never survive because nobody tried hard enough!"

Kristin was taken aback by the controlled rage she saw suddenly burning within the man.

"I'm not going to argue with you, Brian, because to some extent you're right. Just remember, though, there are a lot of people who are trying, and they care as much as you do."

"No they don't," Brian said simply.

"All right, whatever you say. What was the favor you wanted?"

"I was working at one of the urgent care offices not long ago and spotted a Stevie Sanderson on the computer. I remembered the address and I was wondering if you would get hold of Protective Services and have them check to see if it's the same one and if it is, will they make sure he gets some protection this time. Maybe let me know about him?"

"Yes, I can do that."

Brian gave her the information and got up to leave. "Thanks," he said quietly.

He picked up his tray and walked away. Kristin sat contemplating his retreating figure.

CHAPTER 21

Gary Reeser pulled his battered red Chevy into the space in front of the house trailer where he lived. The beat up, dirty looking structure was back-to-back and belly-to-belly with another fifty equally seedy looking "mobile homes". The lot was a graveyard for derelict trailers, aging, weathered hulks that had come there to die. One or two relatively new trailers were conspicuously out of place, like children in a nursing home.

Gary sat for a while, his head resting on the steering wheel. He could hear the baby crying inside and he didn't want to go in. Life was a piece of shit. It always had been and always would be. He raised his head and looked at his hands gripping the steering wheel. The blackened skin, the fingernails that would never be clean, symbolized his whole life.

Gary Reeser was only twenty. Already he felt like an old man. At 5' 9" and 140 pounds, he cut a very unimposing picture as he slouched through life. The face looking back at him from the rearview mirror showed the last stages of the acne that had plagued him since puberty. His hair, which had not seen shampoo in several weeks, was parted in the center and hung, lank, to his collar. A scraggly Fu Manchu mustache drooped down to greet the wispy little beard, as yet barely covering his chin.

A high school classmate had once seen a list of students posted on the bulletin board. The name G. Reeser came to his attention. G. Reeser quickly became Greeser, and ultimately,

Greaser. The nickname stuck. No one ever called him Gary or Reeser or Asshole; not anything but goddamn Greaser.

Greaser was one of six kids, none of whom his parents could afford, mentally or financially. Failure permeated the atmosphere in which he grew up. His father and mother often had violent arguments in which his father wound up beating on his mother, then disappearing for weeks at a time. Once Greaser had tried to interfere and his father had beaten him so badly that he had been out of school for a week. Beatings were nothing unusual to any of the children.

By the time he was sixteen, Greaser was only in the ninth grade. Discouraged and sick of it all, he quit school, left home and got a job pumping gas and working with the mechanic in a service station. He wanted to be more than a lousy grease monkey all his life, and was planning on joining the Army to learn a trade. That's when he met good ol' Beverly.

Greaser stared at the trailer and shook his head. Anything for a piece of ass. He had traded his whole goddamn life for a piece of ass. He opened the door and got slowly out of the car. The closer he got to the trailer, the louder the crying became. He opened the door. His wife was sitting on the couch as usual, with her feet on the coffee table, watching TV.

"Hey, Bev, the goddamn kid is cryin' again! Why don't you take care of her for chrissakes?"

"Don't worry about it. She's okay."

"But I'm not. I can't stand listening to her screaming."

"That's your problem." Beverly's concentration was on the TV.

Greaser looked around the trailer at the stacks of dirty dishes, the dirt, the disorder, and he felt a frustrated rage. He spotted a wet diaper hanging over one of the chairs. "I thought I told you not to leave those wet rags lying around like that. It's fuckin' unsanitary."

Silence greeted his complaint.

"Where's my supper?"

"Wait till after this show and I'll get something."

"Jesus Christ, why did I ever marry you? You're not worth nothin' to me."

"Because you knocked me up, that's why. I didn't want any part of you either, Greaser."

"I didn't notice you havin' your knees locked together yellin' rape. As I recall, you were pretty damn grateful when I jumped you."

"I musta been stone blind drunk in order to stomach you. If I was sober, there's no way I'd let you in my pants."

"You were drunk a whole lotta times if that's the case. I don't even know if that kid in there is mine. I think I was gettin' seconds most of the time."

"You were lucky to get any, Greaser. I took you on as a charity case."

"You go to hell, you stupid broad!"

"You're right, I am stupid. I got stuck with you." She turned away from him and went back to her program. She was tired of arguing. She was sick of the whole cruddy rut she had been forced into. Beverly was eighteen years old and already the mother of a kid, and wife to a greasy loser. What she would never admit was that she was no prize for Greaser either. Diapers, dirty clothes and dreary days; that's all she had to look forward to. Just like her old lady. Her mother had finally gotten a divorce when Bev was twelve. After that, Bev had had a lot of "uncles" who had lived with them for varying lengths of time. Finally one of the uncles had stayed permanently. He couldn't stand Bev or her two sisters and two brothers and they could not abide him.

At sixteen, Bev moved out and went to stay with her father, who lived alone. He never paid much attention to her and she was free to come and go as she pleased. She never went to school and was soon heavily into drugs and booze. She went to bed with practically anything in pants. She refused to remember that there had been very few offers. She did remember that, with the lights out, Greaser had filled her needs pretty well. But she forgot her diaphragm one night, and that damn screaming brat back in the bedroom was the result.

Greaser looked at the back of her head. He longed to punch her out, bad, but knew he wouldn't. He had threatened her once, early in their marriage and she had warned him in return, "If you ever hit me, I'll get you some night when you're asleep and I'll bury a butcher knife so far up your asshole, they'll never get it out."

He was not brave enough to call her bluff.

He turned angrily and stomped off down the narrow hallway to the bedroom. Eleven-month-old Marcia was standing up in her crib, screaming her lungs out.

"Shut the hell up, you stupid little brat!" Greaser yelled at her. His harsh voice only served to make her cry harder. She gazed at him, one hand balancing herself, the other held out, pleading for him to pick her up. With each mind-splitting cry, she squeezed more tears out and down her cheeks. Each time she had to stop to catch her breath, a sob pulled her lower lip into her mouth.

"Goddammit, I said shut up!" He screamed and lunged across the room. He hit the child viciously with the back of his hand. Already off balance the baby reeled across the crib and hit her head against the wall, bringing forth new, intensified cries. The pain-filled shrieks were more than Greaser could stand. He picked her up by the front of her pajamas and began slapping her back and forth across the face. She wouldn't quit crying. Greaser was beside himself with rage. He held the screaming infant in mid-air, and looked around, hoping for some miracle to muffle the terrified, uncomprehending response to his bestial attack. The sliding closet doors swam into focus. Instantly he was across the bed, pulling them open. Like an oversized, unwanted teddy bear, he threw the offending thing against the back of the closet.

"Scream your ass off in there all you want, you stupid little bitch." He slid the doors shut with a bang.

Greaser turned and stormed up the hall. The cries in the bedroom were already dying to a whimper. In the living room, Beverly was still sitting, glued to the TV program. Greaser sped out of the trailer, hurled himself into his car and sprayed gravel against another parked car in his haste to get away from his home.

Beverly finished watching her show and got slowly to her feet. Greaser was gone. Just one less mouth to feed. He'd be back later. He always came back. Too bad. As she wandered down the hall, she realized that the kid wasn't crying anymore. She really ought to look in on the little pest. The crib was empty. Maybe she had fallen out of her bed. The baby was nowhere to be seen. Where could she be? She knew Greaser hadn't taken her, and the room was too small to hide in. Where in hell could she be?

The closet doors were closed, but she vaguely remembered hearing the banging when Greaser was yelling at the baby. With an uneasy feeling, she edged around the bed and tugged open the door. On the closet floor, amid a clutter of shoes and dirty clothes, was the baby, sprawled unconscious, her nose bloody, and bruises forming on the battered face.

Beverly gasped. She knelt quickly and retrieved the little body from the closet.

"Oh my God! The son-of-a-bitch did it again! The mean rotten bastard!"

She took Marcia into the bathroom and tried to revive her with a wet washcloth. She cringed as she wiped at the oozing blood. After a time, Beverly became more and more frightened. Harrowing minutes of indecision passed. At last she grabbed a blanket and wrapped the baby up in it. She ran out of the trailer and across the road to where her friend Sylvia lived.

Sylvia answered her pounding with a quick hello. "Hey, Bev. How ya doin'? I see you brought the kid with you. Come on in. I'll getcha a beer."

"I need a favor, Syl," Beverly gasped. "Marcia fell out of her crib and hurt herself, bad. Can you take me to the hospital quick? Greaser took off with the car and I don't know when he'll be back."

"Sure hon, let me grab my bag and keys and we'll get going right away."

In the Emergency Room of Genesis, the triage nurse took one look at the baby and hurried her into one of the treatment rooms, calling for one of the doctors who was standing in the hall.

One of the other nurses took Beverly back toward the E.R. entrance.

"The doctor will take care of your baby. We need you to give some information to the registration clerk while you're waiting."

Beverly spent the next few minutes giving the clerk contrived details for the registration forms. Afterward, she went into the waiting room, bummed cigarettes, unlit, from Sylvia and sat down to watch television. She lost herself in the make-believe lives until she was surprised to hear her own name paged. She came to her feet with a start and went to talk to the nurse at the desk.

"Mrs. Reeser?"

"Yeah. How's my kid?"

"Let's go in the back where we can talk in private."

Beverly, uneasy about the way the nurse had looked at her, followed down a hallway through the treatment area and into a small conference room.

"Mrs. Reeser, I don't know exactly how to tell you this, but your baby is very badly hurt. The doctor says she has a concussion and very likely a fractured skull, in addition, her nose is broken and she has bruises all over her face. Can you tell me how it happened?"

"Is she gonna be okay?"

"I don't know. Could you tell me how the injuries occurred?"

Beverly looked at the door. She wanted out of the room, away from the accusing stares of the nurses. Marcia certainly hadn't been hurt nearly as bad the last time Greaser beat her up. The nurses in the other hospital had swallowed the story about her falling out of her crib. Beverly was not very imaginative. Again she tried the same excuse, with a few variations.

"Well, I was down the hall getting supper when I heard Marcia scream. I rushed to the bedroom and I found her sprawled out on the floor. She's just learning to stand, so she must have tried to climb out of bed. She probably hit her face on the corner of her crib. Oh, God, I hope she's gonna be all right."

Beverly kept her head bowed and tried to sound convincingly sorrowful.

"Mrs. Reeser, I'm really sorry. I don't want to offend you, but I have a hard time believing that your little girl got hurt so seriously just falling out of her crib. Are you sure that's what happened?"

An indignant protest rose to Beverly's lips, but when she looked up at the nurse, she couldn't get it out. Damn that Greaser! She was taking the heat for something he had done. Well, she wasn't going to. No way!

"My husband hit her. He can't stand to hear her cry so he gets mad and starts hitting her. I beg him to stop, but he won't listen and I'm afraid of him. Can you get the police to help me? I'm afraid he's going to keep hurting her unless somebody makes him stop."

CHAPTER 22

Brian was moonlighting on the second shift in the Genesis E.R. when he heard a flurry of activity coming into the entrance to the area. Just moments before, he had noted the abrupt cessation of an ambulance's caterwauling. By the time he got up front, the ambulance had disgorged its cargo into the triage section. When he got to the triage nurse, she was already in the process of getting the vital signs on the patient lying inert on the stretcher in front of her.

"What's wrong with her, Nancy?" Brian asked

"She's in a bad way, Dr. Tanner. Drug overdose. The ambulance driver said the mother found an empty bottle that had been full of sleeping pills the night before. She's only fourteen and the pills must have been in her for quite a while. She's hardly breathing. I get only a faint pulse and the pressure is falling rapidly."

An oxygen mask and portable tank from the ambulance had accompanied the O.D. victim. Brian grabbed his stethoscope and put it to the girl's chest. The heartbeat was very faint and starting to flutter like a car engine running out of gas. He knew she was in trouble.

"Get her stomach pumped quick! As soon as you get that done, start an IV with D5W and I want 10 cc's of adrenaline, 1 to 10,000, one amp of bicarb and a half cc of Atropine! Stat! She's going to start fibrillating any second!"

Brian took hold of the stretcher and raced with it to the nearest empty treatment cubicle. While he was getting the medications into the girl, one nurse prepared the lavage kit to empty her stomach.

Brian injected the drugs while a nurse prepared to push an IV needle into the unresponsive arm. Another nurse placed monitor electrodes then called out the decaying vital signs. Brian watched the struggle being played out on the monitor's scope in front of him. The girl was losing the battle. Brian was breathing rapidly, his heart pounding in opposition to the diminishing life in front of him. He looked at her closely now for the first time. A pretty face, marred by adolescent pimples. What happened baby? he screamed inside his head. Why did you do this to yourself?

The breathing was barely discernable by now. Brian reached down and tore away the blouse hiding the just budding young breasts.

"Get her bra off and get the ambu bag on her!" he ordered.

While one of the nurses pumped air into and out of the girl's lungs, Brian began doing heart massage on the pale chest beneath him. He worked furiously, sweating from the exertion and emotional distress.

"Doctor, she's fibrillating!" the nurse called out to him.

"Give me the paddles," Brian snapped. "Give me 200 watts!" The nurse handed him the paddles.

"Everyone clear?" The crack of electricity made the body jump.

"She's not responding, Dr. Tanner!"

"Give me 300 watts!"

Again the snap of the body.

Brian threw aside the paddles and began the heart massage again. "Keep bagging her!" he called out.

He was crying to the little body beneath his pressing palms, "Come on baby, please live! Try baby! Try baby!" Again and again. He would not give up. "Please honey, live for me! Please!" he whispered to the dead body.

Brian walked slowly down the hallway, heading for the soli-
tude of the doctor's lounge at the back of the E.R. He would
never become used to death. He had seen it enough in the last
few years, but he had not reached the point where he could accept
it. One minute a person was there, the next only an empty shell
already starting to cool and stiffen. Where did they go when
they died? Did they go anywhere? The eternal questions.

What a terrible crime to lose a young girl like that; a pretty
little person with a whole lifetime ahead of her. For what reason?
Could she find nothing worth holding onto? Brian thought for
a while. He had nothing he could have offered. It was not that
great a thing to be alive. Maybe she was someplace better.

What's it all about, God? There is so much sorrow. Did you
have to make it like this? He asked silently.

The door opened behind him. He resented the intrusion. It
was Darlene Jackson, one of the RNs. She walked slowly around
the table to the coffee pot in the corner of the room. He heard
the gurgle as she poured the liquid; heard her adding the sugar
and dry creamer and clanging her spoon around inside the cup.
She came and sat down near him in one of the lounge chairs.

"I never quite get hardened to it," she said.

Brian thought she was referring to the girl who had just
died.

"What brings a person to a point where he can batter his
own baby and almost kill her? That little girl may yet die and
for what reason?" the nurse continued.

"What are you talking about?" Brian said quickly.

"Oh, I'm sorry, Dr. Tanner. I was just thinking out loud.
We just treated a baby girl, no more than a year old, who was
beaten by her father. At least that's what her mother said. Can
you really understand it, Doctor? Can you believe a grown man
would beat on a baby until her face is a mass of bruises? And a
fractured skull! I've worked here a lot of years and seen my share
of these things and I still cannot believe they happen."

She sat shaking her head, not really looking at Brian. She had no idea of the effect her words were having on him.

Anger was in him to the point where he could no longer sit still. He levered himself to his feet.

"Where is the baby now?" he asked.

"Up in PICU."

Brian headed for the door. At the end of the hall, he took the elevator to the third floor Intensive Care Unit.

"Where is the baby girl who just came up from the E.R.?" he asked the ward clerk at the chart desk.

She looked up with a start. Brian's expression made her uneasy.

"Over in the crib in the fifth cubicle, Doctor. I'm just processing her paperwork now."

Brian moved swiftly. A nurse was in the process of inserting an IV needle into a delicate vein. He looked down at the tiny figure lying there. The face was swollen from the bruises. Tears obscured his vision as he watched the rise and fall of the little chest. Another tenuous hold on life. If she made it, what then? More beating? More fear? Or worse, a lifetime of institutions because her brain was damaged?

Brian couldn't tear himself away from the crib. He knew the nurse was getting uncomfortable, watching him from across the bed. Brian's fury grew. He needed a release from the anger eating away at him. He turned abruptly, went back to the desk and took the chart from the ward clerk. The address on the registration form was a place he had never heard of. He shoved the chart back at the woman.

"Where's this trailer park located? It says Center Road. Where's that at?"

The ward clerk looked down at the chart and thought for a second. "It's on the north end of town. Do you know where Columbia Park is, where they dammed up that little river and made a falls out of it?"

"Yes."

"It's just east of there, about a mile. Maple Road goes by the park. It dead-ends on Center Road. There's a little grocery store on the corner. Turn left and I think the trailer park is just up the road."

Without thanking her, Brian headed for the door at a run. In the locker room he changed out of his whites and into his jeans, sport shirt and winter jacket then headed outside for his car. The air was unseasonably cold, as it can often get in Michigan. A hint of rain was riding on the wind but he didn't notice.

Brian jerked at the car door of the Kharmen Ghia. A few weeks ago, someone had backed into the driver's side door of the old car and left it reluctant to open. He tugged mightily and it shrieked wide enough for him to slide inside. The engine coughed to life as he twisted the ignition key. There was little traffic as he pulled into the street and headed for the outskirts of Lansing.

The night people were beginning to come out of their holes to infest the streets as he passed through the main part of the city. Brian watched with disgust as a drunk weaved her precarious way in front of him while he sat waiting out a red light.

Each time he stopped at a light his car tried to stall and the irritation added fuel to his anger. The rational part of his brain kept asking him what he was doing, but he ignored its warning. He could not stand by impatiently and hope that, somehow, the bureaucracy would stop these people. A vision of the little girl being struck again and again by a grown man, her father, drove all doubt from his mind.

A twenty-minute drive took Brian to the edge of the city. He continued north, passing through an area that had been steadily deteriorating over the last decade. The houses were unpainted and uncared for, with sagging porches and weedy yards. The problem was in the slow process of solution. Houses were being bought by the State, one by one, and demolished. Inexorably, a four-lane by-pass was covering the ground where these saddened homes once stood. The inhabitants had moved on to perpetuate their blight elsewhere.

The road led through a park and gave way grudgingly to the country. One of the last vestiges of the urban area was the trailer park where Gary Reeser lived. Brian turned off the road into the U-shaped park. The place was completely dark, with the exception of a single light hanging from a telephone pole at the back.

Brian put his car into gear and drove slowly around the area. He could find nothing to identify Reeser's trailer. His frustration increased.

A few trailers showed faint glows from TV screens. For a while he toyed with the idea of knocking at one of those doors and asking for information, but quickly rejected the idea. It might be hard to explain what he was doing there in the middle of the night.

He drove through the park again and stopped at the entrance. His car lights passed over rows of mailboxes. At first their significance didn't register. He sat looking at them, an idea trying to form itself in his head. His eyes opened a shade wider. He leaned over, opened the glove compartment and dug out the flashlight stored there. It gave off a feeble, yellow glow instead of a white beam. It would have to do.

Brian got out of the car and went to the mailboxes. He passed the dim beam over the boxes. A few names had been painted crudely across the side, while others had gone first class and pasted stick-on letters to the metal. Many were smudged or faded.

About three-fourths of the way down the row of boxes the flickering flashlight's glow showed him what he wanted. In faded magic-marking pen, the name Reeser jumped out at him, like a pearl in the middle of a dung heap. Still no identifying number or address was on it.

He had seen a lot number written on a few of the boxes. Was there a chance that the park was laid out in some logical sequence? He searched out the numbers again. Near the beginning he had seen a lot #4.

He set about looking for another number farther up the line. The next one he spotted was #15. Starting back at #4, he counted until he got to #15. He was in luck. It was in the proper place. He kept counting up the row. Lot #23 was also in sequence. He continued until he found the mailbox with Reeser's name on it. The lot had to be #31.

The next problem was how to identify which lot was which in the darkened park. Brian approached the first shadowed trailer and began looking for some sort of identification. The stupid flashlight was failing, the beam dying in mid-air, barely ten feet from the bulb. By this time, his eyes were accustomed to the dark, though. He searched for a post, or a marker, anything that would tell him where he was in the numbering system. He passed by more than a half dozen trailers on the left side of the park and was beginning to feel a sense of futility. His anger was abating because of the oppressive feeling of the area and his need to be analytical during his search. Failure nagged at him when he finally found the post near the gravel drive. Lot #15.

Brian turned and looked back the way he had come. Number fifteen was the eighth trailer on the outside of the horseshoe. If that was the case, the outside trailers must have odd numbers and the inside would be even. He began walking rapidly down the drive counting from side to side as he went. He saw no more signs by the time he came to what should be lot #31. It had to be the right one, he thought. He had no choices left. He was trying to rekindle his anger to make the task ahead easier. He tried to visualize an aura of evil emanating from the trailer in front of him, but he couldn't succeed. It was just a sad, dumpy trailer and nothing more.

He closed his eyes. He couldn't stop now. He had promised the kids, and he had promised himself that he would help them.

He remembered the dreams and the pain and the terror, and he knew he must go through with his vow.

Brian moved slowly up the cracked, cement walk and mounted the rusted steps. Each step gave out a rasp of agony as he placed his weight on it. He still could not be positive that this was the right trailer, but he had no other options. Assailed by doubts, he stood with his fist raised before the door. Anger had carried him this far and now he could not turn back. Besides, it was the only way to stop the cries.

Brian rapped sharply on the trailer door. There was no response from within. Someone had to be home. A car was parked out front. Harder this time, Brian assaulted the door. He heard muttered cursing from inside. He gave the door one more shot just to make sure. A light came on in the tail end of the trailer and he felt the vibrations through the structure as someone came stomping toward the front. A porch light blossomed over Brian, making him feel conspicuous. Suddenly the inside door was yanked open and an angry Reeser was looking querulously out at Brian through the tattered screen door. He stood in the darkened doorway, his skinny body adorned only in some ragged boxer shorts.

"Who the hell are you?" Greaser demanded angrily.

"It doesn't matter," Brian replied. "I need to talk to you. Is your name Gary Reeser?"

"So, what if it is? Do you realize that it's the fuckin' middle of the night and I'm standin' here freezin' my nuts off?"

A note of uneasiness had crept into Reeser's voice. Brian sensed that the door was going to be slammed in his face at any second. While Reeser looked uncertainly out at him, Brian quietly opened the storm door wider than the original crack Reeser was speaking through.

"Hey, you son-of-a-bitch, I didn't ask you to come in! What the fuck do you think you're doin'?" He started to slam the inside door. Brian, anticipating it, jammed himself in the entrance. Reeser was frightened and started to push Brian back out the door. Brian knocked the hand away from his chest and in one motion had a handful of Reeser's long oily hair and heaved him out the door, down the steps and onto the sidewalk. He squelched Reeser's scream of pain as he swiftly drove the flashlight into the man's groin. Reeser crumpled in agony. Before he could fall, Brian spun him around and clamped a leather-covered arm around his head and over his yelling mouth.

In this savage embrace, Brian hissed into Reeser's ear, "I want you to understand why this is happening. I want you to feel the pain and know this is what your baby daughter lives through every time you beat her!"

Brian felt Reeser stiffen and released him. As Reeser started to fall Brian turned him and slammed the flashlight into his solar plexus.

Greaser's pain was beyond belief. It engulfed him and rendered him helpless. Fear of the stranger tore at him. Where had this maniac come from? Why was he doing this? The incomprehensibility of what was happening added terror to the waves of pain washing over him. Before he could scream again, a fist smacked into his mouth, splitting his lips and loosening a tooth. The fist came again and again.

Brian stopped suddenly. He could not hit Reeser anymore. The rage was in him still, but he couldn't swing again. He knew the man was in terrible pain but he also knew that no permanent damage had been done. He lowered the stricken man to the ground and bent over the prostrate form.

Reeser was curled into a ball of agony as Brian knelt down and gritted into the man's ear. "That baby of yours may never be the same after what you did to her. If she doesn't recover, I'll make you sorrier than you can believe possible! If, by some miracle, she's all right and they give her back to you, don't you ever touch her again."

Brian, lips pulled back in a grimace of hate, slapped Reeser across the face again. "Do you understand me?"

Greaser nodded once that he had heard. The pain and fear loosened his bowels.

Brian rose and turned to go. "Don't make any more noise or I'll be back."

He left the semi-nude figure lying shivering on the cold cement. As he got to the driveway, Brian broke into a run. He was halfway to his car when the screaming began. They were pain-filled, fearful cries and made him feel - liberated.

He felt in a hurry. The yelling was going to wake people and he wanted to be long gone before all the lights came on. He reached the Ghia, jerked the door open and slid inside. He turned the ignition key. The motor ground but refused to come alive. The battery answered with only a few reluctant impulses. Brian slammed the steering wheel with a disgusted curse.

The car was conspicuous, parked there in front of the trailer park. He couldn't remain there. Already there was a lot of commotion on that side of the park. Brian put the car in neutral and pushed it out onto the road. He remembered the small grocery store a quarter of a mile back. He would shove the car there and hope to hide it long enough to get it started.

He began sweating and straining against the old car. The cold air burned his throat as he pulled it into his panting lungs. His legs were rubber by the time he shoved the Ghia into the parking area at the side of the store. He waited impatiently for his breath and some of his energy to return. He tried the key again. The car sputtered to life. Brian grinned tiredly as he pulled out of the grocery lot and drove back to the city.

CHAPTER 23

The creaking of the rocking chair created a metronome effect, keeping time to her mother's singsong delivery of salvation from the Bible. Judy could not remember more than a handful of days in her ten years of life when she had not climbed onto her mother's lap to be rocked and read to from the Word.

Typically they began slowly, rocking and reading. When her mother found an especially meaningful chapter, her voice rose in evangelical fervor and the chair rocked faster, keeping time with the excitement building in her. Even now, Judy could feel the intensity growing.

"Wherefore, O harlot, hear the word of the Lord. Thus saith the Lord God; Because thy filthiness was poured out and thy nakedness discovered through thy whoredoms with thy lovers, and with all the idols of the abominations, and by the blood of thy children, which thou didst give unto them; Behold, therefore, I will gather them round about against thee, and will discover thy nakedness unto them, that they may see all thy nakedness, and I will judge thee, as women that break wedlock and shed blood are judged; and I will give thee blood in fury and jealousy.

"And I will also give thee into their hand and they shall throw down thine eminent place and shall break down thy high places; they shall strip thee also of thy

clothes and shall take thy fair jewels, and leave thee
naked and bare. They shall also bring up a company
against thee and they shall stone thee with stones, and
thrust thee through with their swords."

Over the years, Judy had picked up the themes that
interested her mother most. Words like harlot, fornication and
whoredom always brought an unmistakable lilt to her voice.
Until recently, she hadn't really understood what the Bible was
talking about. When she asked her mother, she gave vague
generalities that only told Judy that the words were about
disgusting things. She could remember asking, "Mama, what's
fornication?"

"It's a terrible, sinful thing when a man takes you and does
lustful things to your private areas. The Devil will surely take
and burn you for such things."

Or, "Mama, what's a harlot?"

"That's a woman who uses her body for evil. She's gonna
burn alongside the man because she put him inside her body."

When Judy tried to find out how you put a man inside your
body, her mother just evaded the subject. She knew now, though.
Her girlfriend at school, Lizzy Miller, had just learned all about
it from her sister.

"It's really weird, Judy. The guy's thing gets all big and hard
and then he gets on top of you and pushes it inside your twat.
You know the word fuck that we see written all over the place?
That's what that means."

Judy was aghast. "What does he do when he's inside?"

"Well, I guess you just hump around. My sister says it's
really fun. She says you gotta watch out though. If the guy has
a climax inside you, you're in big trouble. You're gonna have
a baby. There are things to keep from having babies, but she
didn't tell me what they were."

"What's a climax?"

"A bunch of white stuff like hand lotion comes spurting out the end of his thing. It's got sperm in it. When it gets inside you, it makes babies."

Judy thought about her mom and dad. She could not believe it. There was no way her mother would let her dad do that in her.

"My mother says that sex is evil," Judy said. "When you give in to sex, you're letting the Devil into your soul." It hadn't made sense before, but suddenly it did.

"Geez, Judy, I don't know about that. It's kinda funny now that you mention it. My sister said that it's so neat that you'd sell your soul for it. She and her boyfriend sneak down in the storeroom and do it all the time. If my ma finds out about it, she'll kill them, I bet."

Judy's memory of the conversation with Lizzy was broken by a new hardness that had come into her mother's voice as they sat rocking and reading.

> "Behold, every one that useth proverbs shall use this proverb against thee, saying, As is the mother so is her daughter; Thou art thy mother's daughter; and thou art the sister of thy sisters, which loathed their husbands and their children: your mother was an Hittite, and your father an Amorite."

Abruptly Judy's mother closed the Bible and set it aside on a small table beside the rocker. She clasped her arms around Judy and continued to rock. Judy sensed her mother nodding some truth to herself.

Her mother always smothered Judy with affection. It sometimes felt as if she could hardly move because of her mother's hovering presence. Her health was constantly monitored, her friends checked and double-checked, and her activities forever reviewed. Her best friend, Beth, had laughed at her when Judy had told her that her mother still rocked her. She couldn't seem to find a way out of it though.

Her mother had begun to hum "Rock of Ages" and to caress the back of Judy's head.

"Mama, why is sex evil?" Judy inserted into the silence.

Her mother was startled from her hymn. A hard edge came into her voice as she said, "Lusting after the flesh is born of the Devil, Judy. It's why the Lord God cast Adam and Eve out of the Garden of Eden. When you're lusting after a man, your mind has no room for Jesus. If Jesus isn't in your heart, then the Devil must be there instead."

As she was about to continue, the front door opened and then closed. Footsteps came down the hall. The hulking form of her father appeared in the living room doorway. As usual his dark countenance was scowling. The blue-black of his beard's daylong growth and the dark eyebrows gave him a forbidding presence. He looked at his wife and child and at the Bible on the stand beside them.

"Been filling her full of your religious mumbo-jumbo again, I see," he said scornfully.

Judy's mother didn't respond, just hugged her daughter all the harder and stared back at her husband.

"I'll be out in the garage. Call me when supper's ready."

He turned and went toward the back of the house. Judy heard the screen door slam. Her father always made her feel uneasy. Where her mother had always been overwhelmingly affectionate, her father was a stiff, unyielding stranger. Judy used to try to hug him, but she had sensed that it made him feel terribly uncomfortable. She had no idea why he didn't love her. She wanted desperately to have him pick her up and tell her that he was glad she was his child. He never did.

Over the years of childhood and adolescence, nothing much changed within the family except that her mother, if anything, became more protective. As the threat of boys became a reality, she became ever vigilant. Judy was constantly warned that men only wanted her body to meet their animal needs. Her mother frequently quoted the scripture from Genesis telling of the punishment that God was visiting on womankind because of the transgression in the Garden.

"Unto the woman He said, I will greatly multiply thy sorrow and thy conception; in sorrow thou shalt bring forth children; and thy desire shall be to thy husband, and he shall rule over thee."

The fights between her parents were distressing, tying Judy in mental knots. They didn't happen often because her father seldom said much. Whenever her mother remarked about the evilness of sex, though, he would be compelled to speak.

"How come sex wasn't evil before we got married? I don't recall you quoting any scripture to me when you were panting in my ear. Your crazy old lady messed up your mind when you were a kid. Between her and the damn evangelist that got ahold of you, they pretty much jacked up your head. I'd like to kill them both."

When Judy began her first period, her mother was visibly upset. When the red stain first appeared in her underwear, Judy was frightened. Her mother's reaction did nothing to allay her fears.

At seventeen, Judy still hadn't had a date. When her mother sensed the inevitability of it happening, she allowed Judy to go out with a harmless boy from the church youth group. Nothing very satisfactory ever came from any of her dates. Subconsciously, she was waiting for the boys to "lust after her body." She began to have fears that she might be homosexual since she was only comfortable around other females.

After graduation from high school, her mother insisted that Judy live at home and commute each day to the college in the city. When Judy was a senior in college, she met Mike in one of her classes. He was so nice and gentle appearing that she felt a need to say yes when he asked her out to a movie. She was an attractive girl and frequently got invitations, which she seldom accepted. She always had to have them pick her up at the house and meet her mother. They never passed inspection of course.

She began to resent her mother a great deal. Fights between them grew in frequency and heat.

Then she fell in love with Mike.

Mike held her like her father never would. She could hardly wait to be with him. They talked by the hour. In a few short weeks, they progressed from holding hands to heavy petting. When she was doing it, she was always waiting for a voice or something to tell her she was on the way to hell. But the voice never came.

One day Mike talked her into going up to his apartment. When he took her into his bedroom, she hesitated. But she didn't want to lose him. She had to do it. As her clothes came off, she became increasingly excited. Before long she was naked and he hurriedly entered her. At least he tried. Nervousness and her hymen made the entry painful for her. Was it supposed to feel like that? It was terrible, she thought. The hymen ruptured and Mike ejaculated almost at the same time. He gave a little moan of pleasure and collapsed upon her.

In a few minutes he rolled over smiling. "That felt so good, Honey. How about you? Did you make it?"

"Make what?"

"A climax. Did you have a climax?"

"No," she said quietly.

He seemed disappointed. He looked closely at her. "This was your first time wasn't it?"

She tried to avoid looking at his penis hanging limply on his leg. "Yes."

Mike suddenly looked a little nervous. "Are you on the pill or anything?"

"No."

He laughed uneasily. "Oh, well, nothing ever happens the first time."

"What if it does, Mike? Will you marry me? I love you, Mike."

Mike looked around like a trapped animal. "I love you too, Judy, but let's not make any hasty decisions."

She didn't see him very often after that. He seemed to have more and more things going on that required his attention. By the time she graduated, Judy was four months pregnant and Mike was gone.

Her mother almost lost her mind. After all her warning and preaching, her little girl had been ruined. After the shock wore off, she became even more attentive to her daughter to make up somehow for having failed her.

"If you ask God for forgiveness, Judy, maybe he won't hold that abomination growing in your stomach against you," she told her daughter.

By the time the baby was born, her mother's sermons transformed the delivery into an exercise in terror. The labor was long and painful. When they finally laid the dark-haired, red- faced screaming boy beside her, she could feel no love for it.

Life got no easier for Judy. Baby Darrel had colic and cried all the time. Her mother constantly reminded her that he was the spawn of the Devil.

The baby began life as an abused child; not physical abuse; instead a victim of coldness from uncaring people. The young seed, falling on barren ground, would create a stunted adult.

Unconsciously, Judy made up for the emotionless void surrounding the child by being overprotective of him. She didn't get a full-time job so she could stay home with him. She did substitute teaching at the local elementary school but accepted nothing permanent until the boy was older.

However, it became increasingly hard to cope with the constant contact with her mother. She began to hate her mother and felt guilty because she did. Her mother's overprotective behavior toward her and hostility toward the baby became harder to bear, day by day.

Judy often felt sure she was losing her mind. One day she could stand it no longer. She had to leave. She couldn't get a full time teaching job in the middle of a school year. Instead she found a clerk's job in one of the department stores in the Meridian Mall. She moved out on a Sunday while her mother was in church. She had almost no money and took only what she could carry, along with Darrel. The taxi deposited her at the cheap little apartment she had found after she had gotten her job.

Life got no better. Money problems constantly assailed her and the guilt of leaving the eighteen-month-old baby alone all day drove her frantic. She still did not love him, nor was he very lovable. The trauma of the womb and the hateful delivery had created a harsh little person. His dark features did nothing to enhance his appeal.

One day Judy started hearing voices. She didn't know where they were coming from, but their message was always the same: "You have sinned, Judy, and now you are paying," they whispered. "That child is the son of Satan," they warned.

Judy could not find the source of the voices though she heard them frequently. They whispered out of nowhere and left her shaking in fear. Her supervisor began to watch her more closely and her job pressure became worse.

Her schizophrenia escalated. Every time she saw a red car anywhere she felt an almost unconquerable need to change clothes. She gave into the need nearly every time. She even took to carrying a second set of clothes with her on the way to work because she knew she would see a red car sooner or later.

She was being followed. They were always very subtle, those elusive beings, but she knew they were there. She would turn suddenly and catch them, just looking away, or turning into a doorway. Fear was her constant companion.

One evening on her way home, one of them got off the bus behind her. She ran as hard as she could but was unable to lose him. She saw his blood-red eyes staring through her clothes as he pursued her toward her apartment. Racing up the stairs, she was just able to close and lock her door before he caught up to her. She leaned, panting and terrified, against the door.

Darrel's crying brought her back to reality. He was ravenous with hunger. She took off her coat and picked him up. Nothing but food would quiet him. She put him in the high chair beside the stove and got out a skillet to fry some bacon and eggs for their supper. The grease was hot and crackling by the time she got the eggs out and the bacon separated.

She tried to shut out the sound of Darrel's screaming, but it suddenly took on an ominous note, a harsh, raspy sound. She glanced over at him. Her breath caught in her throat. His eyes were becoming bloodshot. The eyebrows knit together as he watched her every move. Incredibly, the ears were starting to change shape and become pointed on top. The little baby teeth had sharp edges on them. The smile was evil.

"I've come for you, Judy," the Devil whispered. "It's time for your soul to come back where it belongs."

Horrified, Judy backed up against the stove.

"It's time!" the voice hissed malevolently. The long-taloned fingers reached out for her from the high chair.

A scream arose from deep within her as she backed away. The hand followed her. She felt the heat from the burner near her hand. Without thinking, she grasped the skillet handle and threw the red-hot grease at the apparition in front of her. She began flailing away with the utensil at the grasping, clawing hand. The fear was so great she couldn't cope with it. She passed out.

Judy awoke to cries so full of pain they almost wrenched her heart from her chest. From where she was lying, she could see Darrel sprawled on the floor where he had fallen when his high chair had been knocked over. The grease had burned his hand

and arm in several places. His pain was beyond description or his understanding. He lay there writhing and screaming in agony.

"My baby! What have I done to you?" Judy sobbed. She crawled over to him and cradled him in her arms. There was no soothing him. His skin was fiery red and blistered, with fluid oozing out. She knew she had to get him to a hospital quickly. Her tears mingled with his as she arose and ran with him toward help.

CHAPTER 24

Kristin put the phone back in its cradle. She had just finished talking with the Protective Services Department. The file on Steven Sanderson lay open on the desk in front of her.

She made some brief notations from the conversation she had just concluded. Normally, Protective Services would have made a visit to Steven's parents the next day after a complaint was lodged by a hospital. This was especially the case when a parent took the child home without a physician's discharge directions. But there had been an excessive caseload that had caused five days to go by before a Protective Service caseworker had made a call on the Sandersons.

In that short time, they had moved and left no forwarding address. Inquiries to adjoining apartments had brought no clues as to their whereabouts. All normal methods for tracing the family had also met with failure. The case was still open and assistance had been requested from Centrex, the state's central protective services agency. Any future abuse that needed treatment would get into Steven's file and the family thus located. Until that happened, Stevie was still at his parent's mercy.

Using the information Brian had given her, Kristin asked that the new address be checked and the treated injury at the urgent care center be reviewed. Protective Services would get back with her when they knew more.

Kristin left her office and went up to the third floor of the building to the peds wing. It was 4:15. She had called and found that Brian was working there that afternoon. She stopped at the nurses' station and waited for a short time until the nurse deigned to look up and acknowledge her existence.

"Yes, Miss Grey?" the nurse said.

"I'm looking for Dr. Tanner."

"He's taking care of a patient now. Can I give him a message?"

"No, I don't think so. I'll catch him some other time."

Brian came out of a patient room down the hall just as she was about to leave. He spotted her at the desk and came toward her.

"Hi, Kristin," he said.

It was funny how nice it sounded when he said hello to her. She looked into his eyes. What a sad man, she thought, wondering why.

"Hi, Brian. I was just passing by and I thought I'd let you know that I've been looking into the Steven Sanderson case for you. Sometime when you have a few moments I'll let you know what I found out. It isn't much, I'm afraid."

She saw the interest Stevie's name created.

"I'm really busy right now, Kristin. Can we talk about it over supper in the cafeteria?" he said.

"I'm sorry. I have a meeting with my lawyer right after work or else I could."

She considered him for a few seconds. She looked at the worn pair of running shoes she had seen on him before in the cafeteria.

"Would you like to go running with me sometime soon? We could talk about it then," she said.

Brian looked a little dubious. "It will be a little difficult getting together since I work most nights."

She covered her feeling of rejection with a jest. "It's your loss, Doctor. Seeing these legs in running shorts usually causes most men to cough up a lung."

A smile had almost surfaced on his face, Kristin noticed.

"Maybe I can give you a call," he said.

Kristin was beginning to feel irritated. She felt a little like she was begging and that was something she vowed never to do with a man.

"Okay. Well, whenever you can find some time in your busy schedule, let me know. I'll be around." She turned to go.

Brian saw that she was angry so he reached out and put his hand gently on her shoulder. She turned back to him questioningly.

"If I can find someone to cover my shift tomorrow evening, would you be interested in running then?"

Kristin thought about it for a few seconds. There were the girls. She hated to leave them with the foster grandmother too late. She didn't want Heather and Holly to feel even the slightest sense of abandonment by not picking them up at the normal time. She looked at Brian who was growing uneasy with her silent indecision. For no reason she could explain she wanted to know him better. She hadn't felt that way about a man in many years. She seldom even dated anymore; the experience was often so unfulfilling. She didn't even miss the sex. Her loving emotions were being channeled into caring for the girls.

"All right. What time and where shall I meet you?" she said, making her decision.

"I like to run along the river and through the campus at MSU. Do you know where the IM building is beside the football stadium?" he said.

"Yes. Just to the east of the old Jenison Fieldhouse, right?"

"That's the place. I'll meet you there in the parking lot about five o'clock. I drive an old Kharmen Ghia. You'll probably hear it coming."

"I'll be there. You better rest up 'cause I'm not going to take it easy on you," she teased.

Again, almost a smile from him. A brief softening of the face. She liked him. Why? No answer. She put her hand on his arm, smiled briefly at him then turned and left.

Brian stood staring at her retreating figure. A feeling was reluctantly forming in the back of his mind. He might be looking forward to tomorrow night.

CHAPTER 24

Kristin looked impatiently at her watch. Five-thirty it said. She stared angrily at the road running along in front of the parking lot. The dirty S.O.B. had stood her up. She couldn't believe it. At 5:45 she got out of her Mustang and began pacing the lot, thinking that she might somehow have missed him pulling in but knowing that she hadn't. She was ticked. Another fifteen minutes went by. No way was she waiting any longer.

She went back across the parking lot toward her car. She got in, stabbed the ignition to life and squawked her tires as she left the lot. She had barely left the exit when she heard a car horn bleating just behind her. She looked in her rear view mirror and saw a hand waving from the driver's side window of a Kharmen Ghia that should have lodged in a junkyard years ago. She pulled over to the curb and stopped. She watched Brian squeeze out of the car door and come running toward her.

"I'm really sorry, Kristin. I didn't mean to keep you waiting. About the time I was supposed to leave I got started on a young boy who'd been in a motorcycle accident. By the time we got the gravel all dug out of his skin and his cuts and scrapes taken care of, it was almost five-thirty. I changed as fast as I could."

Kristin was perplexed. Her mind was all prepared to be angry and now she couldn't be.

"That's okay," she said grudgingly, "I didn't have anything else to do anyway."

Brian looked at her a second, then said, "You know, I think you must be a very nice person, Kristin."

Kristin didn't know how to respond to the unexpected compliment so she said nothing for a change.

Brian broke the short silence. "If you still want to run we can take that bike path over there by the river, then cut through some subdivisions and back through campus. It's about four miles."

"All right," she said reluctantly, still feeling the leftovers of her anger with him.

He followed her as she drove back to the parking lot. They got out and walked across the street to the bike path. There was a flock of ducks cruising the river just above a mini-rapids where the water suddenly fell several feet. Even in Brian's emotionally cold state of mind he could appreciate Kristin's long muscled legs flowing out of her running shorts. A young college boy went cruising by on roller blades. He was so impressed by what he saw that while he was staring back over his shoulder, one of his skates left the bike path, caught on some gravel and tossed him to the ground. He muttered an obscenity in his embarrassment, got up quickly and skated off.

Kristin grinned. "Told you," she said.

"Coughed up a lung?" Brian said.

"You got it," she replied.

They started out slowly, letting their muscles and lungs gradually warm. Brian was in old basketball shorts and wore a tattered Cincinnati Reds sweatshirt against the coolness of the evening. Kristin, by contrast, was dressed in light blue Gortex shorts, iridescent lime green windbreaker and new Nike running shoes.

They ran in silence for a while, moving effortlessly east along the Red Cedar River that bisected the campus. Coveys of students were headed back to their dorms or to the library. Occasional hormonally stressed pairs could be seen walking hand-in-hand or lying eagerly by the river.

They had been running for nearly a half an hour and were in one of the subdivisions to the west of the campus when suddenly, from one of the houses, a large German shepherd charged out at them, hackles raised, teeth bared and snarling viciously. Instinctively, without a pause, Brian inserted himself between Kristin and the dog, fist raised. The animal came to the end of the driveway and its chain and thrashed itself continuously into the air in frustrated rage trying to get at them. Brian's move had been a small thing, but it told Kristin a lot about him.

As they continued on, she looked over at him. "I once quit dating a boy when he told me he shot one of the neighborhood dogs with a B-B gun because it was tearing up their garbage cans. He'd have felt really smug if he knew I'd have settled for a cannon a few minutes ago."

Brian gave a little laugh. Kristin noted a small chip out of one of Brian's front teeth, giving his smile added personality.

"That was incredible, Brian! You actually smiled just then. I'm really proud of you. I was beginning to think it wasn't possible."

The smile had disappeared as fast as it had come. "There's not all that much to smile about in this world," he stated simply.

"That's a lot of bull, Brian. The world's a fascinating place. How can you say something like that? No matter how many bad things exist, there is always a ton of good to be found."

Brian merely shrugged.

By this time, they had circled around and were heading back toward the IM parking lot from the south.

Brian and Kristin slowed to a walk as they came back to the river. They ambled along for a while, letting themselves cool down. Sweat glistening on both of them, they went down a short fieldstone stairway to a cement platform setting just above the river. They sat down on the platform to watch the shining water slip hypnotically past a few inches below their feet. Ducks slid closer in hopes of finding a handout. One daring drake rode the mini rapids to the bottom, turned and let whatever food was floating in the river come to him.

"Tell me what you found out about Stevie, will you?" Brian asked out of nowhere.

Kristin had forgotten all about the reason for the run.

"Well, the Protective Services Department got to the original case a little late. By the time they got to the Sandersons', the family had already left the area. The new address you gave me proved to be just as fruitless. They had left there just a few days before with no forwarding address. The agency went through all their possible channels of information to locate them, but there was no trace. The state agency has been contacted to let us know if anything is ever reported about them in the future. Until then, nothing can be done. Are you sure the child was abused? It said on the E.R. registration that some neighborhood kids had shoved the boy down some stairs."

A tangible aura of hatred settled over Brian. "Yes, I'm sure," he whispered.

Kristin watched, intrigued by the intensity of Brian's emotion. "Why are you so interested in this particular case, Brian? Do you always get so involved with the patients you treat?"

"Because I see his eyes at night when I sleep. Because this little boy is all alone with no one to protect him or to love him. His future is being beaten out of him every day. Someday soon, there will be no saving him."

"But what can you do for him? The agency and the courts will do what they can. There's nothing left that you can do."

"You know better than that, Kristin. Those lousy courts only help a handful of children. Instead of a slap on the wrist that the parents get, they should be punished just like they've hurt their children. If they beat their babies, they should be beaten. If they burn them, they should be burned. If they lock them in a closet for days without food, then do the same to them!"

"An eye for an eye, eh, Brian? Two wrongs will make a right? Is that it? It won't work you know. Don't you realize that most of those parents are victims too? You can't put out the fire by throwing gasoline on it. Yes, the parents should be punished but there has to be a solution other than the violence you're suggesting."

Brian looked at her. "There is no excuse for adults destroying their own children. All the nice words and pleadings won't stop these people for a second. Only if they feel the same fear as their children do, will they stop."

"You're wrong, Brian."

Brian returned his attention to the river. It seemed important for him to make her understand somehow but there were only words, impossible tools to convey terror. He shrugged helplessly and got up from the slab of cement.

"We're getting chilly sitting here. We'd better be going," he said.

Kristin could tell that he had shut himself off from her. She felt a keen disappointment at the distance between them now.

She offered to spring for a quick bite at a MacDonald's near campus but he declined, saying that he needed to stop over at the Medical Arts Center to get some mail and get his final rotation schedule.

CHAPTER 25

Kristin read the police report that was an addendum to the Reeser file. It was not a part of the caseworker's activity with the family, but merely included as noteworthy, although probably unrelated to the actual case.

When the caseworker had arrived at the trailer the day after the Reeser baby had been admitted, she found the family extremely uncooperative. Apparently the father had been very severely beaten the night before and refused to talk to the caseworker.

The wife professed to know nothing about why her husband had been beaten. The caseworker noted that the wife didn't seem to care much that it had happened either. The caseworker had obtained a copy of the police report as background on the family.

When the police had interviewed Reeser, he had given no information on why he had been attacked. Essentially no description of the assailant was available, with the exception that, for some reason, Reeser had noticed that the attacker had a chip out of one of his front teeth. The note jarred a thought within Kristin but she couldn't grasp it.

Kristin had half a notion to show the report to Brian. He would be really pleased to see that, by an interesting coincidence, someone had done just what he had wanted to happen. An abusing parent had gotten the hell beaten out of him. Brian would certainly see the justice in that. She debated telling him and finally decided against it. She abhorred violence and cruelty and did not want to reinforce Brian's obvious, gut-reactive need for it in these cases. She wondered briefly why it made any difference to her what was in Brian's head. It was really none of her business.

The intercom on her desk buzzed.

"It's Dr. Tanner on the phone, Kristin."

"Thanks, Marian."

Kristin was both pleased and surprised to hear from Brian. She had felt sure that she would not be seeing him again. She wasn't prepared to make any more overtures toward him and she hadn't thought he would show any further interest in her. She had enjoyed their run. She wasn't sure whether he had.

"Hi, Brian," she said into the phone.

"Hi, Kristin. I'm sorry to bother you at work. I was wondering if you might like to go someplace with me tonight. I don't have to work."

She paused only briefly, thinking of babysitting possibilities.

"I'd love to. Would you like to pick me up at my apartment?" she said.

"Sure. How about seven o'clock?"

"Okay. The address is Johnson Manor, 228 Hamilton Avenue, Apartment 201. Got it?"

"Yes. I'll see you then."

"All right. Bye."

Brian sat and stared at the telephone beside him. It had been a long time since he had taken anyone out on a date. He had awakened early that morning and the loneliness had settled over him like a suffocating fog. He was immobilized by depression. Nothing he could think of made it seem worthwhile to even move. While he lay staring at the ceiling, for some reason he thought of Kristin and he felt better. He couldn't go on the way he had been without someone to talk to. Maybe she was the one.

Kristin put down the phone. She was perceptive enough to realize that the pleasure she was experiencing was not the same she normally felt when invited on a date. For some unaccountable reason, she wanted to get to know Brian Tanner. She didn't have the normal feeling of female superiority around him that other men engendered in her. There was an air of vulnerability about the man which, for some strange reason, didn't make her look down on him as if it was a weakness. She sensed that somehow she would be better off by the experience of knowing him. The raucous buzz of the intercom again interrupted her again.

"Yes, Marian?"

"E.R. just called. They'd like you to come down and talk with a mother who just brought her child in with third degree burns on his face and arm. The nurse said it looks like she did it on purpose. Apparently, the mother won't talk to anybody about it."

When Kristin arrived in the E.R., she was directed to one of the back rooms. She saw the woman sitting on one of the hard plastic chairs, staring into nowhere, all drawn in on herself, with her arms wrapped protectively about her chest.

Kristin sat down opposite the woman and opened up her case folder. It was one of the most unpleasant duties of her job that required her to confront these parents with subtle accusations of child abuse. The reactions ran the gamut of emotions from tearful denial to indignant anger and outrage.

Kristin's interaction with them varied with the response of the parent. She faced a certain challenge to get the parents to reveal what had really happened to their child and, more importantly, the why.

She also had the difficulty of deciding if the parents were telling the truth. Much of the decision was based on the opinion of the doctor treating the injured child. He had to make a judgment as to whether the extent and severity of the injuries could have logically been caused by the event as told by the parents.

Kristin had few doubts about the case before her now. The baby had been severely burned and beaten. The mother offered no reason, no excuse.

"My name is Kristin Grey," she began. "I'm from the Social Services Department. Because of the nature of your child's injuries, I was asked to talk to you and find out more about the situation."

The woman looked mutely over at her. Kristin saw the torment on her face. Kristin talked to the woman for a long time, but could get no response.

At last, the woman said, "I did it. Please forgive me!"

With that, she began to sob convulsively. Kristin could not get her to say anything more.

There was nothing else to do. She would have to call in Protective Services in that evening to interview the mother and take pictures of the child's injuries. Their assessment of the situation, along with Kristin's evaluation, would help the court decide what to do with the mother and child. As yet Kristin could give them little in the way of facts.

The interview had lasted long beyond her normal quitting time. Kristin rushed back to her office and then hurried toward her apartment. The streets were full of the homeward bound rush of workers. As usual there was an abundance of mental midgets wielding their cars as deadly weapons. Using her Mustang's best escape and evasion moves, Kristin made it unscathed to the parking ramp behind her apartment.

She rushed in the front door and was greeted by a big slobbery kiss by little Holly.

"Hi, mommy," the little girl said.

Both girls had changed from calling her Aunt Kristin to just mommy a month after she had started taking care of them. The word never ceased to make her feel both wonderful and vulnerable at the same time. She was long past the time when she could conceive of ever letting go of them. If the father ever came back, she would fight him with every legal maneuver known to man to keep him away. She had already spent time with her lawyer and lobbying a certain judge about the case.

Heather came out of the kitchen, eating as usual. She gave Kristin a hug and a food clogged smile.

Mrs. Benzing, the foster grandmother, came trailing along behind, wiping her hands on a towel. The woman had ceased to be a foster grandmother since Kristin was now paying her for day care services on a regular basis.

"Thanks a million for bringing the girls home, Mrs. Benzing. Sorry I'm late."

"It's no problem, Kristin. Gave me an excuse to have Claude make his own supper. Men are such lazy creatures. I think the only reason he kept me around for fifty years is that I'm the best cook he'll ever find. Well, see you and the girls in the morning."

Kristin looked at the clock. She was expecting the teenager from down the block in forty-five minutes. She knew from a general tacky feeling that a major repair job would be required on her body in a short amount of time. Her teeth felt fuzzy, her deodorant had long since expired tragically and the nubbies on her legs would tear the hide off an armadillo. She dialed up some cartoons for the girls on the TV in their bedroom then headed for the bathroom.

She threw off all her clothes and tossed them into a pile in the corner, then started the hot water for her bath. While she waited for the tub to fill, she brushed her teeth. She spit out a mouthful of foam, looking in the mirror to see if she was keeping the yellow at bay. She glanced at herself and smiled. She seldom looked at her face closely. There was something unsettling about staring into her own eyes. When she did, the loneliness looked back at her. If she refused to face it, maybe it wasn't there.

With a blissful sigh, she settled into the hot water. After a moment's relaxation, she leaned forward to spread lather on her legs. She scraped them clean, then attacked her underarms. With those areas conquered, she let the water out of the tub and turned on the shower. She pulled her hair out of its bun and shook it down to where it fell almost to her waist. The mass of wavy hair was beautiful from constant care and her vegetarian diet. She washed it, then stepped out of the shower, all pink and new. She toweled herself and her hair, then ran the hair dryer for a short time while she brushed it out.

In the bedroom, she sprayed on deodorant and applied a little makeup before deciding what clothes to wear. She slipped into white bikini underwear and put on the extra soft bra that let the nipples show through. She grabbed a satiny, white blouse, red skirt and high-heeled shoes from the closet. Once the pantyhose were pulled on, she put on the other pieces. A dab of perfume and she stood back to look at the result in the full-length mirror.

"Not bad, Kristin baby," she complimented herself.

The buzzer from the outside entrance called from the entryway. She went to the speaker and pressed the button.

"Who is it?"

"Hi. It's Brian."

"Brian who?"

"Come on, Kristin, don't be so weird."

Kristin laughed and pushed the button to open the foyer door. In a short time Brian knocked at her door. He was wearing a pullover shirt, jeans and loafers. Kristin took one look and knew they weren't dressed compatibly. She vacillated between irritation and a desire to somehow get into her grubbies too.

"Can you give me a couple of seconds, Brian? I just got home from work and I haven't had time to change," she said hurriedly.

Brian stood looking at the woman in front of him. She was beautiful! He had seen her only in business suits or running clothes with her hair up in a bun. This was a different person. She looked so incredible with her long dark hair framing her face and hanging down her back! He thought of his own clothes and compared them to Kristin's. She had taken the time to prepare for him that he should have taken for her. He liked her, both for the preparation, and the excuse that she had given to help him save face.

Brian smiled. "Okay, Kristin. I'll just make myself comfortable. Take your time."

Kristin had noticed Brian's involuntary look at himself and then back at her. They smiled at each other as she turned and went back to her bedroom.

She called back over her shoulder, "If you go down the hall to the bedroom, you can meet the girls. The littlest one is Holly. The five year old is Heather."

"Girls?" he stammered. "What girls?"

She understood the perplexed sound in his voice, realizing that he didn't know anything about her personal life.

"They're my . . . er, daughters," she said.

"I thought you said you were a miss. Did you get a divorce?"

"Yes, but they aren't from that marriage. I guess you could say I stole them," she said and laughed. "I'll tell you about it later. Be right back."

A jolt ran through Brian at the phrase "stole them."

Brian wandered down the hall toward the sound of a TV. He tapped tentatively on the door to get the two girls' attention.

"Hi, I'm Brian Tanner. I'm just here to see your, er, mother," he said.

He felt them shy away from him, a stranger, so he did not come further into the room.

"Well, see you later," he said and returned to the living room.

While he was there the intercom buzzer sounded.

"Get that will you, Brian? It's probably Sheri, the baby sitter."

It was and he let her in. After introducing himself he aimed the girl toward the children down in the bedroom.

Kristin reappeared a few minutes later in jeans, running shoes and a red T-shirt with a line drawing of a dancer across the front. She had used a red ribbon to tie back her hair in a long ponytail.

Brian looked her over again. If anything, she looked better than before. The T-shirt and jeans accentuated her femininity.

It was obvious to Kristin that he was having a hard time keeping eye contact with her.

She laughed. "Come on, Brian, they're just boobs. You doctors see them all the time. Just fat cells, right? You have to learn to love me for my personality."

Brian blushed as he grinned at her. "I'm sure I will, but in the meantime, those 'fat cells' aren't hurting your chances any."

"C'mon, sex fiend. Where are you taking me?"

"I don't know. I thought maybe to a movie and then a steak dinner afterward. Is there anything you'd rather do?"

"I'm never going to get to know you sitting in some dark theater. If you wouldn't object, I know of a little Italian restaurant where the food is super and they have a guy that plays a nice soft guitar."

"Sounds fine. Let's do it."

They walked out the side entrance of the building and across the street to where Brian's old Ghia stood. He unlocked the passenger's side and pried the door open. The loose rear fender rattled when he slammed the door after her. She watched him have even more trouble getting in the driver's side door. When he started the car, the hole in the muffler emitted a raucous din.

"Boy, this is a real . . . antique," Kristin chuckled.

Brian nodded. "I probably should get a newer one sometime. I just haven't had . . . time."

"Sure. But what the heck, as long as it gets you from point A to point B, that's all you need."

"I can't guarantee you point B but tell me where the restaurant is and we'll try to get there."

Twenty minutes later they entered the dimly lighted restaurant in Okemos, a suburb of Lansing. A young man was sitting at the back, picking gently at the strings of his classical guitar.

They seated themselves at one of the few empty booths and began to look at the menu.

"What's your pleasure?" Brian asked.

"I'd like some spaghetti, garlic bread, an antipasto salad and a beer."

"I think I'll have the same. Do you want mushrooms and meatballs with your spaghetti?"

"Just tomato sauce. I don't eat cow muscle."

"Cow muscle?"

"I'm a vegetarian. I can't stand the thought of an animal dying so that I can eat."

Brian sat thinking for a few minutes. "Isn't that the way the world was designed? One animal preying on another so that it can live? Isn't the Creator's plan one long chain of dying? Does it make any difference if some cow died so that you can eat?"

"It makes a difference to me," Kristin replied. "I decided a long time ago that hurting another living creature was bad."

"Then God must be bad, mustn't He? He designed this world so that killing is an integral part of our existence."

"I never try to second guess "Her", Brian. When I can finally make a butterfly or a flower, I'll challenge Her about the way things work. I just know that as a human being with a free will, I must never knowingly hurt another creature if I can help it."

The waitress arrived for their order. When Brian had given it, Kristin smiled at him. She noticed he hadn't ordered any 'cow muscle' for himself either. She also noticed that he had ordered a Coke instead of a beer.

"You don't drink?" she said to him.

It seemed he could still smell the vile scent of booze on his father's breath but of course he couldn't tell Kristin about that.

Instead he said, "No, something I learned from my mom, I guess. She said that alcohol is responsible for too much evil in the world so we learned to avoid any of it as a matter of principle."

"Did your mother tell you that women who drank beer were no-account?"

She had meant the comment in jest and she could see Brian struggling in an attempt to make light of the question.

"My mother would have said that beer drinking is for truck drivers and pot-bellied guys sitting around passing gas and telling dirty stories." He grinned ruefully at her.

"I think I would like your mother."

"You'd have loved my mother, Kristin. She was the nicest, gentlest human being who ever lived."

"Since you said 'would have', she must not be alive."

"She died a short time ago."

"I'm very sorry. How about your dad? Is he still living?"

Kristin felt the hatred radiating from Brian as he began his answer. The words were spoken calmly but something very bad was hiding beneath them.

"My father doesn't exist," he said simply.

Kristin wanted to ask him what he meant, but the way he had said it indicated that he would discuss it no further. She quickly returned to Brian's mother. As they talked about her, she could readily see how deeply he cared for her. She understood why, when he got around to telling how she died.

Brian hesitated before he began to talk about the dying. He hadn't said anything about it to anyone and he needed to talk about it.

"My mother died of one of the swiftest but most painful forms of cancer that exists. She was such a selfless person that I didn't know she had it until she was nearly dead. She didn't want me to be sad, or miss the work on my residency, because she knew I could do nothing to help her. She didn't want me to watch her die either because it's a horrible death. She was all the good things of my life. . . And she died."

As Brian sat and confided in her, a single tear dropped over the edge of his eyelid and slid slowly down his cheek.

"Can you understand a world where a person spends her whole life helping cancer patients while they lived with it and died of it and then she has to die of the same thing? How can you believe in a God who lets things like that happen?"

"I can't answer that, Brian. I don't know what the plan is. I just know that being alive is a miracle. It's the fear that we can die at any moment that makes us want to stay alive all the more. If life had no mystery, people would have no appreciation for it either. I truly believe that your mother is in a place where she's always happy."

"I wish I could believe that. How can you trust God to make something good after you die when he created so much hell for the living?"

"It has to be that way. Don't you see, without the bad there can be no good. Without the minus, there is no plus. If you don't experience pain, you can't know pleasure. Without the opposites, there is just one bland, straight line that isn't worth living through."

"There still needs to be compassion for the innocent and the gentle of this world."

"We won't know the answer to these things in this world, Brian. In order to make life worth living through, you have to grab every minute of it, savor it and believe that everything happens for a good reason. Life also demands of you and me, that we choose to be the good guys. People who come in contact with us should be better for the experience. Without us, the bad guys win."

The arrival of the waitress with their food interrupted their discussion. Kristin could see Brian trying to digest what she had said as he ate.

The conversation eventually went to other, less oppressive subjects. Their meal had long since been finished as they talked on. Without conscious effort, their hands had come quietly together on the table. It was the first time Kristin had ever felt a sense of completeness touching a man. It felt strangely as if the flow of her life force continued onward into him and then back to her. It frightened her. She shook the feeling away. There was no way to have those feelings, especially without even really knowing the man.

Brian felt suddenly obtuse. They had passed the entire evening and he had forgotten to ask Kristin about her girls. As he was about to speak Kristin made the mistake of talking about the end of her workday, and her interview with the mother.

"I was late getting home tonight because I received a call from the E.R. just as I was about to quit for the day," she said.

"What did you have to do in the E.R.?"

"They asked me to come down and talk with a woman who had just hurt her little boy terribly."

"What did she do?" Brian asked. Kristin felt his hand stiffen under her fingers.

"She threw boiling hot grease on him and then beat him with the frying pan. He was badly burned and he has a broken arm."

"Why did she do it?" Brian asked brusquely.

"She wouldn't talk to me. She spoke only one time all the while I was there. She said, 'I did it. Please forgive me.'"

Brian's hand returned to his own lap. He was no longer with her. She could see the anger on his face. Kristin suspected that, subconsciously, she had brought the conversation around to this topic to find out his reaction. His intense feelings on the subject told of something in him that she wanted to root out. She needed to know, almost desperately, without knowing why it was important to her.

"Do you think we should throw hot grease on the mother and then beat her?" Kristin challenged him. "Is that the solution to this problem? Do you suppose that would make her quit? Could you do that to her, Brian? Are you capable of doing it?"

Brian didn't answer right away. He wanted to say yes. He wanted to make those people hurt. He thought of his father running free, and he wanted, from the bottom of his heart, to find him and beat him until his arms ached with exhaustion.

When Kristin asked her questions, he could only think of his need for vengeance on his father, instead of the faceless image of a disturbed mother.

"Yes," he said finally.

Kristin was shocked. Here was an obviously gentle man with a streak of violence running through him. He was an enigma to her.

"How did you arrive at a point where you can say 'yes' so easily? Aren't there extenuating circumstances to consider first?"

"Did she burn her baby?" Brian asked stubbornly.

"Yes, but . . ."

"If you did the same to her, what do you think the chances are that she'd have the guts to ever do it again?"

"I don't know. I guess I'd have to know why she did it in the first place. Couldn't there be reasons?"

"I don't care. I just want her to stop. That baby of hers won't have a life worth living unless you make her quit hurting him."

"That's crazy, Brian. You're just as wrong as the mother if you do that. Hurting people is wrong. It's evil no matter who does it."

Brian looked across the table at Kristin, pleading silently for her to understand his point of view. But how could he ever describe to her the feeling of hearing those footsteps come up the stairs, bringing pain and fear and hatred with them? How did you explain being so frightened that you wet your pants at the first scream? Can you put into words how it feels to be tied to a bed post and beaten with a belt until you're sure you can't stand the pain a second longer? Would she understand the nightmares that had shattered so many of his nights with their terror? Could she even begin to understand the hatred that filled him at the thought of his father? The only person he had ever known who was the epitome of love had saved him with violence. If Hazel had done it, then it must be right.

Brian just bowed his head. "I don't think I can make you understand," he said doggedly. "Maybe we should change the subject."

"There you go again, Brian, clamming up on me. At least try to tell me why you feel as strongly as you do. The kind of person you seem to be, doesn't just happen to have a point of view like this without a reason."

"That's okay, Kristin. It's no big thing, really."

Kristin looked into Brian's eyes and shook her head in disappointment. He wasn't going to tell her.

The thread of joy that had been running through their evening came unraveled after that. Both tried to put it back together, but it was no use. After a while Brian asked for the check and they left.

Kristin had been planning to invite him up to her apartment, but that didn't seem like such a good idea at the moment.

They drove silently back to her place, each of them trying to analyze what had happened. Brian escorted Kristin across the street to the side door of her apartment building. She inserted the key and opened it. She turned and held out her hand.

He did not want the night to end this way. It had been a wonderful evening. There was no reason they had to part, feeling so down.

"Kristin, I'm sorry." He took her hand and held it. "It was a beautiful evening. Can we do it again sometime? I really enjoyed being with you."

Kristin smiled up at him. "Yes, I think we should try it again. It will be okay, I think." With that she reached up and kissed him gently on the lips. "Good night, Brian."

"Good night, Kristin."

He was only a few blocks from her apartment when he realized with a shock that they had not talked about how Kristin had "stolen" her daughters. He almost turned and drove back so that he could ask her what she meant.

As he drove home, he thought about all of the things Kristin had said to him. Was he wrong? He didn't think so. There was no changing abusive parents unless they experienced the same fear as their children had. The end more than justified the means. There was *no* excuse for destroying a child. He knew he was right about that.

Brian was awake for a long time after he got home. He lay on the bed, hands behind his head, staring at the darkened ceiling. He knew every crack and line on it. He wondered where Stevie was and whether he was surviving. He thought about the baby Kristin had just told him about. So many ruined lives. "Do you give them extra love when they die, God?" Brian asked of the night.

Sometime after three o'clock, he dozed off. He saw Hazel walking across a green meadow, heading for a stream that was coming out of the woods at the far side. A look of utter peace radiated from her face and she walked along with a lightness as if hardly encumbered by mere earthly gravity. A whole herd of little kids emerged from the woods, racing out to greet her. They ran around her, touching her, shouting and laughing as she hugged them, each one in turn.

"Hey, Mom! Mom! It's me, Brian! Wait up! I'm coming to see you! Mom! Mom!" He yelled as loud as he could and ran toward her but he was unable to get closer to her or get her attention. He had to see her! He had something he had to ask her. And he needed for her to hold him again. Brian was panting with exertion but he couldn't get to her.

He noticed a movement at the edge of the woods. An adult was coming toward Hazel. It was Kristin! My God, how did she get there? He saw Hazel wave to her and then they came together near the stream. They stood engrossed in conversation as Brian saw his mother start to frown. What were they saying? He tried again to get to them, but had no better luck than before. They started to walk away from him toward the woods. He began to scream at them.

"Mom! Wait for me! Mom! Kristin! Kristin!" He awoke with a start. It had been so real! What had they been talking about? He felt a loneliness like nothing he had ever known. He thought of the burned baby and the mother Kristin had talked about. Was Kristin right? Were there reasons to forgive people like that mother?

He had to find out.

CHAPTER 26

The morning sun shone through the east window making it glow and shed freshness into the darkened sanctuary. Row after row of empty pews faced the altar above the stained glass window of Jesus praying in the Garden of Gethsemane.

The church was deserted this Saturday, except for a lone figure sitting in the last row. She was leaning forward with her head on the back of the pew in front of her. Her hands were clasped so tightly on her lap that the knuckles showed white. The sound of traffic going by just outside the windows drowned out the sobbing whisper of the lone petitioner.

After talking to the Protective Services caseworker the previous night, Judy had been allowed to go home. Her baby had been admitted to the hospital burn unit to begin the long process of repair to his body. Judy had spoken very little to the caseworker. The woman had expressed dissatisfaction with what she had been told and had promised that she would have to have a follow-up visit, when Judy felt more like discussing the problem.

Judy had walked slowly back the fifteen blocks the ambulance had earlier covered in its screeching haste. She had not slept that night. She was trying to understand what was happening to her life. Her grasp on her sanity was tenuous at best. Desperation had led her to the church near her apartment.

Her prayers for forgiveness and for understanding left her feeling vaguely better. Her mother said that God heard and answered all prayers. She had prayed again for forgiveness for the fornication that had led to Darrel. Now she needed help in taking care of him and learning to love him. She did not want them to take Darrel away from her. It was not his fault that she had been evil.

She rose quietly from the pew and walked slowly out into the church narthex, then out the front door. She had almost made it to her apartment when she noticed that she was being followed again.

"Oh, Jesus, you were supposed to forgive me!" she cried plaintively.

Her pace quickened as she kept looking over her shoulder on her way back to her apartment. When she arrived at the entrance she caught her breath in sudden fright. Back up the street! He was still there! She ran halfway up the first flight of stairs and waited. The front door opened. He was coming! Hysteria clutched at her throat as she struggled to reach the third floor. She was shaking so badly she couldn't get the key into the lock. She dropped her purse and used both hands to steady the key and slide it into the hole. Her breath spurted out in little, short gasps as the tumblers engaged and the door opened. She kicked her purse into the room, slammed the door behind her, relocked it and slid on the safety chain.

She stood with her ear glued to the door. She heard the footsteps getting louder and louder as they slowly came up the stairs toward her. When the footsteps stopped, she almost fainted. She knew she must not make a sound to let them know she was in there. The sudden knock on the door tore a tiny scream from her lips.

The intruder had heard the cry. The soft voice calling her by name through the door confused Judy. No threat was in the words, just a gentle, soothing voice, seeking to reassure her. Judy didn't know what to do. At first the wavering control on her sanity was not able to comprehend the words' meaning, or who, or what, this person was. Slowly, the rational part of her brain gained superiority and the insanity retreated grudgingly.

Reluctantly, she unchained the door and opened it. A young man stood there, staring at her. Her mind was a blur. She caught only phrases of what he was saying which made her shudder anew with fright. The demon was saying that she had beaten her baby. The man had tricked her! Now he was shedding his disguise! No God, oh my God, it was the Devil coming for her! She couldn't let him take her! Judy was so petrified she could hardly move. The red eyes held her transfixed before their viperous stare.

He was moving toward her now. His hand grasping toward her galvanized her into action. She grabbed the nearest available object, a table lamp, and threw it with all her might at the advancing figure. It struck the Devil a glancing blow on the shoulder as he tried unsuccessfully to dodge the missile. She looked for something else to throw. Before she could spot anything, the malevolent figure had run quickly after her and trapped her in the corner. He had her! Judy was terrified beyond comprehension. She began to scream.

Brian didn't know what to do. He was angry and confused and bruised from the lamp hitting him. He had come quietly into the woman's place and had hardly begun to talk before she tried to brain him. He had not threatened her at all. He just wanted her to talk about what she had done to her baby in order to understand a little about her reason for the terrible thing she had done.

He pinioned her arms to calm her down and to keep her from hurting him more but she continued to scream. He didn't want the neighbors to come rushing in, maybe call the police, but he didn't know how to extricate himself quickly from the predicament. He needed time to think. He clamped his hand over her mouth to quiet her. His hand suddenly exploded in pain as she bit down on his thumb. He shook loose and got a headlock on her as she tried to scratch his face.

He was near to panic. As he grappled with the woman, he noticed a door that looked like it had a closet behind it. Hastily, he jerked her across the room, opened the door and pushed her inside. He slammed the door disgustedly. He yelled at her to shut up, that he was leaving. He ran out the door, down the stairs and out to the relative calm of the street. He squeezed himself into the Ghia and headed angrily for home.

Judy lost all grip on her sanity in the tomb-like blackness of the closet. She didn't understand where she was, or that she could get out merely by turning the doorknob. When the custodian opened the apartment two days later to fix the leaking toilet Judy had been complaining about for weeks, the smell and the quiet whimpering from the closet brought him to where she was enclosed. Two days without food or water and lying in her own urine and excrement had been a part of Judy's journey into Hell.

CHAPTER 27

Brian had solved nothing with his trip. If anything, he was more confused than ever. He was still convinced that people like that mother needed to be punished, but he had found out that he was incapable of mistreating a woman, no matter what she had done. If he couldn't do it, how could he expect someone else to do it for him? He had been secure in his anger before. Now he didn't know what to think. If you could not physically intimidate these parents, how did you stop them? So many children were abused. How could he save them? He felt impotent and frustrated.

Kristin was the only thing that saved Brian from sinking to the depth of the depression he had been in before he met her. He needed a friend to talk to. Somehow, he knew that Kristin had run into him for a reason. Intellectually he knew it was a superstitious assumption, but he couldn't shake the feeling that Hazel had sent Kristin to save him a second time. Without help, he would not survive for long. He needed someone to go to, someone to share affection with, someone to just care about him.

Brian called Kristin a couple of days after his encounter with Judy. She noticed the immediate pleasure his call gave her. She hadn't really cared about anyone, truly cared, other than the girls, in her adult life. People could pass in and out of her life and their leaving seldom made that much difference. Kristin was frequently upset by that tendency in herself. She was a nice person. She never purposely hurt anyone. She knew down in her heart why she had a shell around her. She was afraid to care too much for someone. She didn't want to be hurt again the way she was when her father walked out on her mother. She could not trust people.

Brian affected her differently. He had integrity and an indefinable quality that didn't make her feel afraid. When he came to pick her up for lunch, she grinned up at him from across her desk.

"We ain't gonna ride in that-there four wheeled disaster again, are we?" she kidded him. "Do you want me to drive this time?"

"You must practice being so ornery, Kristin," Brian answered. "Anyway, you don't have to ride in the limo. Let's walk. There's that Chinese place just down the street. How does that sound?"

"Sounds great. Let's get going."

They took a shortcut from the back of the hospital to a service drive that led to Grand River Avenue. On the way to the restaurant, Brian suddenly stopped and picked something out of the gutter. It was a dirt-encrusted marble, purple hued with white swirls floating through it. He wiped it clean on his jeans.

"Here, Kristin. Just in case you lose all your marbles, you'll always have at least one left," he offered.

Kristin looked at the gift lying in her palm. She couldn't describe the feeling. Why did she want to cry? It was just a dumb marble wasn't it? But it wasn't, she knew. It was a symbol. Brian was giving a piece of himself to her to safeguard. She saw it in his eyes, a pleading behind the shy grin.

They continued on to the restaurant, finding a booth in the darkened interior. They gave their orders and sat back savoring the thought of the oriental food coming their way.

"I'm sorry but I forgot to ask you about your girls, Kristin," Brian said. "You were going to tell me how you 'stole' them."

Kristin described how she had found their mother and the condition Holly and Heather had been in when she took them home the first night and how one thing led to another and now she prayed that they would always be hers.

"It's kind of coincidental, Brian, but I got them the first day we met when you came to my office because Dr. Santonio wanted me to let you know how the protective services system works and you were such a know-it-all and left right away."

She winked at him to let him know she wasn't serious about the know-it-all comment.

"I didn't realize it at first," she continued, "but I kept the girls originally because I felt guilty that I had let their mother die."

She had never confessed that to anyone before. She wasn't sure why she said it to Brian other than she needed to get it off her chest.

"How did you do that?" Brian asked skeptically.

"She came to my office as her last plea for help and I didn't recognize it clearly enough. By the time I did, I drove to her house to see if she was okay but of course it was too late."

"You can't blame yourself for her death," Brian said.

"Maybe, maybe not. It's terribly egotistic of me but I think the girls will have a better life with me but I'm sorry their mother died."

"The father?" Brian said.

A chill of fear passed through Kristin. "He was in prison at the time. From his police record and the things Joyce said about him he is a real loser. He cared so much about his daughters that he never even showed up in town after he was paroled. They would have let him out for Joyce's funeral but he didn't care to attend. This was the guy she was so terrified of leaving because he said he would kill her if she did. I have all the legal papers and a friendly judge all set if he ever shows up trying to get Holly and Heather."

"So now you're their mother," Brian said.

Kristin noticed a softening to Brian's eyes, a subtle relaxation of his face.

She smiled at him. "Yes, now I'm their mother."

The day marked a new beginning for both of them. Kristin kept the old marble Brian had given her as a lucky charm. It was somehow illogically important to her. They found they enjoyed each other's company immensely. Because they often worked different times of the day, they were not able to do much together but they ate lunch, walked, sometimes ran and did other things when they could. The moments were always full.

Brian didn't go back to Cincinnati after he graduated. He couldn't stand to face the empty dreams. He earned a living working the E.R. and peds clinics at Genesis. It was enough.

One Saturday afternoon, very early in the summer, he and Kristin were out running along a path that followed a small stream in Okemos not far from Kristin's apartment. A freak Siberian Express had brought near-freezing weather as far south as the Ohio border and they were dressed against the chill. The trail through the city park was soft and muddy, so instead they followed the asphalt path cutting through the middle of it. The track led to a small footbridge that crossed the stream at the far side.

As they ran across the bridge, a sudden opening in the clouds let the sun through and it sparkled off the cold, clean water passing beneath them. She pulled Brian to a halt and they stood leaning on the rail, saying nothing, just enjoying the moment together. Suddenly Kristin spotted an object in the streambed just below her. The whiteness of it was almost lost in the reflected shimmer of the rushing water. She sat down on the bridge, pulled off her shoes and socks, rolled up her pants and got to her feet.

"Hey, weird Kristin, what the heck are you doing?" Brian asked. "You aren't going to go wading are you? That water looks ice cold."

"Don't get hyper in your diaper, boy. I found something for you," she replied

With that remark, she walked to the end of the bridge, tiptoed through the mud and gravel at the edge of the bank and then waded into the water. The first icy clutch of the stream took her breath away and made her feet ache. Resolutely she forced herself forward. It was only knee deep but the current pulled at her, inviting her to fall. Once, stepping on a slippery rock, she almost went down as she windmilled her arms to keep her balance.

At first she could not spot her prize. She searched all around the area where she knew it lay. Finally she walked around to the bridge side to view the bottom from that perspective. There it was! She reached down quickly to retrieve it, getting her rolled up sleeve wet. Laughingly she straightened and extended her arm up to Brian. He reached down and she dropped the object into his hand. It was a pure white marble. There were no words from Kristin. Just a smile.

When Kristin returned to the bridge, she found Brian, naked from the waist up and holding his sweatshirt in one hand.

"Oh, kind sir, are you going to attack me or something equally disgusting and lovely?"

"Judas Priest, Kristin! Just sit down will you."

"Watch your language son, your mother may be listening."

"I know she's listening. Now cooperate, will you?"

Kristin sat down and looked questioningly up at him. He knelt down in front of her and began to wipe the mud and water from her feet and legs.

"Hey, don't do that you big goof! You'll get your sweatshirt all wet and dirty. It'll feel crummy as heck on you the rest of the way."

"I don't care. I just needed an excuse to rub those beautiful legs."

"Now you're talking, partner. What took you so long looking for an excuse?"

"It wasn't time before, was it?"

Kristin agreed. "No, it wasn't time."

She watched quietly as Brian finished cleaning her feet. She laughed as he ran the material between each of her toes. She saw goose bumps on his skin as the cool wind dried the sweat on his tightly muscled body.

"Get your shirt back on, Brian. I don't want some snot nosed kid holding my hand and snuffling in my ear."

Brian did as he was told and then sat down. They were sitting side-by-side, facing each other, knees touching and arms entwined. For a while they sat in silence, savoring the moment. After a short time they began to talk. They were the first moments of contentment Brian had experienced since Hazel had died.

Kristin also knew the time was special. Theirs were two hearts that had come together and for that moment were one, pulsing in sync, no longer hunting for that missing heartbeat.

After awhile, Kristin could feel her muscles starting to cool and her joints stiffening.

"Can I interest you in a big glass of cold apple juice, a hot shower and a nice rub down?" she asked. "The girls are going out for pizza with Sheri after the movie."

"The apple juice sounds good. I'll have to think about the other two."

She could tell from the glint in his eye what he already thought about the others.

"Okay punk, you can't even have a chance at the rest unless you beat me to the park entrance," she challenged him.

With that she got to her feet. As Brian started to get up, she pushed him over onto his back and bolted for the end of the bridge. Not far from the bridge was a set of thirty wooden stairs leading out of the park to the street beyond. Brian caught her just before she hit the last step.

They arrived, sweaty and winded, at her apartment fifteen minutes later. They headed immediately for the refrigerator to quench their thirst. Kristin pulled the frosty jug of apple juice from the shelf and poured two large drafts of the tangy liquid. Kristin had barely raised her glass when Brian had drained his.

"You big hog! Take time to taste it, will you? That stuff isn't cheap, you know."

As she was finishing her chastising statement, Brian grabbed the glass from her hand and proceeded to drink it while he fended off her attack with his other hand.

"I'm going to charge you for that, you creep," she hollered as she tried playfully to punch him in the stomach. He put the empty glass down and grabbed her, turned her around and lifted her in his arms.

"Put me down, you pervert," she yelled laughingly. As he lowered her to the floor, she suddenly bent forward, grabbed one of his legs and tripped him. He went over in a heap. Instantly she landed her whole body on his chest and began to tickle him. Brian was almost helpless with laughter. Finally he was able to pin her arms to her sides and get her under control. They were lying side by side up against the legs of the kitchen table. Little by little the panting and laughter subsided. At the same time they became more and more aware of each other. They looked searchingly into each other's eyes to confirm the happiness they saw shining there. Brian leaned over and gently sought Kristin's lips. They came together tentatively at first. Their sweat, apple juice and joy mingled sensually. Their lips became more demanding, communicating their growing need.

Brian had never known such a feeling. Their kisses, up to this day, had been just friendly moments at the end of a date. As if by unspoken consent, they had never gone farther. They both sensed the importance of knowing each other without letting sex confuse their findings. Lying there on the floor, they knew they had arrived at the next stage of their relationship.

It had been worth the wait.

Brian was just getting out of the shower when he heard the intercom buzzer go off near the front door. He began hurriedly dressing, thinking it must be the girls and the baby sitter returning. Kristin must have thought the same thing because she hit the remote door opener as she dashed for the bedroom and the rest of her clothes.

The knocking on the door was unexpected. Kristin looked questioningly at the entrance as she came back out. She opened it and was surprised to see a man standing there. He stared at her, then up and down her body. There was an aura to the man that made Kristin's skin crawl. He was about Brian's size with closely cropped dark hair. There was a force emanating from him that overwhelmed her. Kristin believed that pure evil existed and this man possessed enough to be almost visible.

"Yes?" she said to the man.

"You named Grey?" he said.

"Why do you want to know?" she said.

"Don't be playing any fucking word games with me lady. Yes or no is good enough."

"Yes," Kristin said.

He started to enter her apartment but she held the door closed to prevent it. He merely shoved it out of her hands and walked past her. He started to go further but Kristin grabbed his arm.

"Where do you think you're going?" she said.

"I'm looking for my kids," he said.

Kristin caught her breath. "Harper?" she said, not wanting to believe it. "Joyce's husband?"

"Fuckin' A," he said. "Where are they?"

"None of your business. You're not to have them. The court has placed them with me for safe-keeping."

"I don't give a god damn what the court says. They're mine and I'm takin' 'em with me."

"How did you find me?" Kristin said.

"Talked to the Social Services lady with the State. Had to kind of 'convince' her that it was in her best interest to tell me." He laughed but there was no humor to it.

"The girls are out of town and by the time they get back I'll have the police here to keep you away from them," Kristin said.

He came toward Kristin, grabbing her by the throat. He felt the tips of his huge hands tighten, slowing her breathing.

A voice from behind them stopped the man. "Let go of her or I'll break every bone in your body," Brian said.

The man turned, smiling and unintimidated. "Well, well, is this the hubby? What's a pussy like you gonna do about it?" he said, walking toward Brian.

Brian came to meet him. "I don't know who you are mister but get the hell out of here right now!" he said.

"In Jackson, we eat pussies like you for light snacks," he said.

Without warning he hit Brian in the face, driving him backward. Brian's foot slipped on a throw rug and he went hurtling backward, hitting his head on a corner of the hall entryway. Pain blossomed in the back of his skull. A different pain erupted in his side as the man kicked him. The rage that always lay hidden in Brian erupted in a blinding flash and before the man knew what was happening, the adversary who had seemed such a pussy was on him. Harper was no coward though and he came back at Brian. He had survived too many fights in prison to let this civilian stop him.

Kristin watched the fight, knowing it was useless to scream as the two men broke furniture in their combined fury. The sound of fists hitting flesh sickened her. The absolute violence and hatred that drove the two men nearly made her sick to her stomach. Each time Brian was struck she would gasp involuntarily. She watched in awe as the blows scarcely slowed him. There was a fierceness, a savageness on his face that she could not believe was him.

At last she saw Brian drive Harper's head against a coffee table and the man went limp. She expected Brian to stop but he kept hitting the man in the face, again and again. She barely recognized the animal who had just a short time been making love to her. Suddenly she was terrified that Brian was going to kill the man and she was afraid for both of them.

She ran forward and tackled Brian, carrying him backward off his prostrate opponent.

"Brian! Brian!" she shouted. "Stop it! Please, for God's sake stop!"

Her crying brought him back to reality and he slumped forward sadly. He looked over at the bloody mass that was the face of his opponent. The man groaned and tried to sit up but his muscles failed him.

Brian didn't want to touch the man again. Neither did Kristin. They sat unspeaking as the man finally regained full consciousness. Little by little he got to his feet. He stared at Brian for a few seconds then turned to go.

"Don't come back," Brian said.

The man nodded as he limped out the door.

Still weeping, Kristin tried to put order out of the chaos in the apartment before the girls got back.

CHAPTER 28

The voice on the other end of the line was purposely muffled. The policeman taking the call had heard it many times before. Someone wanted to report something to tell the police, but didn't want to be identified. It was almost comical; they usually put a handkerchief or rag over the mouthpiece just to make sure.

"Are you listenin', man? 'Cause I'm only sayin' it once," the voice said.

"I'm listening," the policeman replied.

"I'm gonna give you a name and an address. You better send someone out there 'cause a kid's maybe dyin' there. The name's Henry Nelson, 1524 Detroit Street. It's the apartment in the back. Do it today, man. Understand?"

"May I . . ." The dial tone cut him short.

The dispatcher put out a call to a patrol car in the vicinity. The problem was somewhat vague. The two patrolmen were not sure what they were looking for as they headed for the address given them. Pulling up in front, they reported their location, got out of the car and headed for the back of the house. They had to walk between a fence and an old beat up car with two flat tires, it's hood open as if calling for help. Weeds choked the sidewalk and junk littered the yard. A dog was chained to a tree, the circle of beaten earth marking the extent of its universe. The skinny, dirty animal looked too tired and underfed even to react to their existence. The younger cop made a mental note to send the S.P.C.A. out to look after it.

The two men climbed the rickety outside stairs to the doorway on the second floor of the house. The storm door was minus its screen and hung open. The inner door was also wide open, allowing the insects of the area to come and go at their pleasure.

The older cop wrinkled his nose at the smell that greeted them as they came to a halt at the door.

"Goddamn filthy bastards! The poor damn dog out there probably has more class than these assholes!" He kicked the inner door open the rest of the way. It banged loudly against the wall. With his nightstick, he rapped against the windowpane to announce their presence.

A querulous voice came floating from one of the back rooms.

"Hey, what's all the fuckin' noise out there? If that's you Tildee, I'm gonna kick yer ass."

A body soon followed the voice down the hall toward them. The man was startled, then angry when he saw the two cops standing in the doorway.

"What you pigs doin' here?"

He spat a gob of phlegm on the floor at their feet. It was all the older cop could do to keep from smashing his nightstick into the sneering face.

The younger cop stepped forward. "Is your name Henry Nelson?"

The man looked cornered, his face wary. "Nah, he ain't here. Whatcha want with him?"

"There's been a complaint about a child being hurt. Are there any children here? We'd like to look at them if there are."

Henry's look of fear increased as the question was asked. "My - uh - his wife got the kid with her. They out shoppin' right now."

If you don't mind, we'll have a look around, just to make sure."

The older cop blocked the doorway as the younger man began to move toward the other rooms.

"Hey, man, get the fuck outta there! You got no right searchin' this place." He grabbed the cop by the arm.

The young cop shook his arm free and looked into his pursuer's face. "Touch me again and you'll be real sorry."

The quiet force of the statement made Henry back off a pace.

"Long as there's two of ya, ya'll are tough mother-fuckers ain't ya?"

The young cop ignored the question and began his search. The stench soon led him to what he sought. The place smelled bad in general but this room in particular almost made him sick. He flipped on the light switch and caught his breath in disgust, then in pity. He entered the room and knelt before an old, vermin and feces covered mattress. At his approach the cockroaches stampeded back into the walls and the mattress. The little figure lying there was the most pitiful thing he had ever seen.

The baby, curled up on the mattress, was wearing only a diaper soaked in urine and feces. The area of incrustation showed that the diaper had not been changed in a long time. The emaciation indicated that the baby was obviously starving. The concavity of the cheeks, the hollow, lackluster eyes showed that long ago, any body fat had burned away. Infected insect bites were all over the baby, helpless before their onslaught.

The infant did not respond to his touch as he ran his hand lightly over the skull-like head. He could see that it was still alive, but not by much. Unmindful of the filth rubbing off on him, he picked up the dying little creature and carried it from its prison. Tears ran down his face as he approached his partner.

"Bring this animal with you," he said, nodding toward the father. "We need to get to the hospital."

CHAPTER 29

The policeman, escorted by an E.R. nurse, carried his burden down the hall toward Brian, standing in the hallway, watching them approach. The cop had not wanted to give up the victim at the triage area. Noting his emotional state, the nurse had let the policeman carry the child back to the treatment area. She motioned for Brian to join them.

"The kid's starving to death, Doc," the cop said. He could barely speak as he held the baby toward Brian.

The man's voice caught in his throat as he tried to describe the conditions under which they had found him. He laid the baby carefully on the treatment table. The body was so fragile, the cop was afraid it might break.

Brian looked down at the brown bundle on the table. The little creature was scarcely breathing. He knew they would have a difficult time saving it. He was having a hard time controlling his own emotions. His pulse and breathing increased rapidly. Sorrow and hate rendered him momentarily without function. His mind entered that of the dying child and he knew the hours and days of uncomprehending torture the baby had endured. From the moment of birth this small piece of humanity had existed only to stay alive.

How can it happen? My God, how can it happen? How can a human being let a baby suffer and die like this? Brian's mind screamed silent pain and frustration.

The policeman was looking curiously at him. Brian had ceased to move or speak. The nurse placed her hand on his arm. "Dr. Tanner? Is anything the matter?"

At first Brian did not hear the nurse, but a repeated query brought him back. He realized that his emotions were controlling him. If he was going to save this baby, he had to put those feelings behind him. He put the hate and sadness in a place at the back of his mind where they would not interfere with his care of the child.

He nodded to the nurse, then turned his attention to the baby. As he touched the infant, he could feel the bones protruding just beneath the filthy, infected skin. The body was completely devoid of any subcutaneous fat. Insect bites oozed their discharge into dirt that was dried and crusted on virtually every area.

"Get an IV started, five percent glucose. We'll need to do a CBC and check the electrolytes. I want the Lab to tell me just what shape this baby's in," he told the nurse.

Brian put his stethoscope to the tiny chest, listened for a short time and then checked the much-diminished respiration. Together he and the nurse began carefully to clean the dirt from the body and treat the insect wounds. When Brian cut the putrid diaper from the baby, he cringed at what he saw. As careful as he had been, some of the skin had been pulled loose from the small, male genitalia. The diapers had been changed so seldom that whatever skin was still left was ammonia bleached and white on this black child.

Brian and the nurse worked on the baby for a long time, doing what they could to insure its survival. He would have the child admitted and a doctor assigned to its full time care, and then only time would tell.

As he entered the hallway from the treatment room, he saw the young policeman waiting for him.

"Is he going to make it, Doc? It is a he, isn't it?"

"Yeah, it's a he. I don't know whether he'll live or not. We'll do all we can."

"I'll have my wife say a prayer for him."

"Sure, go ahead if you think it'll help," Brian said dispiritedly. "While you're at it, see if she can find out from God why these things happen in the first place."

The policeman nodded in agreement because he too had been wondering how it was possible. The concept of one human starving a helpless infant and ignoring its suffering was beyond his comprehension. In his short time on the force he had already seen so many ugly things, the bestial, darker side of humanity, that he had to fight against the thin veneer of cynicism starting to form around him. He wasn't sure he could stand to see many more things like this poor little, starved baby.

The two of them walked back up the hall together, each glad for the other's presence; silently sharing the horror they had just been part of. The young cop stopped in front of the door to the conference room.

"Can I call you tomorrow to find out how he is?" he asked.

"Sure," Brian nodded, "call after three-thirty, okay?"

"Okay. Thanks. Well, I gotta pick up my partner. He's in here waiting with the piece of shit that's supposed to be the father."

Brian's head jerked up at the word, father. "I want to talk to him," he said.

He pushed past the cop and into the conference room. As he entered, he saw the other policeman sitting in a chair nearest the door, flipping idly through an old magazine. The black man sat next to him, chewing on a thumbnail and looking apprehensive. He came quickly to his feet as he saw Brian approaching. He didn't like the expression on the maggot white face.

Brian inserted himself directly in front of the man. The voice that assaulted the black man was full of rage.

"Tell me what goes on in your mind when you see your child starving before your eyes. That baby is lying there covered by its own urine and shit, being eaten alive by insects, and dying because you don't feed it. What are you thinking about? How do you rationalize it in your head? It is so beyond my understanding that your kind of people exist. I've got to know how you can do that. How can live with yourself? Tell me!"

Brian's face was within a foot of the man's as he yelled these final words. Neither policeman had moved to intervene. The older man did not care about the answers. The young man did. Their divergent feelings left the two policemen where they were, watching as Brian confronted the father.

Ever since the older cop had jerked him out of his house, down the back stairs and shoved him roughly into the back of the patrol car in front of the neighbors, Henry's fear and resentment had been growing. He had no way to strike back at the goddamn cops, but there was no way he was going to take anything from this honky mother-fucker yelling in his face.

"Get outta my face, cocksucker," Henry hollered back.

He gave Brian a shove that knocked him backward. Before either policeman could react, Brian attacked. The cops were stunned. The doctor was assaulting their prisoner! He wasn't just pushing back, he was going nuts. Henry was as surprised as they were. The next thing he knew, he was slammed backward over a chair and onto the floor. Deep scratches were on his face where Brian's fingers had drawn blood. Brian wasn't even trying to hit the man; he was going for the throat. He would scarcely remember the details later, but right now his subconscious was seeking to kill the vermin screeching beneath him.

It took both policemen to stop Brian. Henry would never forget the feeling as the doctor's fingernails dug into his flesh of his throat, shutting off his air. The lights were beginning to go out in Henry's brain before the two cops were able to pry Brian loose.

The younger policeman had Brian in a headlock from behind, holding him prostrate on the floor, talking in his ear and
trying to calm him.

"Take it easy, Doc. Holy Smokes, man, you gotta calm
down!"

Little by little, Brian's hate dissolved and his struggling
ceased. He knew how ludicrous the scene must be as his eyes
focused on the E.R. personnel staring wide-eyed at them from
the doorway.

CHAPTER 30

Kristin was finishing her lunch in the cafeteria as the name, Tanner, pulled her attention to a nearby table. A nurse was laughing as she related her bit of gossip.

"I didn't see it, but Cathie told me all about it," the nurse said. "She was taking a patient back to get a cut sewed up when this yelling and banging started in the E.R. conference room. Just out of curiosity, she looked in the room and here was one of the doctors, Dr. Tanner, just beating the shit out of this black guy. Two cops were in there too and they were trying to get Tanner off him. It took both of them to make him stop. He must have really been mad. Isn't that weird? I wish I knew what caused it. Cathie said that the policemen closed the door and then awhile later, Dr. Tanner came out of the room, talked to the head nurse a second and then left."

Kristin was shocked by the story. She supposed it had to be true. It was not something you expect someone to make up. Embellish upon perhaps, but not just make up. She also wondered what had caused the fight. She felt compassion for Brian. No matter the extent of the fight, he would be feeling miserable right then.

She went back to her office, picked up her purse and keys and told her secretary she would be back in an hour or so. She arrived at Brian's apartment a short time later. A light knock brought him to the door.

He looked at her sheepishly. She could see that some of the old sadness was back. She had not yet found out the source of his pain, but it had seemed to be mostly gone of late. She lightly touched the healing cuts and bruises left from his fight back in her apartment.

Kristin was half joking, half serious, when she mildly rebuked him. "This fighting stuff is getting to be kind of a habit, isn't it? But it looks pretty bad when one of the hospital doctors gets in a one right at work. Especially when policemen are involved, too. Pretty dumb, Brian."

"But, Kristin, this animal has been starving his child to death. If you had seen that little thing, you'd have wanted to do the same thing. HE WAS STARVING THAT BABY! Can you fathom what that means? Can you even begin to know what that baby went through? My God, I can't stand it!"

Tears were in his eyes and his voice had risen almost to a shout. "And it was covered with insect bites and its own excrement. The skin was all raw and white because they never changed its diaper. That man is as guilty of trying to murder that child as if he had taken it out and shot it. Worse, he was torturing the poor little thing as he was killing it. What do you suppose will happen if that baby dies? Life imprisonment for murder? No way. Manslaughter at best. Lots of people don't even consider babies to be human beings yet. You have to grow up before it really matters if you get beaten or starved or mangled!"

Brian slammed his fist into the wall, bruising his knuckles and leaving a dent in the plaster.

The heat of his anger took Kristin aback. He was normally the most gentle man she had ever met. These flares of violence kept surprising her.

"Brian, when you get into a fight with people like that, you've reduced yourself to their level. Violence and hate will not prevent violence and hate. If you really care about these children like you say you do, you'd better find a another way to save them."

Brian looked at her. Inadvertently Kristin had brushed against the truth. She would never understand, though. She could never know how it felt. She had no knowledge of the word fear. All she had was some nice bright and shiny theory which, in the real world, did not mean a thing.

"Okay, Kristin, I'll try."

Kristin watched him carefully as he spoke. She knew he didn't believe a word of what she had said. He had shut her out again.

CHAPTER 31

Kristin sat at her desk, daydreaming. She was concerned over the subtle distance that had grown between Brian and herself. It was nothing she could put her finger on, but she could sense its presence, even when he was holding her. It was a growing chasm which she could not bridge to get to him. Sometimes, when he didn't realize she was watching, she would see him staring off into space, his brow furrowed as though he were searching for something.

She loved him so much. But nothing could ever come of that love, not until that final barrier between them came down. The problem was, the barrier was not even definable. She knew it existed but didn't know what it was.

Something was wrong with Brian's life and until he told her what the problem was, they were in limbo together, unwilling for their love to go backward but unable to let it go forward. She knew she had somehow been destined to share her life with him but she was frustrated that a flaw still existed in the relationship.

The intercom interrupted her thoughts.

"Yes, Marion."

"Jean Hamilton from Protective Services is on the line. Do you want to talk with her?"

"Sure." She pushed the flashing button on the phone and picked up the receiver.

"Hi, Jean, how are you doing?" Kristin said.

"Crappy, same as usual."

"Well, consistency is a virtue they say."

"If it is, it's my only one. Listen, Kristin, the reason I called is to give you some information on that case you asked me about several times."

"You mean Stevie Sanderson?"

"Yeah. I just talked to the people down at the Centrex office. There was another report last week on the boy. I guess he was messed up pretty good. He's still in the hospital."

"Which one?"

"Sparrow."

"That must mean the parents still live in the city."

"Apparently they moved back recently. The report we got from the hospital indicated that the child had been abused a lot. The x-rays showed a lot of healed bone breaks and they could tell he'd been beaten frequently."

"He isn't going to go back to the parents, is he?" Kristin asked.

"I hope not, but you know these darn courts. They do some strange things. Anyway, I asked the lady down there to make a copy of everything in the file and send it to you."

"Thanks, Jean. I really appreciate it."

"Heck, that's okay. Oh, one other thing of interest in this case. The lady down at Centrex was telling me about the different excuses and stuff these parents tell the caseworkers. It seems that this Mr. Sanderson has a new wrinkle. He's threatening to sue us. Obviously he denies he's been abusing his son. Some doctor has it in for him, he claims. He said the last time he lived here when he had his boy in at one of the hospitals, one of the doctors came out and beat him up. Showed them a hospital bill where he'd had a broken shoulder repaired. He said the doctor beat him up because he threatened to sue him for malpractice from taking care of his son. Sanderson said he couldn't work for months. Some story, eh?"

"It sure is," Kristin said. As Jean had been talking, a vague uneasiness came over Kristin.

"Anyway, the report is in the mail. You should have it tomorrow," Jean said.

"Okay. Thanks again."

"Anytime. Keep your knees together."

"Always. See you."

Kristin returned the phone to its cradle. She sat doodling on a scratch pad, thinking. After awhile she began to write a few names down and some comments after them.

> Sanderson - Brian treated son, father beaten up.
>
> Reeser - Father beaten up - attacker had chipped tooth - Brian has chipped tooth.
>
> Harris - discussed with Brian, mother shoved in closet by someone (apparently), mother institutionalized. Broken lamp and overturned chairs indicated an intruder had been there.
>
> Nelson - Brian treated son, attacked father.

She sat mulling over her list for a few minutes then picked up the phone and called Medical Records. After several rings, one of the clerks answered.

"Medical Records, Miss McConahay speaking. May I help you?"

"This is Kristin Grey in Social Service. Will you do me a favor and look up the file on a baby girl by the name of Reeser? I can't remember the first name but she was about a year old when she was admitted with a fractured skull. I'd like to know the date she was seen in the Emergency Room and the doctor who treated her in E.R. and then admitted her."

"Okay. It'll be a few minutes. Do you want me to call you back?"

"No. I'll hold."

"All right. I'll be back in a jiffy."

The "jiffy" turned out to be five minutes before the girl came back on the line.

"Mrs. Grey?" came the voice.

Kristin didn't bother to correct her on the 'Mrs.' "Go ahead," she said.

"Was the name Marcia Reeser?"

"Yes, that's it."

"Then the date was November thirteenth and the Doctor was Endicott."

Kristin was relieved when she heard the name Endicott. She still had to make another check. With a quick 'thank you', Kristin hung up the phone and then dialed the peds department at the Medical Arts Center.

"This is the Social Service Department at Genesis calling," Kristin said when the phone was answered. "Will you look on one of your old schedules and tell me if Dr. Tanner was one of the residents on duty in the E.R. last March thirteenth?"

She heard the banging of a file cabinet in the background and then the voice returned to the phone. "Yep, he sure was."

"Thank you."

With a sinking feeling, Kristin hung up the phone. It could all be a coincidence. She knew it wasn't, though. Why does he do it? How can he risk his career, doing such stupid things?

Kristin worried about the problem all that afternoon and evening, but did not come to any conclusion. She knew when she woke up the next morning that she would have to confront Brian with her questions.

Mid-morning the mail came and brought the file on Stevie Sanderson. She read through it but it told her little that she did not already know, except the parents' new address. She thought for a while, then picked up the phone to call Brian at his apartment.

After several rings, "This is Brian Tanner."

"Hi, Brian. It's me."

"Nice timing, Kristin. I was just taking a shower."

"You only shower once a month, twerp. It's just a big coincidence. I only wanted to call and tell you that I've got some extra money to blow and I want to buy you supper tonight."

"Okay. How about I come by and pick you up at your office about five o'clock?"

"All right. Make sure you eat a big lunch," she said.

Brian laughed and said goodbye. Kristin was perplexed. Was that lovable person really capable of beating up people like that? Ask the black man in E.R., she thought. Not to mention Holly and Heather's father.

It was a long day for Kristin. At a quarter 'till five she heard Brian come into the outer office and then walk down the short hall to her door.

"Hey, Kristin. You in there?" he said.

"Come on in, Brian."

"Are you ready? I'm starving."

"Yes. Just a minute and I'll be all set."

Brian knew something was wrong, just a feeling from the way she was looking at him. It was subtle, but there was definitely something the matter.

"Okay, what's wrong?" he asked.

"You're really perceptive, Brian. I thought I was covering up pretty good." She looked down at her scratch pad for a moment and then said, "Do the names Gary Reeser, Bob Sanderson, Judy Harris and Henry Nelson mean anything to you?"

Brian looked at her without speaking. She had seen the frown begin as she was saying the names.

Finally, he said quietly, "You know the Sanderson name means something to me. What makes you think the others do?"

"A coincidence or two, plus some deductive reasoning. I read the follow-up report on the Marcia Reeser case. The police report attached to it said that some anonymous stranger beat up the father. The only identifying mark the father mentioned was that his attacker had a chipped tooth in front. Coincidences one and two - you have a chipped tooth and you worked the E.R. that night."

Brian didn't respond.

"Judy Harris. A woman with a bad mental problem. It wasn't diagnosed the night we talked about her, and how she burned her baby. She was found in her closet completely lost from reality. It will be a long time before she is cured, if she ever is. When I first read the follow-up report, I thought she somehow closed herself in that closet even though there were signs of a disturbance. Now I don't think so."

"Henry Nelson. It's public knowledge that you beat the hell out of him so I didn't have to wonder about that one."

"That brings me back to Bob Sanderson." She picked up the folder in front of her. "When the caseworker interviewed Stevie's father after this latest incident, he threatened to sue the hospital here because he said one of our doctors beat him up after his son was a patient in our E.R. Normally you could ignore a comment like that, couldn't you?"

Brian was looking at the file.

"What the heck are you, Brian, some self-appointed vigilante? Why do you do something this stupid? You have to tell me what's going on in your head. This is the one thing that's always been between us, that we have to resolve if we're going to love each other."

Brian was not listening. "Does that file tell about Stevie? Something recent?"

"Yes. He's a patient over at Sparrow."

"Was he beaten up again?"

"Yes."

"Damn the man! Damn him to Hell! Let me see the file."

"I can't. It's not going to help you solve anything."

"I want to see that file. I have to find out how that little boy is."

"Is that it, Brian, or are you going to go beat the shit out of his father again?"

"Give me the file, Kristin." Brian reached across the desk and took the folder from her hand.

"If you open that file, Brian, you might as well leave, because there won't be anything more for us. I fell in love with a gentle man. I can't live with the other part of you."

Kristin looked at him in silent appeal. Please don't go, Brian. I need you to love. Please don't leave me!

In the end it came down to too much pride and too much anger. Brian took the folder and walked out of the door.

CHAPTER 32

When Brian awoke the next morning, he was alone again for the first time in a long time, not only physically but mentally. It was a terrible feeling. He had made the wrong decision. Life without Kristin was not going to be worthwhile. He would have to go back and explain to her about his childhood. It was strange how he had always been ashamed of being beaten, like something was wrong with him. It had always been there at the back of his mind, that he was somehow afflicted or diseased. Intellectually, he realized the feeling was ridiculous, but, other than the high school cross country coach, he had never told anyone about what had happened. He had tried to bury his pain in the far reaches of his mind and pretend that he was normal but something was always coming along to resurrect the feelings and remind him that he was branded.

Kristin would help him work it out. That's what she had come for. He knew it now.

The previous night, as he sat reading the file on Stevie, his rage had continued to grow. Then he began to realize the anger was futile. It merely destroyed his peace of mind and would, ultimately, destroy him. It was obvious from the file that his beating of the father had done nothing to protect Stevie. The abuse had continued anyway.

Why did the man do it? Why did anyone do it? He still had to talk to Stevie's father. If he could glean just one piece of knowledge, it would be a beginning. If he could somehow find out the reasons, he could at least make a start on finding some cures. He might make only a small dent in the problem, but it would be better than burying himself in frustrated hate and ignorance. Kristin could help him.

Brian sat around all day, just thinking about his life, trying to put everything into perspective. There was this one thing left to do, then he would go back to Kristin. He had the day off work since he did not have weekend duty so he could take his time. Sometime in late afternoon he got off the couch where he had been lying, grabbed his jacket and car keys and headed for the door.

The sun had shone in his windows all day, but as he got to his car he could see gray clouds moving in from the west. By the time he was part way across town, the sky had darkened and a fine mist was in the air. It really was not rain, just enough moisture to force him to turn on the windshield wipers every few minutes. Brian knew the road he was looking for, a decaying highway that had once been a major artery leading motorists east before the expressways had eliminated the need for it. All the businesses and homes along it suffered from the same disease of disuse as the highway that had spawned them. Old, abandoned or misused motels, used car lots, Dairy Delights and the like, littered both sides of the road for several miles before the freshness of the farmlands eased the pain created by these eyesores.

It was in one of these old motels that Sanderson and his wife and Stevie had come to live. The run down place, no longer attracting tourist trade, had been converted. Each 'apartment', consisting of a bathroom and bedroom, became permanent homes for people on the underside of life. The cars parked out front reflected the people inside, worn out, rusted and dented, with missing hubcaps and balding tires.

Brian pulled into the cracked, weed infested cement of the Elms Motel. A faded sign advertised, 'Rooms by the Day, Week or Month'. A touch of sympathy for Sanderson, the man, passed briefly through his mind and was gone. He drove along the front until he came to apartment 10. He pulled up and got out of his car.

He wasn't sure what he was going to say. He knew Sanderson would remember him, which would definitely be a problem. First he would have to convince the man he was there for a different reason than the last time. Why *was* he there? He wasn't sure himself. He only knew that he had to talk to the man. No threats this time, he just had to find out something - anything - about why he beat his boy so often and so brutally.

Brian knew he was being irrational and naive. But he had to prove to himself, and to Kristin, that he could solve his own problem without hurting anybody.

He had to help that little boy, too. That was the ultimate driving force behind what he was doing. The first time he had looked down at Stevie, he had seen himself. Hazel had saved him and he owed the world a life. It was strange, how he felt guilty because he had survived and he had not helped some other child do the same. He couldn't begin again until he had paid his dues.

Brian walked up to the door and knocked. He knocked again. Apparently no one was at home. He went to the window and peered through a slit in the Venetian blinds. He could detect no movement within. Acute disappointment assailed him for a moment. Then he thought that maybe Sanderson would only be gone a short time. He would go back toward town a ways and get a sandwich, kill an hour or so and then try again.

Brian got into his car and drove off. Fifteen minutes later, Sanderson parked his car in the drive after having delivered his wife at an all night Coney island restaurant where she worked as a waitress. It didn't pay much but she could steal a lot of hot dogs and hamburgers. They sure as hell wouldn't starve anyway.

The mufflerless Buick Regal ceased abusing the evening and Sanderson got out.

"Hey, Sanderson," a voice hailed him.

"Yeah, what d'ya want, Eubie?" he replied.

Eubie Coffelt, his neighbor, came shambling up. Sanderson couldn't stand the busybody son-of-a-bitch.

"I jist wanted to tell ya that there was some guy knockin' at yer door a while ago."

"Cop?"

"Nah. Couldn't tell what he was. 'Bout yer height, sandy hair, jeans and a tan jacket. Looked harmless, but he didn't look like he belonged 'round here."

"Wasn't no fuckin' bill collector, was it?"

"Nope. Like I said, I couldn't tell what he was after. He looked real upset when there weren't no one home though."

"Okay. Thanks for tellin' me."

"Hell, that's all right."

Sanderson walked slowly back to his room, thinking as he went. Like all people of his kind, he hated strangers nosing around - especially those goddamned social workers prying into how he raised his kid.

Sanderson was not especially bright but the thought occurred to him that the guy who had beat him up last time they had the kid to the hospital in this no-fuckin' good city looked like the guy Coffelt was talking about. Sanderson at first was afraid, then he began to hope that was who the guy was. He had a score to settle. He'd be ready for the son-of-a-bitch this time. With surprise on his side, he just might make the fucker wish he'd never messed with ol' Bob Sanderson. He smiled in anticipation as he went inside the apartment.

The last, gray light of the evening was passing away as Brian drove back toward the motel. The greasy hamburger and fries he had just eaten lay in his stomach, daring his body to try and digest them. He thought again about his mission and about Kristin. He suddenly felt regret that he had not bought into the cell phone generation. His mother had said they were too intrusive and separated people from each other. Kristin had said that physicians of all people should be connected. Maybe she was right because he wanted more than anything right then to hear her voice. One last thing and then he'd go see her.

As he drove in and approached apartment 10, he noticed with satisfaction that a light was on in the back. Then his nerves began to betray him. The gloom of the evening and the butterflies paddling through his undigested food, were making him think twice about his mission. He almost put the car in reverse and went home. He uttered a curse for his failing bravery, then shut the motor off and got determinedly out.

From a darkened corner of the room, Sanderson peered out at the man coming toward the door.

"It *is* that lousy bastard again!" he whispered to himself. Fear nibbled at him for a moment. "What does the guy want? What's in it for him? It don't make no sense!" he said quietly to the empty room. No matter. He'd fix the guy's wagon good this time. He'd never know what hit him.

Brian knocked at the door. Sanderson had left it purposely ajar causing the door to open part way. Unsure what to do, Brian stepped just over the threshold and called out. "Sanderson? Are you in there? I have to talk with . . ."

A star exploded in the front of Brian's forehead as Sanderson hit him with a broken two-by-four he had fished from a pile back of the motel. Brian collapsed on the floor with an agonized moan. The club came down on his back, breaking two of his ribs. A red mist clouded his vision as Sanderson hit him again.

The man loved the sight of his victim thrashing around on the floor. He bent over him, gloating.

"Hey, asshole, how does it feel to be on the receivin' end of the beatin'? I don't hear no instructions comin' outta yer mouth this time."

Brian lay there, groaning. He wondered what the man would do to him next. The two-by-four waggled back and forth in front of his face as Sanderson got ready to hit him again. Brian knew he couldn't take many more hits with that club.

Sanderson, confident of his enemy's helplessness didn't bother to keep a firm grip on the handle of his weapon. Despite the vise of pain squeezing his ribs, Brian reached out and embraced the club and the man's leg in a desperate bear hug. Surprised, Sanderson couldn't move fast enough. The club was effectively pinioned. Sanderson couldn't pull it free so he started pounding Brian's back and the side of his head with his free hand. Brian's head rang from the repeated blows to his face. Still he held on. The man was hitting left handed, which diminished the force of the attack.

Sanderson still felt in control but was enraged by his inability to loosen the two-by-four from the man's desperate grip. The chicken-shit at his feet was gonna hold on all day like some fuckin' leech or somethin'. He pulled his left leg back and delivered an off balance kick to the vulnerable rib cage.

Brian gasped from the savagery of the kick and the additional damage to his broken ribs. As the leg swung toward him a second time, Brian rolled forward. Sanderson, off balance, toppled to the floor, releasing his hold on the club as he fell. Brian, still gripping the club, and the leg, wound up staring directly at the man's groin. Instinctively, he raised his head like a battering ram and slammed it into the man's testicles. Sanderson cried out and clutched his damaged, aching balls. For the moment nothing mattered but easing that terrible pain.

Brian slowly rolled over and tried to get to his feet. A violent trembling rendered his body incredibly weak. Several moments went by before he could get up. Using the bed to pull himself upright, he was able to get to a sitting position on the mattress. He sat there sobbing from the hurt and the craziness of it all.

Using the club as a crutch, he finally pushed himself to his feet. He approached Sanderson on his way to the door.

The groaning man mistook his opponent's intentions. Sure that Brian was going to bash him with the club he rolled over and staggered to his feet, in spite of the consuming ache in his groin. At the same time, he reached in his back pocket.

In the darkened room, Brian heard an ominous click, then saw a glint of the bathroom light reflect off the switchblade.

Brian raised the club to protect himself. The thrust of the razor sharp blade was partially deflected as it passed over the back of his wrist and laid open the flesh. Brian dropped the club and clutched his injured hand. Stumbling slightly, Sanderson stabbed at him again. Brian grabbed the knife hand, a white-hot anger replacing the terror and pain.

The two men fell to the floor and grappled with the knife. Sanderson forced the blade toward Brian's stomach. The blood flowing down Brian's hand made it increasingly hard to hold onto his assailant's wrist. A quick turn of Sanderson's arm and Brian felt the jolt as the blade slid through his skin, deflected against his rib cage and plunged into his side. The pain consumed him.

Fear for his life shot more adrenalin into his system. He fought, out of control now, oblivious to the pain. He forced the blade and hand back out of his body and began turning it toward Sanderson. The man shrieked in fright as the knife came inexorably toward him. Sanderson's strength and will power deserted him. The knife plunged toward his face. At the last second, he turned his head aside and the blade sliced downward, gashing open a long wound on his cheek and lodging, point foremost, through the cartilage of his ear.

The pain paralyzed him. He had no fight left in him. He began to scream. He lay there just screaming and screaming . . .

Brian forced himself up. Blood was all over him. It was falling from his fingers and puddling on the floor. The front of his shirt, jacket and pants were soaked from the wound in his side. His life was flowing out before his eyes.

He had to get to Emergency in a hurry or he was going to die. He grabbed a shirt lying wadded up on the dresser and shoved it onto the surface of the wound. Painfully, he pulled his belt from his jeans and strapped it tightly around the shirt. The flow of blood barely slowed.

He left the groveling, sobbing man behind and staggered out to his car. When he pulled on the dented door, he felt the wound open wider. He didn't notice Eubie Coffelt standing in the shadows. Eubie had been watching the fight through the slit in the Venetian blinds.

The keys were still in the ignition as Brian collapsed on the seat. The stick shift was going to be hell but he had to get going. Clutching the shirt more tightly to the gash, Brian backed out and then headed for the highway, his free hand first shifting, then steering.

Traffic that time of the evening was light and he made good progress for a while but the loss of blood was making him increasingly weak, impairing his judgment. The car began to weave slightly, drawing angry honks from the few passing cars. He vaguely noted a scraping sound as he sideswiped a car. He kept going but he knew it was already too late.

"I'm going to die! I'm going to die without Kristin ever knowing how much I love her!" he said aloud. "I have to talk to her but there isn't time."

Brian began to weep, knowing he would never see her again. Through the disorientation, he spotted an old phone booth on the corner and without thinking, pulled over and stopped. Would it still be working? The Ghia stuck dangerously out into the traffic lane. Cars blared furiously as they swerved and passed. One car careened into a fire hydrant. Oblivious, Brian staggered from the car, his shoes leaving small, red blots on the pavement. He would call Kristin and then he would call an ambulance. He could go no farther. He reached carefully into his soaking pants pocket and pulled out a coin. It was a quarter. He dropped the reddened token into the slot and dialed.

The phone on the other end of the line rang and rang. "Please be there, Kristin! I have to tell you."

Kristin extracted herself from the shower and came muttering and cursing to the phone, little puddles of water forming at her feet.

"Hello. This better be good, whoever it is. You just got me out of the shower."

"Kristin, it's Brian."

She almost put the phone down. He had walked out on her. But there was a halting, whispery quality in his voice that had grabbed her attention.

"Brian, is something wrong?"

"Kristin, I had to tell you I love you before it's too late. You have to know that." His voice could barely be heard.

"Brian, what's wrong! I can tell from the way you're talking that there's something the matter."

"I got in a fight and got stabbed. I'm bleeding to death." His voice trailed off into silence.

Fear clutched her insides. There was no time to ask many questions. "Where are you, Brian? Why haven't you called an ambulance?"

The voice was almost inaudible. "There wasn't enough time, Kristin."

Brian slowly slid to the floor of the phone booth. "Bye, Kristin," he said with a little smile.

He didn't hear the police sirens wailing up the highway toward him.

CHAPTER 33

The small face looking up at him still had a sadness about it, but at least the fear was finally gone. They were walking along hand-in-hand across the park overlooking the Ohio River. The white scar across the back of Brian's wrist reminded him of how precious each day had become. He had barely survived the flight to the hospital in the back of the police cruiser. He remembered little of the rescue; brief snapshots of movement; disconnected bursts of activity; the wail of the siren as the police rushed his body through the night; the urgent commands of the nurses; the lights of the operating suite in the E.R. . . . and then oblivion.

Brian smelled the air, sensing that winter was hiding out there waiting. He loved the fall, the nip in the air, the smell of burning leaves. Autumn had a special, nostalgic quality all its own but for now Indian Summer had come to brighten their days for a short time. Winter would be fun, though. He could hardly wait to share it with Stevie. There might even be a couple of Red's games left they could go to.

By next year at that time he hoped to have completed building the Hazel Tanner Memorial Clinic. He had worked out a joint venture with one of the Cincinnati hospitals that was seeking more primary care admissions and an architect had been hard at work with the plans.

Brian saw Kristin across the stream at the edge of the woods, getting the picnic ready for them. Holly and Heather were running around, sort of helping her. He waved to her and she waved in return. While he had lain recuperating in the hospital, he had shared with her some of the tragic moments from his early childhood, the scenes frozen forever in his mind because of his nightmares. And he had told her how Hazel had saved him; of the miracle she had given him.

The excessive abuse by Stevie's father led the court to seek a foster home for the boy. Brian and Kristin Tanner had been allowed to provide that home. Brian's fight with Sanderson had made the application difficult, but in the end, his profession, along with Kristin's former connection with the State Social Services Department, had convinced the court to allow the placement on a trial basis. The Court had chosen to disbelieve Sanderson's plea that Brian had attacked him before. The man had no credibility.

Sanderson's neighbor, Eubie Coffelt, had been a big help, describing how Brian had been attacked and had only fought back in self-defense. Eubie had loved every minute of the attention while he told his story, condemning Sanderson who had always treated him like shit anyway.

It would be a long, difficult fight for Stevie, Brian knew. The boy would need love and understanding but together, they would make another miracle.

Brian stopped for a second. He was sure his eyes were playing tricks on him. At the edge of the woods, he saw an older woman watching them. She had a smile on her face. As quickly as she had come, she disappeared. But, she **had** been there.

"Mom," Brian said softly.

She was out there waiting. She **had** promised. Someday he would see her again.

A tear gathered at the edge of Brian's eye and wandered gently down his cheek. He knelt down and looked at Stevie. Ever so tentatively the little boy reached up and touched the tear.

And Brian smiled.

Proof

Made in the USA
Charleston, SC
16 June 2010